Red Clay
Ashes

A NOVEL

Julie Tulba

ISBN-13: 978-1-7339118-4-9

Printed in the United States of America

OTHER BOOKS BY JULIE TULBA

The Tears of Yesteryear
The Dead Are Resting

For my "buck private."

To the American men and women who served in Vietnam—those that made it home and those that didn't. Your supreme courage and ultimate sacrifice will never be forgotten.

AUTHOR'S DISCLAIMER:

PROLOGUE

Saigon
The morning of April 29, 1975

"The temperature in Saigon is 105 degrees and rising."

The woman shot upright in her bed, her body still drenched in sweat, the ancient wooden ceiling fan that circled above her head offering nothing more than an annoying and unwelcome rattling sound but certainly no cooling relief. Her sleep that night and all the ones before it was nothing but an endless cascade of troubled restlessness as she tossed and turned back and forth on her all too tiny bed.

Life anymore felt like a tableau to the woman, one in which she was no longer a part of, no longer living in, but rather one that she was watching with acute detail and perhaps even fascination from the outside, from somewhere far, far away from the place that the world knew as Vietnam.

Just as she was about to tell herself that she must have been dreaming, that she had imagined hearing those words, "the temperature in Saigon is 105 degrees and rising," the unmistakable sound of a past she no longer claimed filled the apartment, "White Christmas," the song that would forever link Bing Crosby and Christmas together.

And she knew then with the utmost certainty that it wasn't a dream. For to hear the words of that timeless Christmas song sounding in her small apartment on the other side of the world, in a land where such things as freshly baked gingerbread and Douglas firs were as crazy and unimaginable an idea as a man walking on the moon had once been, she knew then that it was all over. That the final act was being performed and very soon the curtain would be coming down for good, one final time. And there was nothing she could do about it.

Saigon-The American Embassy
Early morning hours of April 30, 1975

"Lady, if you don't get your fucking ass on this helo in the next 10 seconds I'll personally hand you over to Charlie as soon as he gets here for being so stupid," the young Marine staff sergeant screamed at the woman, his words surprisingly clear considering the deafening sound of the Huey's rotors which were furiously spinning precariously close to them. Along, of course, with the screams and wails and every other conceivable noise a human being was capable of producing from the hordes of people that were vying to get onto the waiting helicopter and the Marines who were attempting to board them in as orderly a fashion as possible considering the circumstances.

For a brief moment the woman stared at the staff sergeant and he at her, the latter waiting almost expectantly for her to say something back to him, even to defy his orders. He looked to be no more than 20. His skin and face still had a youthful, almost angelic look to them; it was only his eyes that betrayed an advanced emotional age well beyond his living years. A haunted and wearied soldier in a boy's body, a sight as common to her as the smell of the omnipresent *nuoc cham*, fish sauce, that she had even come to love after all this time here.

But she said nothing. Just as the American military had given up its fight here two years earlier, she knew she had to give up hers. That it was time. That he was never coming back. So she placed her hand in the staff sergeant's outstretched one and found herself being roughly pulled up into the Huey and barely a second later, felt it lifting off from the roof, slowly ascending into the night sky.

The woman became impervious to everything around her- the other passengers, a mixture of Americans and South Vietnamese. The latter were fleeing in advance of the North Vietnamese Army, which by all accounts was at the gates to the city by then, ready to mentally conquer and destroy their fellow countrymen for having been on the other side during the war, the wrong side.

When she looked down at the embassy's courtyard and saw the hundreds, perhaps even thousands of people still there, all scrambling this way and that, an image that brought to mind ants on an unattended piece of watermelon at a summer picnic, she wondered how many would make it out? And how many more would be left behind, their fate almost certainly already decided upon from their connection to the Americans.

And then she wondered if one of those scrambling ants down there was him. That if at this very moment he was telling the Marines on the ground that he too was an American, that they needed to let him through and let him board one of the helicopters before it was too late.

But the Huey turned direction then, heading towards the South China Sea, where the fleet of U.S. Navy ships awaited the evacuees, heading away from the final bastion of what had once been the

Republic of Vietnam. And so her last image of Saigon, the city that had birthed her identity, the only place she had ever really thought of as home, was nothing more than a blackened canvas interspersed with shooting red fire balls, presumably from an exploding ammunition dump. The curtain was coming down but America was damned if Charlie was going to get its cache of ammunition.

The woman knew one thing- she would never be able to hear the words of "White Christmas" without reliving the sheer heartbreak of this day.

PART I

"How long do you Americans want to fight? One year? Two years? Three years? Five years? Ten years? Twenty years? We will be glad to accommodate you."
— **North Vietnamese Prime Minister Pham Van Dong,** to the *New York Times*, December 1966

"It was my idea to go to Saigon. If there was a war out there, I felt I had an obligation to go cover it. If I didn't, I would spend the rest of my life regretting it. I don't know to whom I owed anything, but I felt like I needed to do it, because somebody has to do this. But I also have to admit that I found it a rush."
— **Richard Pyle** was the AP Bureau chief in Saigon from 1970 to 1973.

CHAPTER 1

BEE

When Bee smelled the plumeria candle at the Bath and Body Works store in the mall one cold Saturday in January, she immediately felt a jarring sensation, almost as if someone had whacked her on the head like you do to a *piñata* when you're at a kid's birthday party. She couldn't quite describe it but it was a scent that smelled instantly familiar to her, but also one that seemed to bring to the surface undistinguishable memories of a time and place that were entirely foreign to her.

It wasn't the first time Bee had experienced this sensation; over the years there had been certain places and things that had triggered a reaction within her, a feeling she never knew why or from where it came. There was the time she had been backpacking in Costa Rica and one of the locals she had been traveling with urged her to try *jugo de tamarindo*, or tamarind juice. That first sip, Bee was shocked to find, tasted vaguely familiar. But she was at a loss as to where she could have possibly tried such an exotic drink since back home in Butler, the small, rural city she had grown up in just north of Pittsburgh, well, Butler didn't do exotic.

Then there was Dan, the former Peace Corps volunteer she had dated for a couple of months who liked to constantly espouse his knowledge and authority on all things Southeast Asia, even though Thailand was the only Southeast Asian country he had ACTUALLY been to. But one night he had surprised her by cooking her a homemade meal in her studio apartment. The moment she walked through the door she was immediately hit by a pungent fish smell, one that seemed better reserved for an alley behind a hole-in-the-wall Chinese restaurant and not where she slept. But all the same it was still eerily comfortable and familiar to her. When she had asked him what that smell was, he took almost immediate offense at her calling his dinner "a smell" but finally answered, *"nuoc cham,"* (like that meant anything to her). When she continued to look at him with an utterly blank expression, he said snidely as if she were a philistine, "It's a Vietnamese dipping sauce."

Dinner that night had been surprisingly good but the *nuoc cham* smell (or the skunk-like odor as she came to think of it as) lingered for weeks and no amount of frigid air from the outside or countless spritzes of Elizabeth Taylor's Black Diamond perfume made it go away. She hated this foreign smell that had invaded her apartment, that had taken up residence there without her permission. She couldn't deny the truth—she had breathed in the scent of this foreign invader before. But where?

And then there were the dreams. It was in the deep recesses of slumber that images of fuchsia colored bougainvillea and bright yellow buildings that looked like they were from another time, something out of a Somerset Maugham novel, appeared most often; dreams where the faces of the people were always blurred, their words foreign sounding and undecipherable to her ears.

When Bee had asked her mother if they had ever been anywhere during her childhood that would have had bougainvillea trees and bright yellow buildings, her mom had responded with a curt, "of course not." Equivalent to, "why would you ever ask such a ridiculous question?"

Her mother hadn't approved of Dan, feeling he was much too hippie in his ways, never mind the fact that he now worked for the IMF in New York and wore a three-piece suit each day to his office, now almost entirely unrecognizable from the young man with the long hair in his bell bottom jeans and leather fringe jacket she had once known. But that was her mom, unyielding in her opinion of someone or something to her very core and having no time for nonsense (ridiculous questions definitely fell into THAT category).

Pittsburgh, Pennsylvania
2005

Bee had bought a small bottle of plumeria lotion since candles weren't allowed at work in her job as reference librarian at the Carnegie Library (irrespective of the fact that patrons routinely brought in articles from the outside they weren't allowed to). But Bee found that the lotion smelled just as good as the candle. She never applied any to her hands, but when she knew no one was around, she would open up the bottle and just smell it. She'd close her eyes and immediately be transported to that exotic place she still wasn't sure even existed outside of her mind's subconscious.

The phone on her desk sounded then, breaking Bee from her *Heart of Darkness* style dreaming, as if she were Charlie Marlow himself sailing up the Congo River about to fetch Kurtz and not sitting at a desk in a cold, gray office on Forbes Avenue in Pittsburgh's Oakland neighborhood as she herself was doing that very moment.

"Yes?" Bee said into the phone semi-dismissively.

"Is this Beatrice Cerny?" a deep male voice asked.

Bee immediately sat upright in her chair, surprised that it wasn't Ida on the other end, the library's stalwart secretary who was responsible for fielding all outside calls to their respective destinations. Ida had been with the library for what seemed like forever; Bee often joked that Mr. Carnegie himself must have hired her when he decided to become Santa Claus for bibliophiles with his starting of the Carnegie Libraries. But Bee was perplexed. She never received any outside calls, well, that is to her personally when she was at her desk in the office and not at the reference desk on the main floor.

"Yes, this is she," Bee replied hurriedly, a wave of anxiety starting to wash over her for the man on the other end did not sound as if he was in the library world trying to sell her on new spine label stickers.

"Ms. Cerny, my name is Officer Kovalenko. I'm with the Butler City Police Department. We picked up your mother, a-" there was silence on the line then, as if he was looking down at his notepad like you see cops carry in the movies, as if he made so many calls like this a day he couldn't possibly keep track of all the names. "Yes, a Hazel Cerny."

"Why was my mother arrested?" Bee asked standing up, the anxiety she had been feeling now transforming into a wave of bile at the back of her throat that threatened to rear its ugly head at any moment.

"Oh, my apologies Ms. Cerny," Officer Kovalenko said. "I didn't mean to say she was arrested, no, she was found wandering on Main Street and-"

"Walking the streets in the daylight is now a crime?" Bee angrily interjected, not caring in the least how rude she was being to this complete stranger. "I didn't know Butler had become a police state like Rangoon."

"Ran what?" Officer Kovalenko replied, clearly confused. "Ms.

Cerny, if you'll please let me finish," he said, sternly and loudly, all traces of pleasantness gone from his tone. "I never said she was arrested. We picked her up because she was walking on Main Street without a coat on, without any sort of outer layering or gloves or a hat. She was also in flip flops."

Her mom had been walking outside without a coat on the first day of April wearing flip flops. She retrieved today's *Post Gazette* from underneath a pile of books on her desk and on the front page saw that today's high was 37 degrees. Bee felt stricken then, immediately collapsing back into her chair. When she still said nothing, Officer Kovalenko continued.

"Someone inside Miller's Shoes spotted her dressed like that and took her in where they then call us. She had been carrying her purse with her, which is how we knew to call you."

"Is she okay, she's not hurt or anything right, I mean she doesn't have frostbite or...?" Bee trailed off, not knowing what to say or ask, at a complete loss for words.

"Healthwise she seems okay," he said with an air of someone who wasn't a doctor. "She of course was quite cold but we've given her a few cups of hot coffee here at the station and that seems to have helped, along with some blankets. Mentally, umm, I'm no doctor but she seemed very disoriented. She couldn't tell us her name, or where she lived, said she didn't have a daughter after I saw the emergency contact card in her purse that listed a Beatrice Cerny as her daughter. She just kept saying the name Vince over and over." He paused then, before asking, "Does she suffer from dementia or Alzheimer's?"

"No," Bee sputtered into the phone. "She's never done anything like this before. This doesn't sound at all like my mother."

"Well, those things," Officer Kovalenko began solemnly, "there's always the first time."

Silence then with neither of them speaking.

"You'll keep her there…safe?" Bee asked, adding the last word as almost an after-thought, as if she wasn't a good daughter, as if this was somehow her fault even though this kind stranger had never once insinuated that. "It's just that I'm down in Pittsburgh, in Oakland, and it will be a little bit before I can get up to Butler."

"Of course," he told her, his pleasantness back, now speaking to her as a father would to his grown daughter. "She's not talking at all, but sitting entirely calm, looks almost at peace."

And at that moment, perhaps she was. But Bee would never know. For her mother, her stern, always disapproving mother who never once exhibited an ounce of maternal tenderness even when Bee was little, suffered an aneurysm that day at 2:29PM (or so the coroner would later tell her) while sitting in the chair at Officer Kovalenko's desk. But when she passed, there was definitely a faint smile on her now cold lips, something that was still noticeable when Bee arrived at the morgue at Butler Memorial Hospital. Cold from death and not from living.

CHAPTER 2

BEE

2005

With the death of her mother, Bee truly was all alone now. Sure, she had scores of friends, many of whom she was quite close to, but there were no siblings to share this emotional weight, not even an aunt or cousin to ask for help with the funeral luncheon. It all fell to her. And unlike her daughter, Hazel Cerny had no friends to speak of, not even a casual acquaintance or two that Bee could recall. But that's how her mother had always wanted it to be. She wanted no contact with the world outside of what was required, and her own daughter naturally falling into the "required" category.

As her mother's home had long since been paid for, Bee had found no rush in clearing it out and disposing of Hazel's few things. Her mother had been a minimalist long before it had been dubbed cool by trendsetters. The few times she had had friends over as a kid, Bee had been embarrassed by the home's stark, almost austere interior. She had stopped inviting friends over after one of them had asked Bee in all seriousness if they had been robbed. Bee had never told her mother this, nor had her mother asked why friends stopped coming. It just wasn't Hazel's nature to care about what she deemed to be the trivial nature of little girl socializing.

The one and only thing that Hazel Cerny kept, collected even, were books. Bee knew a lot of this stemmed from what had been Hazel's job for as long as Bee could remember, a translator of English books into French. And so Hazel would have undoubtedly considered the books a "necessity," and not a materialistic indulgence, the latter including Bee's many personal articles such as purses and cassette tapes and later CDs. Books, however, were the one thing that escaped Hazel Cerny's disapproving words, a good thing considering Bee was a librarian after all.

And so nearly a month after the funeral, Bee made the drive up to Butler for what she thought would be the last time. Per her will, her mother had been cremated, although Bee hadn't the faintest idea what to do with the ashes. Her mother had always been very detail-oriented, matter of fact about nearly everything in life, except for the disposal of her ashes, it seemed. That's one directive Bee would have appreciated from her. For now, the ashes were in a small box in the upstairs hall closet, slightly creeping Bee out every time she passed by it.

It had only taken Bee five hours to clean and empty the house, the driveway filled with a few trash bags that would be collected in tomorrow's pickup, the trunk of her car laden with boxes of kitchen goods and bags of clothes she would take to the local Goodwill. She had left the sorting and disposal of her mother's immense book collection until last, knowing that this out of everything was what would take the most time to do. But thankfully as a result of both her studies and professional experience as a librarian, she was highly skilled in the art of weeding, with no more than a cursory glance at a book's physical condition but also its thematic matter and currency to know if it should be saved or tossed.

Hazel had bookcases in just about every room of the house but it was her bedroom where she'd kept her French book collection, all the titles she had translated during her life, arranged of course in alphabetical order. Bee noticed a feeling of warmth moving across her for the person who had rarely displayed maternal affection for her only child when Bee was growing up.

"Cathy's daddy doesn't live at home anymore so her mommy works in an office now. I don't have a daddy so how come you don't work mommy?"

"But I do work Beatrice," Hazel said to her seven-year old daughter, not lifting her eyes from the page of the book she had open before her to her left, her typewriter immediately in front of her.

"But you don't leave the house," Beatrice said, not understanding how her mommy had a job if she was always at home.

Hazel sighed then, filled with both exasperation and annoyance. She removed the red pen she had behind her right ear, made a marking in the book in front of her, then placed the black and white bookmark in the page she had just marked and closed the book. Turning to face her daughter she said, "I do work Hazel. I do have a job that I work at five days a week, sometimes more, often for more than 40 hours a week. Just because I don't leave the house and work in an office as a secretary doesn't mean I don't work or that what I do isn't important."

"Your job is to read books?" Beatrice asked in a child's innocence, because her mother's desk was in fact always littered with books.

But Hazel, who routinely treated her seven-year old daughter as more of an adult than the small child she actually was, got annoyed thinking

15

her daughter was being fresh. "No, my job is to translate books from English into French. I read them in order to translate them."

"What does 'translate' mean?"

Hazel just looked at Beatrice then, a look on her face that could have been read as "how the hell did I get here?" But instead she pulled Beatrice onto her lap and pulled out the paper that had been in the typewriter. "What does this say" *she asked pointing to the words on the sheet.*

Il peut plus me souffrir. Ça se voit. Il dit que je suis de la mauvaise graine et que j' fais jamais rien de propre.

Beatrice squinted at the words, her mind not understanding what she was looking at. She knew she was a good reader, all the teachers and the school librarian always told her so. But looking at the words on the sheet, it was as if she didn't know how to read and she wanted to cry but wouldn't because her mother didn't like it when she cried.

"I don't know," *Beatrice said, her little lip starting to twitch, a sign she was upset.*

"Of course you don't," *Hazel said matter of factly.* "That's because these words you see here are in French, not English. So translate means I take words that are in English and put them into French. So I read books that are in English and change them so people in France can read them."

"You speak French?" *Beatrice asked, thinking her mother must be a superhero or something to know another language.*

"Yes, I do. But run along now and go play. I have more work to do before I make dinner," she said, gently pushing Beatrice from her lap and turning her attention once more to putting the sheet of paper she had removed back into the typewriter.

Beatrice ran her finger across the spines of the books, a mixture of hardback and paperback, and pulled from the shelf the one on which her finger had stopped. *Les vestiges du jour* by Kazuo Ishiguro. She flipped to the title page and smiled when she saw the words-

Traduction par Hazel Cerny

Her mother's life's work summed up in one sentence with the words, "Translation by Hazel Cerny." She put *Remains on the Day* back on the shelf and pulled out another title, *La couleur pourpre.* Bee had always loved Alice Walker but *The Color Purple* was a particular favorite. She started putting the books into the box then, knowing undoubtedly that's how her mother would have wanted Bee to remember her, holding onto her books.

Upon reaching down to pick up the box, Bee happened to notice a small book on its side at the very back of the shelf. She reached in and saw that it was the French language version of Jules Verne's *Around the World in 80 Days.* She leafed to the title page thinking this was perhaps a rare exception of her mother having translated a French title into English, never mind the fact that it had been written more than 100 years ago. But instead of seeing her mother's name there at the bottom, beneath the listing of *Le tour du monde en quatre-vingts jours,* there was a handwritten message.

October 28, 1968

*To my little Frenchie. You'll have to translate this for me
one day when we're on our own journey around the world,
although our journey will last a lifetime, not just 80 days.
I love you baby, buku.*

Before she could even wrap her head around the fact that someone
had once called her stolid, no-nonsense mother "baby," a thin brown
envelope fell out of the book. Opening it, Bee discovered a series of small
black and white photographs. The first one she picked up was of a man
and a woman wearing sunglasses at the beach, she in a bikini, he in swim
trunks. When she turned it over she read the words *Da Nang, 1968.*
The second picture was of two women, both dressed in army fatigues
complete with helmets atop their heads, a massive helicopter in the
background, each of them with huge smiles, as if the funniest joke had
just been told. The inscription on this one read *Me and Suzy Q, Saigon,
1970.* When she placed the two photos next to each other, she realized
that the woman in the beach photo was the same woman in the other
picture. And then it dawned on Bee, the "me" from the inscription on
the back was her mother. She studied the photos again and instantly saw
her mother in each one. The next photo was of a nondescript four story
building except the street was lined with palm trees and everything
around it looked chaotic. When she turned it over she read the words
Rue Pasteur. But it was the last photo that Bee felt stricken by, for it was
of her mother presumably, and her? The little girl in the photo appeared
to be about a year old, the man in the photo was holding her. Even in
black and white, Bee could tell the man was dark haired like she was.
When she turned it over she read the words, *With our little bumble bee,
Saigon 1970.* How old was she here, one maybe?

Bee felt dizzy then, sinking to her feet in a state of sheer bewilderment and shock. Saigon? As in Vietnam? As in what the hell was she doing there as a baby during the war? The war was still going on then, right? But wait, she thought to herself. When DID the war end? 1974? 1973? The anal retentive part of her wanted to at that very moment get an encyclopedia and find the answer. But the picture that lay on the ground, the three faces in that black and white photograph staring up at her, Bee knew her factoid curiosities would have to wait. She needed to get to the bottom of this…somehow.

Sitting on the carpeted floor Indian style, Bee was now eye-level with the top shelf of the squat, two-tier bookcase and saw there was something else at the back of the shelf. Reaching her arm back she removed a thin, brown manila envelope, one clearly weathered with age. She opened the envelope and removed what appeared to be a series of newspaper clippings. Unfolding the brittle newsprint, she read the headline on the first clipping-

"Vietcong attack U.S. Embassy in Tet offensive"

And then gasped when she saw the byline- Hazel Baxter.

She picked up the next two clippings and saw they were all written by a Hazel Baxter-

"U.S. and South Vietnamese forces are ultimate victors in Tet Offensive but at high cost of life"

"U.S. combat deaths in Vietnam exceed total number of men killed during Korean War"

"Direct U.S. Military involvement in Vietnam ends with Paris Peace Accords"

"Bringing them home, all POWS to be freed within 60 days"

"Operation Babylift ends after artillery attacks by Vietcong on Tan Son Nhut Airport"

"Longest war in American history finally comes to an end"

But when she got to the final four, she noticed the byline now read Hazel Cerny, not Baxter. From the 1969 clipping about the number of deaths in Vietnam being more than all those killed during the Korean War to the Paris Peace Accords, her mother had gotten married?

Bee laid each of the seven clippings on the ground in front of her and stared at them, her mind reeling from all that she had just discovered about the one person she thought she had known all there was to know, when in fact, she had no idea who her mother really was and now, never would. Her mother hadn't just kept her past a secret, but she had kept Bee's earliest years a secret from her too. And Bee wanted to know why.

Hours later, Bee sat in her bed, knowing there was no way in hell she'd be able to sleep that night. The black and white photographs rested atop the copy of *Le tour du monde en quatre-vingts jours,* while the seven newsprint clippings were once again spread out before her, as if having them arranged in such a manner would somehow make her mother manifest and logically explain everything to Bee, make sense of her existence which she now doubted and had no idea what was fact and what was fiction.

As she picked up the clipping about Operation Babylift coming to an end, she flipped it over and saw a thin sheet of stationery stuck to the back of it. Unfolding it she read-

February 1, 1979

My dearest Hazel,

How are you? How is little Beatrice although she's not so little anymore. There's not a day that goes by where I don't think of you and wonder how you're doing, how you're adjusting to life in the U.S. once more. I won't ask if I can come and visit or even hope that you'll reply to this letter. I understand why I can't and why you won't. But just know that I am always thinking of you regardless of the number of years that pass by. We lived five lifetimes over in Nam, you and me, and shared something that only the people who were there will ever truly know. You'll always be my sister, my dear girl.

Suzanne

P.S. I'm stateside once more. Had enough of rice and fish heads! Here's my address and new number-
Suzanne Quaglio
210 E. 12th Street Apt. 3A
New York, New York 10003
212.814.0333

Suzanne Quaglio. Why did that name seem familiar, Bee wondered as she stared at the handwritten note. And then it dawned on her, Suzy Q! Yes, from the photo! That had to be her. She picked it up and studied the two women in the picture, one whom she thought she knew and the other a stranger to her, but not a stranger to her mother apparently.

Walking into the guest bedroom that also doubled as a home office, Bee turned on her computer and waited for it to boot up. Once it had she pulled up Google and typed in the name "Suzanne Quaglio." She was both surprised and yet not from the results that greeted her-

Suzanne Quaglio, Pulitzer Prize-winning journalist

Suzanne Quaglio, award-winning Vietnam War and Khmer Rouge correspondent

Suzanne Quaglio, retiring after covering more than 10 foreign conflicts during her illustrious career

Bee didn't see any obituary, which she took as a good sign. She reasoned that a woman as famous in the journalism field as Suzanne Quaglio, there would undoubtedly have an online obituary posted if she was indeed deceased.

Bee picked up the phone and dialed the number on the note, thinking to herself there was no way in hell this Suzanne Quaglio would still have that same number, considering the note she had written to Hazel was more than 20 years old.

The phone rang and rang and just as Bee was about to hang up in defeat, someone picked up.

"Hello?" an older woman with a deep, husky voice answered.

"Oh, hi," Bee replied, startled after thinking she'd never get a live person. "Um, I probably have the wrong number but I was looking for a Suzanne Quaglio."

"That's me," the woman replied. "What can I help you with?"

"Um, sorry to bother you but my name is Bee, I mean Beatrice, Beatrice Cerny and I'm-"

"And you're Hazel Cerny's daughter," the woman said, cutting Bee off before she could get the words out.

CHAPTER 3

BEE

2005

"You still remember her after all these years?" Bee asked incredulously into the phone.

Suzanne laughed then, a deep sound one that seemed to reverberate all the way from New York to Pittsburgh. It was a laugh that made Bee think of the picture of the two women, the one where her mother was smiling in a way that Bee could never remember her doing when she was growing up or even when she was an adult. But clearly she had at one time, in a life and place that had been as far away as possible from her existence in Butler, Pennsylvania.

"Of course I do, Beatrice," Suzanne answered. There was a pause then. Bee sensed the other woman wanted to say more but was hesitant to. "She's gone, isn't she?"

"How'd you know?" Bee asked in total surprise. By all accounts the two women hadn't been in touch in decades and per her mother's wishes, there hadn't been any public obituary printed.

"Because I always knew that the day I heard from you, Hazel

Cerny's daughter, I knew that she'd be dead."

"Look, I discovered these pictures and newspaper clippings that my mother wrote and-"

"Let me stop you right there," Suzanne said, cutting Bee off mid-sentence. "This isn't some talk to be had at 8 PM on a Sunday night or 8 PM on any night. How soon can you get here?"

"Here?" Bee asked, not following.

"New York, the Big Apple," Suzanne answered.

"Um, but I'm in Pittsburgh. I have a job."

"And what exactly is it that you do?"

"I'm a librarian," Bee said, a wave of inferiority rushing over her considering she was speaking to a Pulitzer Prize-winning journalist.

"Right, well your mother and I back in the day the same age as you survived mortar launchers and Agent Orange. You can find a way to get your ass to Manhattan. The dusty books and stupid questions from stupid people can wait. Your mother is gone and you need to know everything now."

Bee blanched at that, even though everything Suzanne had said was true. But especially the part about Bee's needing to learn about her newly found bombshell past, hers but especially her mother's. The predictable parent who was now an utter stranger to her.

"I can catch a train tomorrow," Bee said meekly.

"Good. I'll expect you tomorrow. My address is still the same. Goodnight Beatrice." And she hung up, allowing for no further discussion…whatsoever.

And so the following day Bee found herself riding eastbound on the Pennsylvanian, her stomach awash with a mixture of not only feelings of excitement but also ones of nervous jitters over what Suzanne would tell her.

When the taxi she had gotten at Penn Station pulled up in front of 210 E. 12th Street, Bee thought about telling the driver to keep going, that she'd made a mistake, gotten the address wrong, that it was really 210 W. 12th Street. There was a small part of her that didn't want to go in, that didn't want to hear what Suzanne had to say. She had lived this long without knowing about this past of hers. She was 36 years old, why possibly change the course of her life now? But the image of her as a baby in Vietnam, her mother having been a war correspondent there for years, she knew these things would always haunt her if she didn't find out the truth. And that's how she found the nerve to be buzzing Apartment 3A even though her stomach made her feel as if she was awaiting her executioner.

"Mhm" was the first thing Suzanne said to Bee upon opening her front door. Studying Bee she said, "You look just like…" but then trailed off. "Listen to me, an old lady babbling away. Come in, come in."

She stood aside to let Bee enter. Bee was sure her mouth dropped wide open upon entering Suzanne's apartment, for it was the most glamorous, sophisticated, and original home she had ever been in. She knew nothing about Asia but every square inch was bedecked with what appeared to be expensive looking Oriental antiquities. Samurai swords and Japanese woodblock prints adorned the walls while ceramic vases and figurines that looked like they could have come right out of Beijing's Forbidden City graced tabletops and other surfaces. The interior matched Suzanne in every way, she thought. Although in her 60s now, Suzanne still had a youthful figure, her face free of the wrinkles and age lines that had abounded on Hazel's face in her later years. Her blond hair was cut in a bob that was angled right at chin length and she wore classy gold hoops in her ears. She was a stunner now and Bee could only imagine what she must have looked like during the war. I mean, even posing in army fatigues Bee thought, she could see that the woman had been beautiful.

"Your home is stunning," Bee said, hoping she didn't sound too much like a country bumpkin. She thought of her own rowhouse back in Pittsburgh that was furnished almost entirely with Ikea and thrift store purchases.

"Thank you, my dear," Suzanne said, walking towards a liquor cart. "I spent nearly a decade on the Asian continent, acquired and discarded two husbands during that time," she said over her shoulder. "But my Asian homewares made for much better memories, wouldn't you say?"

"Um, yes," Bee said, not sure of what else to say. This Suzanne was not only an award-winning journalist but clearly a sophisticate too. And calling these beautiful priceless antiques homewares, as if you could just pick them up at Kmart. Bee knew that's something only a person who had grown up with or was surrounded by money would say.

"Drink?" Suzanne asked, already taking a sip from the highball glass she had just poured herself.

"Uh, sure," Bee replied. "Whiskey soda, please."

"Good girl," Suzanne said approvingly. "Believe me when I say I'm as a modern as you'll get for having been born in 1943 but I just can't stand girls who drink beer. It just seems so unbecoming, so gauche. But I suppose that's my mother talking. She was a deb after all who never consumed more than three glasses of sherry in her lifetime if you ask me," Suzanne said, rolling her head back in laughter.

"Deb?" Bee asked, feeling somewhat gauche herself.

"Debutante, my dear," Suzanne said, appearing at her side and handing her the whiskey soda.

"Oh. That wasn't a thing in Butler, or at least I don't think it was," Bee said.

"No, only the top echelon of the crème de la crème of societies in the big cities. But you didn't travel all this way to talk about debutantes debuting and society balls. So how much do you know?"

Bee took a big sip of her whiskey soda and then pulled out the copy of *Le tour du monde en quatre-vingts jours* from her purse and then from the book's pages, the seven newspaper clippings and the three black and white photographs. And finally she opened to the title page of the Jules Verne book, the one where the handwritten inscription had called her mother "baby."

"I knew none of this," Bee said, waving to the articles before her that she'd placed on the glass coffee table "until two days ago."

There was silence then, Suzanne clearly channeling her journalistic skills and letting her subject continue.

"I, I don't know where to even begin, what I should be asking you," Bee said, her voice quivering with all the emotions she had bottled up the last couple of days.

"Start anywhere you want, and we'll go backwards and forwards and this way and that until you know it all," Suzanne said, warmly patting Bee's hand.

"I lived in Vietnam?" Bee asked, pulling out the photo of her mother holding her as a baby.

"Yes, you were born there," Suzanne said.

"Wait, what? I wasn't born in Vietnam, I was born in a military hospital."

"Yes, and where do you think this military hospital was?"

"The U.S. of course."

"And you never thought to ask where it was?" Suzanne asked, rather wryly Bee thought. "My dear, do you know how many hundreds of military hospitals there are outside of the grand ol' US of A? First rule of thumb for any good journalist, you're never for a second provincial or inward in your line of thinking, no matter the topic. You think on a global scale, not a domestic one." A pause then before she asked, "Do you even know where your birth certificate is?"

"I don't need to know, I've had a passport for as long as I can remember," Bee said feebly, attempting to sound confident and in control of the situation where she was more or less being ridiculed but knowing she was falling well short of said goal. And then thought to herself, my god, I truly don't have a clue where my birth certificate is. What if I accidentally threw it out? How would I even get a copy now that I'm hearing I was born in the middle of a war in a country that probably still hates Americans. Bee felt like she wanted to throw up then and there, projectile vomiting onto a rare 18th century Japanese woodblock print.

"Well, I do know one thing," Suzanne said sarcastically, a smile appearing on her face.

"What's that?" Bee asked.

"You'd have made a horrible journalist."

"Why do you say that?" Bee asked, somewhat hurt that a woman, even one with a Pulitzer Prize, was judging her so quickly, especially since she now knew her mother had been one, a rather good one judging by the well-written newspaper clippings she had read over and over the last few days to the point where she could almost recite them verbatim.

"You don't ask a single goddamn question when it really matters. And shit matters if it concerns you. Trust me."

Suzanne softened after that, perhaps sensing that Bee was one step away from completely losing her shit, figuratively and literally. They also switched to Diet Coke, a fact that Bee greatly appreciated since even with the nearly 30-year age difference between them, Bee had no doubt that Suzanne could drink her under the table.

"Before I start telling you, well, everything there is to tell," Suzanne began, "I want you to see the visuals, to have faces to the people and stories you're going to hear. So come on, I have it all laid out on the dining room table," as she got up and started walking from the room.

Bee dutifully followed, the feelings of anxiousness and excitement she had felt on the cab ride here all coming back. She stopped short in the doorway when she saw the table. Every inch of it was covered by photo albums that had been opened to specific pages but also by stray photographs and more newspapers, almost as many as in the periodicals room at the Carnegie Library.

"The world is your oyster, or at least my dining room table is," Suzanne softly laughed while taking a seat at the head of the table. "Look," she said, waving her hand at the table, "and then the storytelling begins."

Bee walked towards the table, approaching it as if she were at a museum, not wanting to get too close to the works of art for fear of being scolded by a security guard. She looked down first at the open album that was on the far side of the table. At the top of the page was written the words, "Saigon 1968" and Bee immediately recognized a young and very chic Suzanne (who she thought could have been a doppelganger for the French actress Catherine Deneuve) in the first couple of photos. And then Bee saw her mother. Her mother dressed in a tiny mini skirt and what appeared to be go-go boots, her long blond hair in pigtails that made her look like Mary Ann from *Gilligan's Island,* a massive historic-looking building in the background. Her mother crouching in what appeared to be a trench, a Kodak Brownie around her neck, an almost haunted look on her face. Bee turned it over to read the words, *Khe Sanh, 1968.* Her mother and Suzanne, both dressed in evening gowns, their up-dos resembling a Marie Antoinette poof, each on the arm of a handsome soldier. This one read, *American Embassy bash, New Year's Eve, 1969.* And then she saw him. The man from the photo at the beach, at Da Nang. She instantly knew it was him. Her mother dressed in a white dress, a stylish white hat with a lace veil perched atop her head, he in a light suit, a stark contrast against his dark hair and tan features. She didn't need to turn it over to know what it would say.

"This is my father, isn't it?" Bee asked, holding the picture in her hand so Suzanne could see.

"Yes."

And Bee realized then why her entire life her mother had treated her as she had, why she had never held Bee close when she'd had a bad dream or skinned her knee, why she had never kissed her goodnight at bedtime or the sheer fact that there had never been a single photo of her father in the house. Bee looked exactly like him.

"All right my dear, sit," Suzanne said, pointing to the chair immediately next to hers as she got up and walked back with a handful of photographs that were in a clear plastic bag. "What did your mother tell you about your father? We'll start from there and begin the process of dispelling any of the lies, mistruths, and omissions of truths."

"That he was a Marine and that he had died in Vietnam before I was born," Bee dutifully answered, parroting what she had been told as a child by her mother at a very young age and then parroted herself to anyone who asked about her father.

"Hmm," Suzanne said. "Well, did you know you had an uncle?"

"What, on my dad's side?"

"No, your mother's."

"My mom always said she was an only child."

"Well, she was one after he was killed. In Vietnam. A fallen

Marine." Suzanne then reached into the baggie and pulled out an almost sepia toned photograph of a very young looking, clean shaven man sitting on a mound of sand bags, holding a rifle in his right hand, a row of palm trees in the background. She handed it to Bee who turned it over and read *Milton Baxter, Leatherneck Square, 1966.*

"I don't understand," Bee said. "Why keep something like this from me? Why keep a 'dead uncle' a secret from me? And why make what happened to this uncle the story about my actual father?"

"The first obligation of a good journalist is to tell the truth. And your mother always did that, the entire time she was in Vietnam. She was one of the best goddamned journalists I've ever known. And I mean that. But what happened over there, the loss your mother suffered, the never knowing, she stopped being a journalist and instead became an enemy to the truth. It was easier to block the truth out than remembering. Remembering even the good."

Neither woman spoke then; even the tough as nails Suzanne Quaglio fell silent. Not even she, it seemed, was immune to the memories that surfaced when seeing the past put in front of you.

"I saved these photos, you see," Suzanne quietly said. "Your mother planned to leave Saigon with nothing, with no memories of what had once been."

"Except me," Bee softly said, "the most painful memory of all that she couldn't get rid of."

"Yes," the other woman replied. "I had always hoped that one day we would meet, that you would track me down and I'd be able to give you these in person. Because for better or worse," she said, indicating the albums and photos before her, "this is your history and you deserve to know it."

Taking a deep breath then, Bee asked, "What was his name?"

"Vince. Vincent Cerny."

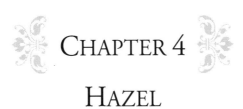

CHAPTER 4

HAZEL

April 1967

Today marked the second time that Hazel had pulled out her Rand McNally World Atlas. The first had been after receiving her brother Milton's letter from Vietnam, the one he had written to her shortly after arriving "in-country" as he called it. It had been rather brief (a writer he was not, unlike her), a few lines of his almost illegible text in which he wrote that "it was absolutely, physically, humanly possible to go from being completely dry to soaked in sweat in just a minute's time," that the noise was chaotic due to the constant taking off and landings of planes and choppers and nearby artillery fire, that everybody in his squad called him "newby," since had had just gotten there and "still had his cherry" and that from Da Nang he had flown to a place called Dong Ha.

Da Nang, Con Thien, Dong Ha, Khe Sanh. Hazel had remembered staring at these names on the map's pages, quietly saying them over and over to herself, as if somehow they would manifest before her. As if just like that, she would see what Milton was seeing, she would feel the intense heat he had described, and hear the deafening sound of all those planes and helicopters taking off. She would be transported to Vietnam just as he had been.

Quang Tri. She had pulled out her map again now to find just one place, one name that would forever haunt her. Barely two months after arriving over there, her brother was dead, killed in battle in "Operation Prairie III in the Quang Tri province, Republic of Vietnam."

The names of those places no longer sounded exotic to her. All she could think now was of the pain that emanated simply from seeing them in print and knowing what they represented for her family and every other family whose son or brother or husband or dad was killed in a place they couldn't even pronounce.

"I need you to stay with your mother, to move back here, I mean, and help out."

Hazel looked up to see her father standing in the doorway of her childhood bedroom, her fingers pausing in mid-air from the keys of her Remington typewriter she had just been using, the room suddenly falling silent without the clickety-clack sound of the keys.

"What do you mean 'move back here'?" she asked, not entirely sure what he was getting at.

"Move back home, pull your weight, help your mother, keep house. What you're supposed to be doing."

There it was, Hazel thought. Those words, "what you're supposed to be doing." As in, your predetermined destiny for the mere fact that she was a woman, not a man. That she didn't deserve an education beyond high school. That she should be long married by now, complete with a baby or two.

"I can't. You know I can't," she told him, saying this with a smile even though a deep pit was forming in her stomach. "I graduate next month. I'll have finals and besides, I have enough work now trying to play catchup with the extensions I've been given for my classes."

"I'm not asking."

Hazel was stunned. This she had not expected. And knew she would have to tread very carefully with what she said next. She could remind him that for the last three weeks she had in fact been "pulling her weight." For it was she, not him, who had done all the cooking and cleaning in the house, who had made sure her mother got a shower at least every other day, and who took her to Mass each morning at St. Paul's even though that was the last place she wanted to be. All of this while trying to finish papers and start studying for finals which were mere weeks away.

"And I'm not throwing away all that I've worked for the last four years," she said quietly with an air of determination but also defiance. But then as a conciliatory offering, she added, "After graduation I can move back here for a bit, but not before."

Her father looked at her with disgust written all over his face. "You're as worthless as that piece of paper you'll soon be getting," he told her before stomping off to the living room.

She turned her attention back to her typewriter then, but all thoughts of what she had been trying to say next in her comparative analysis paper of Albert Camus' *L'etranger* were quickly forgotten.

It was Milton who had pushed for her to go to college, to secretly apply for the scholarship at the University of Pittsburgh, and who had seen to it that she was properly drunk with the bottle of cheap champagne he had mysteriously acquired on the day she found she'd received a full ride.

"To my brain of a sister," he had said toasting her glass as they sat outside on the back steps of their Miller Avenue house, their mother long asleep, their father working the night shift that week in his job at Armco Steel. "May she not spend her entire time at Pitt with her nose in the books, but also learn a little bit about the opposite sex while she's at it too."

"Anything for research, eh brother dearest?"

"Absotivoli," he responded, laughing as he took another swig of champagne right from the bottle, his feet dangling off the edge. After she had told him that she wanted to study creative writing at Pitt, along with French, he had looked at her dead seriously and asked, "Tell me whatever you write will be as good and juicy as *Peyton Place*."

She laughed then, remembering how shocked she had been to find her younger brother reading Grace Metalious' scandalous novel, not even caring that he had clearly been snooping in her room to have discovered it in its hiding place, for it was a book that Hazel's mother would have absolutely forbidden her to read. And to date, that was the only book Hazel could ever remember her brother actually reading.

"You get it," Hazel said then, staring off into the distance. "You get that just because I'm a woman, that doesn't mean I'm only good enough for marriage and babies. I don't want to be like mom."

"Of course I do, Haze. I'm not book smart like you are, I can't stand school, but why do you think I want to join up once I graduate? I want my own chance to see the world and I'll get it through the military AND" he said, flashing her one of those famous megawatt smiles of his, "on Uncle Sam's dime too." He paused then before quietly adding, "You don't want to be mom and I sure as hell don't want to be dad, working at Armco like his dad did before him and his dad before him. Slaving away in those mills day in and day out and then getting drunk most nights at Pelliccione's."

"Well, just don't go getting yourself sent to Vietnam. From what I've read it sounds like it might be another Korea in the making," Hazel said, not wanting her little brother to go anywhere near Vietnam. She knew the world around them was drastically changing, that the old world was giving way to the new, that the age of empires and their fall flung colonies was a thing of the past, as evidenced by France's sound defeat in Vietnam in '54 and their ultimate withdrawal from Indochina. But Hazel also knew that the United States wasn't going to let another region of the world, even if it was one that was thousands of miles away from America's shores and had no bearing whatsoever on the lives of the American people, become part of the Communist wave.

"Well, there's your first problem sis, you read too much," Milton told her, ruffling her hair in a way that he had been doing since they were kids and was just as annoying. "And besides, how much do journalists really know?"

May 1967

As Hazel tried to focus on what the Chancellor was saying, she couldn't help but feel crushed that no one was here for her today. The first ever college graduate in her family and she was all alone, with no one there to support her, to congratulate her on her achievements, to tell her that they were proud. When she turned around in her wooden seat, she gazed at all of the guests in attendance- all of the moms and dads and brothers and sisters and grandparents whose smiling faces showed how immensely proud they were of their 1967 University of Pittsburgh graduate. Hazel's own parents were not in attendance. Ever since her fight with her dad the month before, he had basically said nothing to her the past few weeks and knew that had she reminded him of her commencement ceremony he might have very well told her to go to hell, her and her uppity, high class ways. Hazel's mom, well, Hazel didn't think she knew what day it was, not that it would have mattered to her anyway. Every time that Hazel was there at the house, her mom was numb, as if the Western Union telegram telling them of Milton's death had just come. And besides, Hazel's mom didn't drive.

Milton would have come if he were alive, been here for her sitting amongst the crowds, cheering her in a totally loud and brash way that would have undoubtedly elicited shocked looks from the audience when her name was called and she walked across that stage to get her diploma. If he were alive, Hazel knew he would have gotten her parents to come too, to help them see how truly proud they should be of their daughter who graduated Magna Cum Laude, majoring in both French and Creative Writing.

Hazel hadn't really been listening to what was being said to the graduates but then she clearly heard Chancellor Kurtzman say, "I challenge you to continue to show fresh and vigorous concern for the quality of American life."

The quality of American life. Hazel couldn't help but think, what did that **really** mean in 1967 if a 19-year old American boy is sent by his country to fight and die for another country on the other side of the world, one he most likely couldn't have found on a map, barely two months after getting there?

Hazel had grown up speaking some Ukrainian; her mom's parents were from the Old Country and they had never bothered to learn

English since everything they needed could be done or had within their rather large Ukrainian-speaking enclave of Lyndora, the town immediately next to Butler. As a child she had hated how backwards her grandparents seemed, especially her grandmother with the same headscarf she'd always wear tied under her chin that made her look so foreign, so un-American. But she did love when her grandmother would take Hazel with her to St. Michael's when she and all the other old ladies would make dozens upon dozens of *pierohi* for an upcoming wedding or funeral that was being held there. The other old ladies always loved when ten-year old Hazel would speak to them in her broken Ukrainian and then reward her with a slightly flawed but delicious doughy dumpling.

Hazel had never planned on majoring in French at Pitt. She had known from a young age that she wanted to be a journalist. When she was little she loved creating stories in a small black leather notebook she had bought at Woolworth's with her babysitting earnings. And in her senior year of high school, she had even been named editor of the school's paper, the *Skyliner*. It was the paper's advisor, Mr. Boyle, who had written Hazel a glowing recommendation for her application to Pitt. But from the first day of her French class in middle school, she had fallen in love with the French language. She had taken it all throughout high school and had been absolutely crushed when her dad told her she couldn't go with the French club on a school sponsored trip to Quebec City her spring break of junior year even though the club had raised funds so that out-of-pocket costs on the part of students and their families were minimal.

She could still remember him saying, "You're not leaving the country so you can come back and become a beatnik," to which Hazel had responded by yelling, "God, could you sound any more like you're from the last century!" to which Milton had started to laugh until their father shot him an icy stare and their mom started to wring her hands even more, so much that her knuckles were beginning to turn white.

It was her full scholarship to Pitt that meant her parents had zero say in what Hazel would study. It was the first time in her life that she'd had complete control over her future and when it came time to declaring her majors, she had happily written in Creative Writing AND French in the designated box. It was an insane amount of work, plus she worked a part-time job the entire time she was a student at Pitt, working as a hostess at the Park Schenley, but she was deciding her future, and not a future automatically being decided for her simply because of the life her parents had and the place where she'd grown up.

When her French advisor had recommended she study abroad, Hazel had politely demurred, knowing that there was no way possible she could do that with her Creative Writing major requirements and still graduate within four years, a prerequisite of her scholarship. But then he had mentioned a "summer abroad," six weeks spent studying at the Sorbonne, one of Europe's oldest and most prestigious universities. Pitt would cover the costs of tuition and room and board while she was there; she'd have to cover everything else including the cost of a plane ticket. But she had done it- the years she had spent babysitting and working as a waitress at Woolworth's lunch counter on weekends and summers throughout high school, gave her the money to get her ticket even if it had meant nearly draining her bank account.

In her time at Pitt, Hazel had felt she had been undergoing an internal transformation, each day shedding more of her small-town roots and becoming more the worldly sophisticate she aspired to be one day. But the moment she stepped through the doors of the Pan Am Terminal at New York's JFK Airport and saw the cadre of Pan

Am stewardesses dressed in their beautifully tailored blue jackets and skirts, their trademark pillbox hats resting on their heads at just the right angle, Hazel thought to herself "that could be me." They were all young women just like her and perhaps many came from a small town just like her too. It wasn't that Hazel wanted to be a stewardess, but she wanted to go out and see the world.

The six weeks she spent in Paris had truly been magical for Hazel. Her classes had been rigorous and at times exhausting but she had thrived in her new environment, far away from the societal demands and restricting confines that were placed upon girls her age, ones Hazel felt were more than 50 years outdated. When she was not hunched over her books studying, either in her closet-size garret that she rented in the city's 5th *arrondissement* or the Sorbonne's *bibliothèque* which reminded her a little of the ground floor of Pitt's Cathedral of Learning, Hazel would walk the streets of different *arrondissements*, sometimes for hours at a time, periodically stopping at a random street café for either a café au lait and croissant or a glass of *vin rouge* and some olives, depending on the time of her strolls. The only time Hazel communicated in English was when she wrote her two weekly letters home, the obligatory one to her parents (but really her mom since Hazel highly doubted her dad cared to hear from her), and to Milton, where she was a lot more forthcoming with things she wanted to share. Otherwise, she was living her life entirely in French.

The day before she was to fly home, Hazel made a sojourn to Ernest Hemingway's first apartment in Paris, the one he had lived in as a struggling 22-year old writer with his first wife Hadley after arriving in the French capital, wanting to leave his stolid and uninspiring American upbringing behind. Standing outside 74 rue Cardinal Lemoine, a copy of his *A Moveable Feast* tucked under her arm, Hazel looked up at the building and wondered if she too would ever become "someone" one day like Hemingway had become, a name spoken on the lips of people of all ages. She didn't know if she wanted that kind of popularity and success but she did know this. She was meant to be out there in the world, the new world order that was seeing the dismantling of centuries' old colonial empires and the election of the country's first Catholic president. This new world was drastically changing and transforming with each passing year and Hazel Baxter wanted to be a part of it.

"Today's Vietnam story in a moment."

Hazel glanced up at the mention of the word Vietnam coming through the television set, as if Walter Cronkite was saying it directly to Hazel and her dad, and not also to millions of other American homes across the country who just like them were tuning in for their nightly "nation building" report, but for a nation they knew nothing about except what the politicians and now journalists were telling them.

And then they and all the other homes across America at that moment were there in Vietnam. The correspondent's voice cut in saying that "the Marine scout detail had been sent out to look for North Vietnamese encampments." She watched with rapt attention as it showed the leader talking to his men and then the camera panning out with them going up a dense wooded hill. Even from as far away as Butler, Pennsylvania, Hazel could hear the sound of machine gun fire off in the distance emanating from the television screen. She wondered if this was what Milton had experienced, what, on a weekly basis? A daily basis? Did he ever have a moment there where he wasn't hearing gunfire, knowing that those shots were intended for him and every other American boy fighting there?

The film took a chaotic turn, the camera whipping up and down, Hazel not sure what had happened until her dad said, still looking directly at the television screen, "mortars," as if she knew just what that was. But once the camera had righted again, it panned in on a young Marine, making her heart stop. For even though he had blond hair and blue eyes, he looked to be no more than 18 or 19, his eyes, as he turned looking right into the camera, showing exhaustion and an almost eerie hollowness to them. Is that how Milton looked over there she wanted to ask her dad. She had thought him incredibly brave to enlist, especially in the Marines, knowing without a doubt that's where he would be sent. But "in-country" as he had always called Vietnam in his letters to her, had Milton been as incredibly scared and afraid as the young boy did in the camera shot just shown?

"They're doing a good job, those boys over there. Making this country damn proud," Hazel's dad said as he took a swig of his Iron City beer, his eyes never straying from the television screen.

Things like that we're all that Hazel's dad said to her anymore. Nothing to do with her, but all about "those boys over there." And Hazel wondered how many of "those boys" that she saw each night on camera would come home on their own, or come home in a body bag like Milton had, or not come home at all for there was nothing corporeal to bring home.

Since graduation, Hazel had gotten some per diem assignments at the *Butler Eagle*, but almost always on topics related to "women's things." It's as if her experience being the editor of her high school newspaper, her four years of writing for the *Pitt News,* and the fact that she had graduated magna cum laude with a degree in Creative Writing, didn't count for anything. That only her gender did, which meant she was only qualified to write on areas that she would "personally" know about as a female, never mind that she had never gardened a day in her life, or was the worst housekeeper and most subpar cook in recent history. What else could she possibly know about outside of those feminine realms?

"They give me absolutely nothing of merit to write about," Hazel dejectedly told Betty, her friend since childhood, as they sat at Betty's kitchen table, utter quiet now since Betty's three children had finally gone down for a nap. "I'm capable of so much more than that. I mean when I was at Pitt, I interviewed students who went on Freedom Rides down south, I made the front page when Dr. King came to campus and spoke in '66. But to the *Eagle,* I can write cleaning columns and the next big wedding recap."

"What is it that you want to write?" Betty asked her.

Hazel had always thought it a shame that Betty had never gone to college. She was so intelligent and curious, not in a nebby way but rather that she had an insatiable desire to learn. But she had gotten pregnant a few months before their high school graduation and Hazel silently thought, her fate was sealed shortly after, what with marrying her high school boyfriend and then having two more babies over the next three years. Hazel had never cared for Betty's husband John, though they had all known each other since they were kids. He reminded Hazel too much of her dad, which was made all the worse since he was at least 20 years younger. But in John's outdated societal ideology, the job of his wife was to keep house and mind the children, not to have a job, education, or even her own personal views (on matters she knew "nothing about").

Without even thinking, she answered, "The war. Vietnam. What it's like over there."

With a slightly mischievous yet encouraging look in her eyes, Betty said, "Then find a way to go. And let me see your name in print," as she squeezed Hazel's hand.

CHAPTER 5

HAZEL

November 1967

It was the heat that struck Hazel first, literally and figuratively. Upon exiting the lush, cool interior of the Pan American 747 that had carried her across the wide and open Pacific, making stops in Honolulu, Guam, Manila, and finally Saigon, an exhausting journey that had taken more than a day, she squinted up at the fierce sun and couldn't believe that she was really here, here in Vietnam, on the other side of the freaking world. Of course only moments before she'd had this same sensation (only a lot more jarring) when the aircraft had more or less nosedived straight onto the runway. She had gripped her armrest as if her life depended on it and had even heard some people throwing up in one of the other rows. It was only when a deep, baritone voice arose from the row adjacent to hers that Hazel's thoughts of imminent death momentarily were forgotten about.

"Don't worry, they do that on purpose, the deep diving I mean," the man told her, giving her a warm smile. "They do it to avoid any possible fire from below. After a couple of years flying into Tan Son

Nhut, they're more or less pros at it. Nothing to worry about," he said as he returned to collecting his papers, like it was the most natural thing for a plane to dive into the tarmac upon landing. Hazel was still too shaken from the plane's planned nosedive that she hadn't even bothered to get a good look at the man who had succeeded in at least temporarily distracting her.

The smells came next. As she started to sweat profusely through her coral colored mini dress, waiting to descend the steps onto the runway, her nose was immediately assaulted by a foul and almost abrasive smell. She could detect motor oil and gasoline fumes, but there was something else she was smelling, something rancid almost. Was that fish?

"You get used to it," a voice said from behind. As Hazel whipped around to see who had said it, her heel twisted. She was about to lose her balance entirely on the steps of the plane, perhaps even causing a literal human domino effect with the bodies in front of her, when a hand reached out and caught her around her waist, more or less pulling her back up against him. Steadying her, Hazel looked up to see that her hero was the man from the adjacent row.

"Okay?" he asked, looking directly into her eyes.

"Um, yes, thank you," Hazel said looking down at the man's shoes instead, embarrassed to have been such a klutz but then realizing he still had his arm around her waist and back which was undoubtedly soaked through with sweat. The line started to move then and the man dropped his arm from Hazel's waist while she made a concentrated effort to focus on her steps, lest she embarrass herself a second time and really seem like she didn't belong here.

"First time here I'm guessing?" the man asked, suddenly appearing at her side.

"Is it that obvious?" Hazel answered with a nervous smile.

"Yes," saying this so quickly they both laughed. "I'm Vince," he said, extending his hand towards hers.

"Hazel." It was then that Hazel studied the man. On the plane she had thought him to be someone in his late 30s, maybe even 40s but now upon closer examination, she could see he must be around 30. He had dark hair, almost black, and was incredibly tan. There were bags under his eyes, age lines too, which is why Hazel had thought he was older than he was but up close to him, she could see he wasn't that much older than her.

"So what brings you to the Pearl of the Orient, or former, I should say," he asked, looking so intently at her she was almost unnerved.

"Um, I'm a journalist. I want to cover the war," a line she had rehearsed in her head countless times yet upon delivery of it, she knew she must sound like the equivalent of a child playing dress up with her dolls. She wanted to say, "I'm going to cover the war," but right now that was entirely uncertain.

"Are you here for a newspaper?"

"A freelancer," she answered timidly. "But I don't know if I'll be able to stay."

"Why's that?" he asked.

"You need three news organizations vouching that you'll be writing for them. I was only able to get two," she told him, her voice fraught with a defeatist air. "So as of right now, this is more of a vacation than a job. I can only stay here without a visa for less than seven days."

"And you came all this way anyway, knowing that if you don't get a third, you're FUBARRED?"

"Excuse me?" Hazel said, no idea what fubarred meant.

"Fucked up beyond all repair," he said, laughing at her semi-shocked face, "more or less."

Hazel paused then, letting the enormity of what this man, this stranger, had just said really sink in. She had traveled halfway around the world by herself, using up the bulk of her savings to purchase her plane ticket, on the off-chance she'd be able to become a reporter here. Not to mention the unspoken understanding that in doing so, she had perhaps permanently severed any last tie to her dad, no matter how tenuous it was.

"Yes, I guess I did," she said, suddenly at that moment feeling older and very much wiser than her 22 years.

"Well, here's the thing. Everyone who comes here on a 'whim' as you did, they all think they can write, that they can tell the award-winning story that people back home will salivate over and talk about for years to come. But what matters is what sets YOU apart, what makes you different from all the rest."

"I speak French…fluently," she said, adding the fluent part as she didn't want him to think she was embellishing her language skills.

"And that there is your ticket to 'Nam," he told her.

It was only later over a meal of frog's legs and Chablis at the Caravelle's rooftop bar, did Hazel learn that Vince himself was a journalist, and as her idol Ernest Hemingway would say, "a damn fine one" judging by the fact that he served as the *Washington Dispatch's* Saigon bureau chief.

"Don't look too impressed," Vince told her laughingly as he licked his fingers clean of the cream oozing out of the miniature éclair he had just eaten. "I only got the promotion a few months ago. Not to mention, it's probably wise not to ask HOW I got it either."

"Yeah, but you were still a correspondent for the *Washington Dispatch*," Hazel said, the last two words uttered with reverence, something she did for any big name newspaper she dreamt of writing for one day. "And you're so young!" she added, her voice taking on a higher pitch, an effect of perhaps too much Chablis and too many time zones crossed while getting here. She wondered what time it was back home, back in Butler, and what her parents were doing at that very moment as here she sat with a man, a stranger really, in the capital of South Vietnam.

"How old do you think I am?" he asked her, sitting back in his wicker chair as if he were appraising her.

She studied him then just as she had done hours earlier on the tarmac at Tan Son Nhut. God, was that really just hours ago? She thought she'd pass out from sheer exhaustion but then the sights and sounds of Saigon would give her a new jolt of energy, just what she needed to keep going for every sight and sound was entirely new to her, one hundred percent exotically different from anything she had ever known, let alone imagined. And, of course, the fact that she was sitting across from a very handsome gentleman also didn't hurt.

"30?"

He smirked then in a way that were anyone else doing it would have annoyed Hazel, but on him she found it endearing.

"36 actually. So, still think I'm some boy wonder?" he asked, in earnest now she thought with almost a trace of sadness. He paused then before saying, "I'm no boy wonder. At the end of every long and mentally exhausting day here, I'm still just a reporter wanting to give the readers back home the honest story of what's really going on. Spend one week here and you know what you see and come across, is not what the people back home are seeing."

She said nothing, the lighthearted tone from just moments before seemingly vanishing into the hot and humid night air.

"So tomorrow I'll take you to see Ann, Ann Bryan. She runs the bureau of *Overseas Weekly*, the Pacific edition I mean," he said as he picked up his tiny espresso cup and gulped it down in one sip, oblivious to the fact that he was drinking a hot, steaming beverage in 90 degree weather.

"Ann Bryan?" Hazel asked, hoping to sound casual and not appear completely ignorant as to who this Ann Bryan was, especially since Vince spoke about this *Overseas Weekly* as if it were a publication she should already be familiar with. She took a sip of her own espresso then, burning her tongue in the process.

He studied her again now, that serious look coming across his face once more which seemed contrary to the man he seemed to be most of the time, Hazel thought. "Oh sorry, I keep forgetting you've literally just got here and weren't coming back from an R & R stint."

"R and R?" Hazel asked, knowing now she did sound completely ignorant but she didn't want to feign understanding something she hadn't the faintest idea about, especially if it was something illegal or worse.

He smiled at her then as if she were the most adorable child he had ever seen. "*Overseas Weekly*, well, it's no *Washington Dispatch*," he said, making them both laugh, "but Ann Bryan's a solid reporter and writing for it, well, it's a way to get your foot in the door even if their approach to journalism is more on the muckraking side. But seriously though, it could be your ticket to obtaining your MACV ID."

Before she could even ask what MACV stood for, he replied, "military assistance command in Vietnam."

"Thank you," she said quietly, hungry to hear more.

"No joke, you don't have a MACV ID here, you might as well go home," he told her seriously. "It's what gets you into the daily briefings, rides in helicopters, well, essentially the 'right' to go into battle with the soldiers. Without it you're-"

She cut him off then and said, "FUBARRED?" laughing as she said it.

"Frenchie, you're one quick learner," making them both laugh and Hazel feeling a warmth in her stomach at him calling her 'Frenchie.' As if they had known each other for years and hadn't just met earlier as strangers on a plane whose runway was riddled with the daily remnants of enemy fire. "But back to Ann. It's basically a military paper but one that the brass doesn't write or put out. *The Stars and the Stripes,* that's 100% controlled by the military brass. *Overseas Weekly,* it's a paper for the servicemen stationed here. Ann and her writers, they're committed to telling the truth about what's really going on here and *The Stars and Stripes* sure as hell doesn't do that, they tell whatever will keep Johnson and the top brass back home the happiest about their 'stop Communism' dead in their tracks campaign and that the US of A is valiantly helping the 'yellow man' in his fight against evil."

There he was again, saying things like "what's really going on here." What did he mean by that, Hazel wondered? Newspapers always told the truth so why was he acting like the stories they printed about the war weren't factual?

"Just as much as Ann's a great journalist, she's also a highly formidable opponent. She went up against McNamara and won."

"Wait, the McNamara as in Secretary of Defense McNamara?"

"The very same."

"Why? How? Over what?" Hazel sputtered in disbelief.

"When the Pacific edition of *Overseas Weekly* first came out, it wasn't allowed to be printed in Vietnam, let alone sold on the streets or in military PXs. Ann always thought that McNamara personally hated it. They sought permission to have it printed but kept being denied. I mean Ann even rented a facility in Hong Kong to print it, then had it FLOWN back to here and then sold. But officials caught on, and the Vietnamese, always happy to do Uncle Sam's bidding, they started meeting the planes from Hong Kong right at Tan Son Nhut and getting rid of the papers."

"So what happened next?" Hazel asked, eager to hear more, almost as if she was being caught up on the latest episode of *Guiding*

Light.

"They filed a lawsuit against McNamara last year in the District Court. They lost- "

He stopped upon seeing Hazel's eyes widen. She loudly exclaimed, "I can't work for some illegal, underground paper in Vietnam. I'll be thrown in jail and God, my father really would never speak to me again," saying the two things as if they were mutually exclusive and equally horrific.

"At the district level," Vince said, glossing over Hazel's outburst, "but won at the appellate level just last month. You always this impetuous?" he said, asking the last part with a wry smile.

Ignoring his barb she asked, "So everything's kosher now?" Hazel said, using a phrase she had first learned from a Jewish classmate of hers at Pitt, one that she loved and had quickly adopted herself.

He looked quizzically at her for a moment as if she had just uttered the craziest thing ever but then laughed, "One hundred percent hot dog kosher." He paused then before adding, "But seriously, the win was huge. Not just for the paper but for First Amendment cases everywhere. A tabloid pape started by a woman took on the Pentagon and won, if you can believe it. And now it's distributed and sold all throughout Asia. And besides, unless you're here and you see what's really going on day in and day out, I don't think anyone can grasp the significance of the win. Journalists the victors in court, and for once not the military brass."

Just then a flash in the distance caught Hazel's attention. "Is there some sort of local festival going on tonight?" Hazel asked, her eyes mesmerized by the visual light parade off in the distance.

"There's a steep learning curve here for anyone who comes but you won't last a day out there if you think fighter planes dropping flares onto enemy ground are friendly fireworks," Vince said, his tone entirely flat and devoid of any feeling. "You know you're in the middle of a war, right? That this isn't some game. For the Vietnamese, for the soldiers, hell, even for us sometimes, it's a matter of life and death out there," he said, waving his arms to indicate the country.

Hazel felt chagrined then, mentally berating herself for being so stupid, for sounding so utterly naïve and green. She hadn't thought she was. All this time she thought she was so worldly, so brave, so daring for getting on a plane by herself and flying to the other side of the world, into a war zone, when really she was nothing more than a schoolgirl with a steno pad.

There was silence between them then, only the sound of muffled conversations at nearby tables and the occasional boom off in the distance. Was stuff being blown up deliberately, she wondered? She kept her gaze averted from him so he wouldn't see the tears that had started to pool in her eyes. She didn't need a "hysterical woman" being added to her list of naïve faults tonight.

"It's no 'make believe' out there," he said, his tone softer and kinder now. "Hey," he said, leaning across the table and gently cupping her face in his hand so that she would have to look at him. "I'm sorry, I didn't mean to be so—"

"No, you're right," she said cutting him off, quickly wiping at her eyes. "If I'm going to make it here," pausing before adding "successfully," almost as if it were an afterthought, "my school girl innocence and naiveté needs to be shed tonight."

"Just don't go shedding all of it too soon," he told her.

"Why's that?" she asked, not understanding his meaning.

"Your schoolgirl innocence look. It's kinda cute."

Hazel wasn't sure if Vince had been flirting with her or not because when he said she could spend the night with him in his suite at the

Caravelle, she swore her mouth dropped wide open. But then he added that she could have the bed and he'd take the sofa in the other room and knew that he hadn't been flirting, he had merely been trying to buck her spirits up and probably watch out for her too, especially when she learned that rooms there cost $80 a night and without saying or asking, knew that she couldn't have afforded to stay there on her own. But she was okay with that. She hadn't come to Vietnam for love or romance or even a one night stand. Hazel had admittedly not given any thought as to where she would stay once she got here and so was just happy for the offer of his bed, at least for her first night in-country as Milton would have said. If she didn't succeed in getting her MACV ID, well, she'd spend the rest of the week she was allotted to be here pretending she was a character in a Graham Greene novel and go home with one helluva story. Namely that she slept in the very good looking *Dispatch* Saigon bureau chief's bed.

CHAPTER 6

HAZEL

November 1967

"When a woman comes to Vietnam to cover the war, she's called a 'girl reporter.' When a man comes here, he's just called a reporter. I want to change that."

Hazel liked Ann Bryan, a lot. In the short time she had known her, she could tell that Ann was very good at keeping up "with the boys." She didn't know if it was the older woman's red hair or her impressive height, or her clearly no-nonsense approach to journalism, but she was clearly the boss here, a female boss in a wholly male dominated war zone.

"When I first got here," Ann continued, "I did it all- reporting, taking pictures, editing, handling circulation, PR, even playing the role of the errant copy boy, anything to get the Pacific edition of the *Overseas Weekly* up and running. I'm not saying this to brag or make myself seem any more important than anyone else here. But it's more to show every single man who feels that 'we don't belong here,' that we do. It's a war zone, but so what? My mission is solely to give our troops a voice without fear of being punished for doing so. I want us to write for the soldiers in their own language, not the language of politicians and top military brass, the same people who at the end of the day, don't really give a damn about your average draftee or enlisted man here like they should, the ones **they're** sending **here**."

It was at that moment in the Newsweek Villa, in the office that the *Overseas Weekly* rented and shared with the *Washington Post,* that made Hazel think of something she had read recently in an op-ed piece against the war, a line once spoken by Herbert Hoover, the former president whose legacy would be forever and infamously linked to the Great Depression- "Older men declare war, but it is youth that must fight and die." It wasn't men her father's age or even older fighting the elusive enemy in jungle warfare, no, it was young boys like her brother Milton, barely out of high school, who were fighting an elusive enemy in what seemed to be unforgiving terrain, and who died before ever having had the chance to really live.

"And then those same idiot buffoons, namely a certain chauvinist four-star general tried to get us barred from the front line."

"I'm sorry, say again?" Hazel asked Ann, worried she had been lost in her thoughts longer than she had thought and would make a bad impression and most naggingly, not get the highly coveted MACV ID she so desperately needed.

"I keep forgetting you literally just got here...yesterday," Ann said to Hazel, smiling. "Not to mention, I have no doubt that Westmoreland's attempt to bar female journalists from reporting on the front-lines didn't necessarily make the hometown papers."

"So what happened? I mean, you said 'tried' which is past tense which to me means it failed, didn't succeed." Hazel asked this with unabashed curiosity, one step shy of idolizing the woman before her, the woman who also seemed like a force to be reckoned with.

"Failed they did," Ann said with a smirk. "Basically, Westmoreland being the antiquated relic that he is, was afraid that us women would inconvenience or endanger soldiers who would rush to our sides to protect us when we became scared at the sound of mortar fire or the sight of enemy soldiers."

"But that's ridiculous," Hazel responded indignantly. "Every female reporter out there is where she is because she wants to be there, not because she was made to."

"You're a quick study. And then the absolute kicker, and confirmation that the male sex really does not have much in the way of smarts, was his compromise edict."

"Which was?" Hazel asked, wondering why the older woman had taken now of all times to pause.

"Which was banning us 'gal reporters' from spending nights with troops in the field, which more or less meant that a commander had to guarantee that any female reporter would travel to and from a battle in a single day."

"Wouldn't that be impossible?" Hazel asked incredulously. "I mean in the thick of a battle wouldn't a commander have more pressing needs than ensuring transportation back to Saigon by 7?"

"Absolutely, positively, one hundred percent freaking impossible," Ann said, words that Hazel assumed she must have uttered countless times before. "He thought we'd be too distracting in the field among his soldiers if we stayed the night or longer with them, encamping amongst them, but if there's a mechanical issue with that helo that was supposed to take you back that night or enemy fire was too thick to take off without being shot down, no, that wouldn't prove distracting at all for the men who have to arrange those 'minor' details," Ann said, her tone oozing with sarcasm over the word minor.

"And for the second time in less than a year, I found myself going up against the Pentagon, this time with all the other female journalists here. We were all strangers to each other, but we had these two things in common—we were women, and we were journalists. And our livelihoods, our hearts and souls were here in this very place. And no man, especially someone who wasn't even a journalist, wasn't going to tell us that we didn't belong here."

Silence filled the room then. The cacophonous sounds of life remained outside the villa's wall, a reminder to all how Saigon's population was exploding in such a way that it couldn't possibly keep up with the influx of refugees who were fleeing the countryside and pouring into the capital and the steady arrival of more American troops.

"The ban was lifted for the mere fact that it was unsustainable. There's no such thing as a 'good day' here in Vietnam as you'll come to find, so when you have more bad than good ones, you can't ask for the impossible to happen. But MACV officials, always eager to do the Pentagon's bidding, well, they did add a stipulation to show Westmoreland and his cronies that they took his concerns seriously, the one on how us damsels could prove a liability for the fightin' men. Every female journalist here, whether she's a resident or just here temporarily, signs a letter to any new female journalist working here, to 'not place the burden on the field commanders on whether it's safe for the girls to stay overnight in battlefields.' Basically, we have to promise we're not going to ask for special treatment or protection."

"We don't ask for anything that the male journalists wouldn't," Hazel said, oblivious to the fact that she had used the pronoun 'we' to describe Vietnam's female journalists and thus was including herself in this group, feeling like she already belonged amongst this cadre of adventurous spirits who were dedicated to reporting the truth.

"Bingo," Ann said, her eyes returning to the papers on her desk. "So Vince told me on the phone that you've got two news orgs vouching for you, but you still need a third."

"Yes, um the *Pittsburgh Catholic* and the *Butler Eagle*, that's my hometown paper. I've written for them a bit over the years, more in the way of—," Hazel trailed off, feeling at that moment incredibly inadequate next to Ann, who was by all accounts a seasoned and clearly respected journalist, not to mention a female warrior.

"Ladies' topics?" Ann said, smiling as she did. "Housekeeping, child rearing, cotillions, how to get that nuisance spot out of your husband's best dress shirt before dinner at the boss's house?"

"It all feels so trivial," Hazel said, "so inconsequential," the words echoing around in her head that nothing she ever did would really matter.

"It is, but it's not your fault," Ann told her. "At all. You're a product of the times, which is something entirely out of your control. But you took control simply by coming here. And the good thing is this war is changing everything—a war with no frontline, a war waged from helicopters, a war where women are reporting right alongside the men and where the words that we write and the photographs that we take are just as good if not better than the men's. It's a war where we're finally mattering in terms of us showing it to the world through our work."

In the very brief time that she'd been here, Hazel already felt like she was getting an education richer and more complete than what any of her classes at Pitt had taught her.

"We don't do breaking news stories for the sheer fact that we can't compete with the wire services. But what we do is this. We write about the impact of the fighting on the soldiers, whether it's in the form of that week's court martials at Long Binh, flying on a medevac mission, interviewing someone from the Psyops group-"

Seeing Hazel's confused look, Ann clarified, "Psyops group, the army's psychological operations. Basically it's their job to win the hearts and minds of the VC."

"And are they?" Hazel asked, as if she were conducting an interview, already on the clock.

"Spend one night in the field with the men and you'll have your answer. The U.S. is treating the VC as if they are another Germany, that in time they'll have another victorious 1918 and 1945 on their hands. But while they wage their futile war of attrition against the enemy, the enemy is waging guerrilla warfare, which is a type of warfare as foreign to us as the Vietnamese language. The Vietnamese spent almost a decade fighting the French. A decade, can you even imagine? They didn't tear off the yoke of one colonial oppressor only to be replaced by a new one. Because that's how they see us. Everyone who honestly believes we're winning the war here, we're winning over the hearts and minds of the North Vietnamese people, one hundred percent underestimates the nationalist fervor, the desire for Vietnam to be completely free from the West, their complete will to fight and never give up."

If anyone back home delivered the impassioned speech that Ann just had, the person would have been called a defeatist, an anti-American even. But Hazel knew that was not the case. When you say something like that here in Vietnam, you're just speaking the truth.

"Still interested?" Ann asked Hazel.

"Yes."

"Then I'll be your third. Welcome to Vietnam."

And just like that, Hazel Baxter was here to stay.

As she left the Newsweek Villa it dawned on Hazel that she had no idea where she was going, let alone how to get back to the Caravelle where her suitcases were. When Vince had dropped her off at the Villa over an hour ago, he hadn't said anything about meeting up and she hadn't thought to ask, too physically exhausted from jet lag, too mentally nervous over her meeting with Ann. Were it not for the fact that everything she owned was locked in his suite at this very moment, she would have taken this as a sign that he considered his duty towards the naïve, inexperienced young American girl complete. It wasn't as if he owed her anything; on the contrary. Hazel thought she would be forever indebted to him for all he had done for her over the last 24 hours.

Hazel decided perhaps she should wander for a bit, taking in the sights and sounds of Saigon as she had once done in Paris on her daily afternoon walks through the different *arrondissements*. She had barely been here but she already knew that cheap wine was plentiful. Perhaps she could fine a nearby café and nurse a glass of *vin rouge* while writing down her thoughts in her journal. But then she stopped herself. This wasn't Paris. This was Vietnam. And its people were at war.

But then she spotted the church across the street. She started to step off the curb only to have the jarring sound of horns emanating from a cluster of advancing motorbikes, making her jump back in fright, her heart pounding furiously over what had almost just happened. God, wouldn't that just be the kicker if she too fell in Vietnam, but not from a downed helicopter or enemy fire, no, simply from crossing the street.

"First rule of thumb here," a deep voice said from behind, one that she immediately recognized. "Never think they'll stop for you."

Hazel whirled around to see Vince standing there, a look of amusement on his face. Or was it concern. She wasn't entirely sure.

"And second rule of thumb. You get hit, don't think they'll stop, get off their bike and help you. They won't."

"I wasn't sure if I'd see you again," Hazel stammered, her heart still pounding a bit erratically although she wasn't sure if it was from her near-death experience moments before or the sight of Vince again.

"Why'd you think that?" he asked, slightly bemused.

"Well, you never said where I should meet you, or a time or…" Hazel's voice trailed off then, realizing how needy she must sound, not to mention quasi-possessive, the latter which she had absolutely no right to be.

"Yeah, I'm sorry about that. I was meeting a source at the Continental and they were late in meeting me. Otherwise, we would have rendezvoused perfectly after your meeting with Ann. Which by the way, how'd it go?"

We. That one simple word that made Hazel's mouth go dry. Like they were a unit, a couple. She didn't understand how she could feel this way about someone she had just met, someone she knew hardly anything about. Was this what it meant to fall for someone at first sight?

"Um, good. She's taking me on, so I'll be writing for *Overseas Weekly* too. So I can stay."

I can stay. Three simple words that validated the feeling that she actually belonged here.

"I know you must be busy and all, but I was wondering if you could tell me how to get to the post office? I was hoping to send a cable home, letting them know I arrived safely."

"Sure. We can do that and then we'll get your MACV ID."

"Oh you don't have to do that. I mean, you must be busy, have work to do, not be my-"

"Guardian angel?" he interjected. "Maybe I want to be, Frenchie. I do seem to keep having this uncanny ability to appear just when you need me the most."

Hazel wasn't sure if he was joking or being serious; she just stared at him dumbly.

"Don't worry, Frenchie. I actually got back to 'Nam a few days earlier, before my leave was up. So my time is my time."

"But why help me? I mean, I'm not the only newly arrived journalist who's green around the edges."

"Because I can tell you're no buck private."

"A what?" Hazel asked, laughing at what he had just called her.

"You're an honest to goodness private first class."

Hazel's mouth went dry. Private First Class Milton Baxter. That one she knew.

"Hey, you okay?" Vince asked her, concerned. "You took on a thousand-yard stare just now."

"Yes, of course. Just thought of something, that's all," Hazel said, hoping she sounded convincing.

He didn't look convinced. At all. But all he said was, "And because I like you."

Hazel was stunned. Had she heard him correctly? Had he really just said he liked her? Liked her as a woman? As a friend? Which one was it? Should she say something back to him? That she liked him too? She was dying to ask which was it, but not wanting to sound like a girl with her first school-yard crush, instead she asked, "Can we actually go in that church first?"

"I'm not quite sure what I was expecting but it wasn't this," Hazel said as she and Vince sat at a small café, drinking cups of strong black coffee and sharing a couple of semi-stale but still flaky croissants. After she had successfully obtained her MACV ID, he had spent the rest of the morning giving her a tour of District 1, which she learned had once been the heart of the French colonial world here in Saigon. If you looked beyond the never-ending dust and fumes that were virtually impossible to not inhale from the glut of ancient buses with their faded blue paint and French lettering on the side, reminders of a bygone era, and of course, the military jeeps which seemed to clog every inch of road space there was in an already too congested city, Hazel could imagine closing her eyes and picturing how it once must have looked. The glittering fashions from *La Belle Époque* on display at the newly built Opera House, a scene straight from a Toulouse-Lautrec painting. The timeless elegance of a building like the Central Post Office which, were it not for its bright yellow ochre façade, could have easily been found on the streets of Paris. But that, of course, was what the Empire had wanted, what all colonial empires throughout the world, throughout time, had always wanted—to bring a taste of "home" to a place that never really belonged to them.

"What's 'this'?" Vince asked curiously.

"There's a war going on in a country that's been divided for years, and yet here I am sipping a café, munching on a croissant, albeit a stale one, with a handsome man to boot."

"So you think I'm handsome?" Vince asked, flashing her one of those mischievous but also incredibly captivating stares.

"You know what I mean," Hazel retorted, lowering her gaze so he wouldn't see her crimson cheeks.

"Yes I do. But first things first. The café and croissant are as common here as a donut and cup of joe back home. The French ruled here for decades and a lot of French came over and stayed. So you'll find in no time that French food here is nothing overly exotic or luxurious, it's just prevalent. And often a safer bet than what you'll find on the streets, not that I advise partaking there. Besides, not a lot of Americans know of this place. And I hope it stays that way. Yeah, the war's still out there, but not in here, not when it's just French and maybe a Western-educated Vietnamese person or two."

"Yet you took me here," Hazel said softly.

He stared at her so intently for a moment that Hazel couldn't look away. But then the moment was broken when he laughed and said, "Yeah, but you speak French. Oh, here's Jeanne, the owner," he said, looking to the back where a tiny, gray haired woman now appeared. "Prepare to impress me, Frenchie."

Five minutes after Hazel and Jeanne's conversation, the latter firing away in rapid-fire French in what sounded like a *Marseillais* dialect to Hazel, as she noticed the endings of words were often dropped, all the while Hazel struggling to keep up and appear intelligent, Vince smiled at her and made the motion of tipping an imaginary hat atop his head towards her.

"What?" Hazel asked, blushing.

"You know what, Frenchie. I meet a lot of people who say they can speak another language and really can't speak a fig of it. You really can. Color me impressed."

"Yeah, but you don't speak French. And besides, Jeanne did most of the talking."

"I know body language, any good journalist does. And I could tell you weren't feigning anything in terms of understanding what she was saying. And besides, you know what she whispered into my ear?"

"No, what?" Hazel asked, slightly nervous.

"She said, 'she eez good.' And you know something? I'm inclined to agree with the old Madame."

"I hate to ask, after all you've already done for me, but do you know of any leads on housing? I just…" Hazel trailed off, feelings of anxiety and shyness suddenly overwhelming her. "I just wouldn't have the faintest idea on where to look."

"Are you finding your current accommodations not up to snuff?"

Vince asked jokingly. "I mean, I know *les rats* are hardly the most agreeable of roommates."

This made her laugh then, his utterly ridiculous and overexaggerated French accent. Although the rats were not a joking matter. In the two days she had been here, Hazel had seen more rats than she had in her entire life. Ones so large, their bellies so distended, they looked the stuff of nightmares. And they were everywhere, running along the streets, combing through the mounds of garbage that littered the sidewalks, even in the hallways of the Caravelle, Saigon's most modern and Westernized hotel. Their scurrying noise, especially when there was a gaggle of them, never failed to send a shiver down Hazel's back.

"Tell me this, Frenchie," Vince began. "What did you think was going to happen when you got here?"

"I never thought I'd make it this far," Hazel said honestly. "I thought I'd get here and they'd take one look at me and call me an imposter, tell me that I didn't belong here, that I was just a kid. That they'd echo every sentiment my dad ever thought about me. That I should stop trying to be someone I wasn't."

"Which is?" Vince asked her.

"A woman trying to make it in a man's world."

"So I take it he doesn't approve of you coming here."

"Not by a long shot."

"And yet you came anyway."

"Yes."

"So are you here to prove something to your dad? Or to yourself?"

"Both I guess? Is that wrong?" Hazel asked, suddenly feeling insecure that she had said the wrong thing to someone who was probably here for all the right reasons, none of which involved an overly critical parent or feelings of self-worth.

"To succeed at anything in life, including being a good journalist, you have to really want it, you have to feel that passion deep within you. If you didn't really want to succeed here, you never would have gotten on that plane back in the States in the first place. You never would have traveled halfway around the world by yourself with no guarantee of anything once you got here if you were doing this as just a capricious whim. Me enlisting at 18, now that was a ca-"

His words dropped off then, his attention now focused on a man who had just entered the bar. Vince called out to him, "Hey O'Laughlin, come here a moment."

A tall, lanky man with ash-colored blond hair walked towards them slowly.

"Hazel, I'd like you to meet Dan O'Laughlin, one of the best photographers you'll ever meet. *Life* just bought another one of his photos this week, he's already had three make the front cover. Dan, this is Hazel Baxter, a recently arrived journalist by way of the Keystone State."

"Oh yeah? Whereabouts in Pennsylvania?" Dan asked with a friendly smile.

"Um, Butler, it's a small city north of Pittsburgh."

"And when did you arrive?"

"Yesterday?" Hazel replied, saying this as both a question and an answer.

"Very cool," Dan said, and then it dawned on Hazel that he was high, his eyes red, his words unsteady and drawn out when he spoke.

"So Dan," Vince said, cutting in. "Roshner told me you're headed home. Your place still free?"

There was silence for a moment, the other man not realizing that Vince was speaking to him.

"Oh yeah, I am," Dan finally said. "Can't keep fighting the jungle fever anymore. Docs say I may not recover if I get it a third time. But yeah, I gave the landlords rent for this month and next. Told them

I'd try to find someone to take it. They've been good to me," every word and syllable he spoke drawn out.

Hazel shot up at this, all feelings of drowsiness and exhaustion soon forgotten. Was her new life really coming along this effortlessly and seamlessly, she thought to herself? Would getting an apartment in Saigon truly be this easy? And one where she wouldn't have to attempt browsing newspaper advertisements or inquiring at the American Embassy or worse, trying to negotiate directly with a Vietnamese landlord.

"How much a month?" Vince asked, sounding as if he were negotiating a major business deal.

"$250."

Hazel inwardly blanched. That was nearly $100 more a month than she had paid for her one-bedroom apartment in Oakland. And she had no doubt that it was probably not nearly as nice, not to mention not rat-free. $250 a month, she'd run through her savings by the following summer if she didn't start writing like crazy and more importantly, have her stuff picked up.

"Sound good to you, Frenchie?" Vince asked her, smiling broadly.

"Absolutely," she said, extending her hand to Dan who just stared at it a moment like it was some foreign object he wasn't sure what to do with. But then he shook the proffered hand, giving it a weak, unfirm handshake her dad would have described as, "someone you don't do business with…ever."

Hazel took the small, two room apartment that was furnished with plastic furniture, complete with a narrow army cot for a bed, sight unseen. It reeked of a combination of both pot (presumably from Dan) and the smells of Aterbea, the restaurant below that was known for its pepper steaks and whatever fresh produce had been trucked in from Dalat that day that the French-style cook would ultimately prepare. And then, of course, there was the adjacent coffee-shop whose jukebox emitted loud, coursing music long into the night, making sleep virtually impossible most nights, but it was hers. It was home. 63 Rue Pasteur was home now.

Her Royal portable typewriter that sat atop the low to the floor plastic table further cemented this.

But as she would learn from Vince and see for herself, housing in Saigon was at a premium. Each year more and more people arrived in the South Vietnamese capital— Americans, aid workers and businessmen from other countries, and the majority of them, Vietnamese refugees fleeing the destruction of their native villages- all pouring into Saigon by the thousands making its clogged roadways a mess to navigate, its reputation as the Pearl of the Orient now deeply recessed in the annals of history as a former beauty queen that was no more. And so what available housing there was never stayed available for long.

"Here's to you, Frenchie, and may you have the next big story fall into your lap," Vince said, toasting her can of French Beaujolais with his that he had picked up at a nearby Corsican market.

"Or just any story that pays enough to keep me afloat," Hazel said. She had said this to be funny but the truth was, her staying depended on her writing and writing well, that publications would want to buy her articles.

Earlier that day Vince had taken her to Cholon, home to a large population of ethnic Chinese who lived in Saigon. It was here where the black market thrived; buying stolen goods in Vietnam was highly illegal but routinely done. This included the purchasing of military-issue fatigues. Reporters weren't allowed to buy them and yet most unit commanders wouldn't let reporters travel with them unless they were outfitted in the appropriate attire. One of the many annoying and frustrating idiosyncrasies of life in Vietnam if you were a reporter.

Hazel hoped her face hadn't shown her fear and apprehension when they got out of the cab and walked around the back of a small house onto a side street. Vince knocked to what sounded like a code, the door was opened ajar and they were quickly ushered inside, frantic hands then swiftly closing the shutters, plunging the room into almost complete blackness until a small lightbulb that dangled precariously from the ceiling was illuminated.

She was quickly measured for both green camouflage fatigues for when she was with the army, tiger stripes for the Marines and then found herself purchasing boots, a blanket roll, poncho, web belt, and two canteens. All things she had never used before in her life but was now the owner of, all coming at a hefty price.

"You came here for a reason," Vince said, looking down at her as he spoke. "Let that reason come through in your writing. You do that, and you will make it here. You will belong."

CHAPTER 7

HAZEL

December 1967

"This here's the Oscar Deuce."

The man said this to Hazel as if he almost expected her to actually say, "nice to meet you," back... to a plane. But the way the Air Force major had patted the front of the plane, Hazel could tell he was immensely proud of his aircraft so she responded, "she's, eer I mean, he's a beauty." Did one actually think of airplanes as beautiful Hazel thought to herself, especially if one considered it to be a he?

"And its official name?" Hazel asked.

Major Callaway looked at her confused for a moment until recognition dawned on his face and he said, "Oh, a Cessna O-2B Skymaster."

Hazel furiously jotted this down in her reporter's steno pad before asking, "I take it there's an A version?"

"Yes ma'am," Major Callaway responded, even though he was at least 10 years Hazel's senior. "So the O-2A was designed to carry ordnance whereas the O-2B is strictly for PSYOPS."

"Ordinance?" Hazel asked. She was loath to ask anything that made her look completely new and ignorant of both her new surroundings and job, fearful of being told, "you don't belong here," but knew she couldn't do her job as a journalist if she didn't know what the hell the person she was interviewing was actually talking about.

He looked at her then, the expression on his face saying, "and this is why war is a man's business," but politely answered, "ordnance are mounted guns, artillery."

A flush of embarrassment rose to her cheeks and for the first time since she had arrived here, Hazel was glad for the country's miserably high temperatures, hoping that her face only appeared red from the heat and humidity and not her inward humiliation of not knowing something so utterly basic.

"So you're telling me when you go on missions, you don't have any protection?" Hazel asked incredulously, not caring this time if she sounded green or not. They seemed like straight up suicide missions to her.

"Yes ma'am," Major Callaway answered. "The O-2B is equipped with nothing but a loudspeaker and leaflet dispenser." Noting Hazel's perhaps now greenish pallor, he added, "Still interested in going up?" He didn't ask this cruelly, nor even tauntingly. He said it matter of factly, because this was war and when did war ever really make sense?

"Have you been shot at before?" Hazel asked him.

"Not for the last couple of weeks," Major Callaway replied. "Summer was a bit rough, took six hits in two months."

Hazel was stunned. She thought coming to Vietnam to pursue a professional dream on what was more or less a whim was an act of bravery, but no, it was nothing to what Major Callaway and the other pilots here did every time they climbed into their pilots' seats and took to the skies.

And then he said the exact thing that Hazel was thinking.

"Every time we're up there," Major Callaway said, tilting his head up to the sky, "we're a dead target for every single VC who wants to see us dead." A downed plane with the words USAF on its side and a captured American is the ultimate crowning achievement when Ho Chi Minh is the guy you're saying your nightly prayers to.

But then they were up, off the ground, flying high above the treetops and all thoughts Hazel had of the plane being shot down were momentarily forgotten when she saw the Vietnamese countryside before her- rice paddies appearing like an endless viridescent sea on the horizon, the occasional sighting of ant-like figures of people making her wonder who they were. Were they glad the Americans were here, did they support what America was doing, or would they run to tell others in their village about an imperialist plane in the sky and help to bring it down?

"It's not always like this," Major Callaway was saying in Hazel's headset.

The Oscar Deuce was fitted for just two passengers, the pilot and an observer, in the fore and aft seats respectively, so she couldn't see his face and wasn't sure what he was referring to.

"What do you mean?" Hazel yelled into her headset's microphone, the noise of the aircraft almost deafening to her.

"The terrain," he said. "Most of the time what you'll see is scorched earth, razed trees, you know, that kind of stuff." And then, adding in an almost philosophical way, "Nothing to suggest life untouched by the ravages of war."

"From Agent Orange you mean?" Hazel asked, referring to the herbicide and defoliant chemical the American government had been using to defoliate rural and forested land for the chief aim of depriving the VC of food and concealment but also clearing sensitive areas such as around base perimeters.

"Some of the time yes, other times, it's ground units that had gone in and flushed out villages."

Hazel was going to ask flushed out from what but then he said, "Here we go, Baxter."

And then the sky was awash with the color white, the leaflets no longer in the belly of the plane but now raining down onto the countryside, the papers fluttering this way and that as they slowly floated down onto the ground.

Hours later back in her small apartment in Saigon, the whirring of the ceiling fan offering more noise than cool air, Hazel was nearly literally burning the midnight oil. The lone lightbulb housed in a socket that she knew would be deemed not up to code back home, weakly illuminated the room as she sat Indian-style on her narrow cot, the leaflets Major Callaway had given to her spread out before her. She didn't know what any of the Vietnamese words on the leaflets said but assumed the one showing an American medic administering aid to a small child being held by his mother was one of a positive message. But the one of a young boy crouched amongst dead bodies laid out on the ground haunted her. For his look wasn't one of tears or anguish but rather a harsh, stark reality that this was his life, this was what life was like in Vietnam for a 10-year-old boy. Where sitting near a row of dead bodies was the norm and not the stuff of nightmares.

Would words on a page that were written by American men, the same people who most likely knew little about the Vietnamese culture, really win the hearts and souls of the North Vietnamese people? Would the image of an American medic administering aid to a North Vietnamese child convince them of the good the American military was doing or rather just serve as a reminder that their child needed medical care in the first place BECAUSE the Americans, the latest occupying foreign force, were there in their country. And the heartbreaking image of the Vietnamese child amongst dead bodies. The North Vietnamese could just as easily manipulate that image and claim that this is what the Americans were doing to the Vietnamese people.

Hazel was glad her article on going on a PSYOP mission was for the *Overseas Weekly* where her mission, as Ann had told her the day they met, was to "write for the boys," and "not the Washington brass." She had only been in-country for barely two weeks but understood that this wasn't 1944 Normandy, France or the Dutch countryside in the spring of '45 when the local civilians eagerly awaited the liberation of their towns and villages from Nazi rule by the Allied forces. No, this was Vietnam, a country and people not unaccustomed to the suffering and depravities of war. It had spent nearly a decade fighting one Western enemy and emerging victorious only to eagerly take up arms again against a new one, determined to not just oust the latest foreign occupier but also be granted self-government. Hazel knew that Major Callaway and others like him were deeply rooted in their conviction that PSYOP offered the greatest potential of not just turning the enemy, but perhaps even turning the tides of war in America's favor.

But how could the tides turn when America couldn't even find the enemy it was fighting? Or win the war when there wasn't even a front to take?

JULIE TULBA

"Hey, Frenchie!"

Hazel turned around, not because she answered to "Frenchie" but rather, she immediately recognized the voice. Vince. She hadn't seen him for nearly a week, not since he had taken her to the rooftop bar of the Rex Hotel for the military's daily press briefing or as he told her what he and the other journalists referred to it as, "the Five O'Clock Follies."

Vince had introduced her to a slew of people before the briefing started, some who were freelancers like her, but many from the major networks and papers like the legendary Peter Arnett, who Hazel knew had won a Pulitzer Prize the year before for his reporting in Vietnam, and ABC correspondent Frank Marino, who she had recognized from watching TV back home. They were all polite, feigning cordial interest when she told them who she was writing for. But a few had looked at her, their expressions implying, "she must be sleeping with him, someone so young and green not to mention pretty fraternizing with someone at Vince's professional level." But then there were some who wanted to say, "Who the hell is she?"

Vince had warned her that what she heard in the briefing should be taken with a grain of salt. That JUSPAO (which he had jokingly broken down in a maddeningly slow sort of way when telling her it stood for Joint United States Public Affairs Office) was still, at the end of the day, a propaganda wing for the United States in Vietnam. "Charlie has Hanoi Hannah, we've got JUSPAO," he'd said. "But do yourself a favor and get out here, hop on a Huey and see the fighting firsthand, spend some time with different combat units. You want to be a good reporter, then your eyes need to see this war firsthand. Not going on the word of the American war machine. All Johnson and his generals at the Pentagon care about are numbers, low casualty numbers for our side, high casualty numbers for theirs. But it's not true, none of it is."

"Then why attend?" Hazel had asked, not understanding.

"Because the fundamental difference between communism and a truly free society is being able to see and hear both sides for yourself, not just the side your government wants you to experience. And that's the simple fact that LBJ and his cronies don't seem to understand and why it makes them more akin to Ho Chi Minh and his crew than they'd ever concede. Hearing just one side, especially when it's filled with lies and spun mistruths, is not an open and free society. Not to mention, it's A-rate free entertainment."

So as she sat next to Vince that day, notebook and pencil ready to take notes, the professional briefing had in no time turned into a three-ring circus, a nod to Vince's describing it as "free entertainment." It was a scene Hazel felt was right out of a Shakespeare play- military briefers playing the roles of the actors whereas the press was the unruly and unimpressed audience, a combination of hooting, hollering, shouting, and even hissing taking place at regular intervals. When a military official with four stripes announced, "the Department of State has sent a diplomatic note to Prince Sihanouk of Cambodia, pledging that the United States will not cross into Cambodia to pursue PAVN/VC forces fleeing from South Vietnam. We promise to respect Cambodian neutrality, sovereignty, independence and territorial integrity," someone in the audience immediately yelled, "the goddamn lying machine takes the cake with this one boys." To which someone yelled back, "The U.S. doesn't respect a goddamn anything, at home or abroad." This was met with "except its body counts of Charlie!"

During the entire briefing, Vince never once called out like most of the other reporters and photographers had, only whispering at times into Hazel's ear the names of certain military briefers who were speaking and essentially telling her why they mattered. She had dutifully copied them down into her notebook, determined to have them permanently etched into her head in no time.

"How have you been?" he asked her. "I haven't seen you in a while. It's almost like you've been hiding," adding the last part with a smile, his eyes seeming to say, "hiding from me."

"Oh no, just been busy," Hazel replied, pretending to focus her attention on the motorbike behind him that had not one but two large wooden frames strapped to its side which just boggled her, considering they were longer than the length of said motorbike. But anything to not look directly into Vince's eyes.

"Hey," he said, lightly tapping her nose with his index finger.

Entirely flushed now, she nervously said, "Oh, I'm sorry," as she raised her eyes to meet his. "It's been a good busy though. I filed, well hopefully I should say provided Ann approves it, my first story for *Overseas Weekly*."

"Look at you, ace reporter," Vince said smiling. If it had been anyone else, Hazel would have taken that as a belittling comment, a condescending nod to her gender. But with Vince, she knew he meant it, that he was proud of her. "So, what's it on?" he asked.

"PSYOP," she replied. "I got to go on a mission a couple of days ago."

"Oh yeah?" he said, now sounding disinterested, and his attention focused somewhere else. "So you really believe whatever it is they're smoking over there?" he asked, his tone now sharp, his eyes back to looking directly at her. "It's beyond me why anyone who thinks that white men educated at the Ivies who maybe had a crash course in the Vietnamese language and culture are going to be able to win the hearts and souls of Charlie's people,"

Hazel wanted to say no she didn't, she wanted to share the personal thoughts and doubts she had over what Major Callaway told her and what she had seen in the various pamphlets. But all she said was, "Are you always this cynical?" angry now that he had ruined this proud moment of hers.

"Are you always this naïve? I thought one viewing of the Follies would be enough for you to see through the sham of things here," he said coolly. "And that above all includes the PSYOP group, one of the biggest shams of all in my humble opinion."

"Well, you'll just have to read my article when it comes out." Hazel had said this to be serious but Vince just laughed, there amongst the rotting piles of garbage, the two obscenely large rats scurrying towards said garbage, and the crawling baby who had nothing on his bottom and who the rats would have to crawl by to get to said garbage. A typical Saigon street, but now emanating with the sounds of laughter.

"Oh, indeed I will, Frenchie."

He didn't say anything more, so wanting to fill the silence, well, figuratively speaking since Saigon was never quiet, she nervously added, "And I have my first article for the *Pittsburgh Catholic* all lined up. 'Christmas 1967, Saigon-style.' I'm meeting with one of the priests at Notre Dame along with a few of the parishioners. He speaks French and actually lived for a time in Lyon. So it should be interesting to speak with him."

"Counter it with an article on the Buddhists," he told her.

"What?" Hazel asked him, not understanding.

"Both sides Baxter, always look at both sides."

Vince was often like this with her, cryptic with what he said, but Hazel had deduced by now that it was his way of pushing her towards more—more answers, more ways of being a better journalist.

"Any plans for Saturday night?" he asked.

He was often like this too, doing a 180 on things they were discussing, moving onto the next topic while she was still trying to dissect the previous one. A complete whirlwind of a man.

Not quite sure what he was asking- was he asking her out? Was he inquiring about her lack of a social life as an older brother would?

(Milton often had, which had annoyed her to no end since he had been the social bee.) So she decided to make a joke of it and said, "Well, I was thinking about finally trying some of the rice wine I keep hearing scores of good things about."

"Sean Flynn and Tim Page are throwing a party at their villa Saturday night."

"You say these names like they're ones I should know," Hazel said.

"Well, do you know many people with a film star for a dad?" Vince said, half-laughing.

"Wait, Flynn as in Errol Flynn's his dad?" Hazel asked in disbelief.

"Yeah, and looks just like him too. But for Sean, it's something he could care less about. I don't think he ever saw 'Robin Hood' too much growing up."

"Wait, didn't he star in a movie too?" Hazel asked, trying to remember the name of the film that she and Betty had driven down to Pittsburgh to see since it wasn't showing at the Penn in Butler. "*The Son of...?*"

"*The Son of Captain Blood.* Color me impressed Frenchie, you know your films. Well, these days Flynn wants to be remembered for his photography, not his swash-buckling, rather dismal film career. But all joking aside, he's an amazing photographer, he, Tim, Dana. I mean they're constantly putting themselves in situations to capture that once in a lifetime image but here in a place like 'Nam, those same type of images come around all too often, sadly to say. Every day, week, month, we're always shown some new horror and tragic occurrence to capture and for us, to write about."

Us, he said us, Hazel thought to herself, warm at the thought he was including the green likes of her with the seasoned likes of him.

"So, the party's at Frankie's House-" he stopped, noticing Hazel's confused look before adding, "it's the name Sean and Tim gave the villa in honor of their houseboy 'Frankie,' and yeah, you can bet they couldn't pronounce the kid's Vietnamese name. They're pretty intense and crazy even. But I think it's their way of compensating for all the near-death experiences they've had and continue to have all the time. That life in this form, body, existence, is basically just "free time."

"So in short, what you're telling me is that there's going to be a lot of drugs there?" Hazel asked, half-joking, half-serious.

"The Haight-Ashbury of Southeast Asia basically."

Hazel lifted her hand, just about to knock on the front door to the old French villa on Bui Thi Xuan Street, but then chided herself, thinking that the loud music emanating from the other side of the door was undoubtedly Vietnam's version of a fraternity party. She had attended her fair share of those while she was at Pitt and never once had she knocked on the front door waiting to be admitted, she had just gone in. So that's what she did here, on the other side of the world.

As she stepped over the threshold, the smells of pot, cigarette smoke, and some other exotic odor immediately greeted her, along with the voice of Grace Slick, who at that moment was telling her non-listening crowd that they "better find somebody to love." Hazel took a moment for her eyes to adjust to the darkness of the dimly lit room, laden with thick smoke that she wondered was perhaps opium, when a voice from behind said, "Want to smoke some opium?"

Hazel turned, startled to see a white man who looked to be in his late 30s, early 40s, suddenly standing next to her. He appeared almost manic, his eyes red, his pupils dilated.

She was going to say, "No thank you," but then thought how woefully virginesque that would sound, even to someone as stoned as the man before her. So instead she replied, "Sorry, can't. My party routine for the night at ANY party is to get rip roaring drunk first and then proceed to the drug buffet. But at this very moment, I don't have a drop of booze in me and I simply must remedy that." And with that pronouncement, Hazel walked away from the stoner who in addition to looking manic, now appeared almost befuddled by what Hazel had just said.

"Well said, *ma chérie*," a man uttered from across the room.

"You heard that?" Hazel asked, amazed that he had heard what she'd said to the stoned man considering how loud the music was.

"My hearing is impeccable," the man replied as he got up to come towards her. "Guillaume Allaire," he said, extending his hand towards her. "But you can call me Guy since none of you Americans can say my name without butchering it."

Shaking his hand, Hazel replied in French, "I thought I detected a French accent."

"Well, well, well, will wonders never cease to amaze," Guy said laughing, proceeding to study her as if she were a fresh cut of meat he would be devouring any moment, his eyes slowly trailing down the length of her legs which were perfectly defined in her mocha colored pantyhose.

Wanting to not only break the silence but also distract his roving eyes, Hazel asked, "So I know there's opium readily available. What else are people indulging in?"

Guy took a long drag on his cigarette before answering, "Anything you could possibly want. Come," he said, taking Hazel's hand in his. "Le buffet is this way. The LSD, mushrooms, also the cocaine and heroin, but you don't seem like a hard drug girl."

And before she could protest or extract her hand from his, Hazel saw Vince, their eyes seeming to lock together at the very same time. He was in a conversation with two other people, casually holding a bottle of 33 Beer although she could have sworn he'd tightened his grip on the bottle when he noticed Hazel's hand in Guy's as his knuckles started to whiten. As Guy kept talking, on what Hazel couldn't say because she wasn't listening, her eyes just stayed on Vince's, and his on hers.

"Hey," Guy said, his face right before hers. "*Où es-tu allé?*"

Where'd she go, he'd asked her. To Vince, she wanted to say. The sole reason she had come to this party, where barely five minutes in she felt entirely out of her depth. Sure, she had smoked her fair share of marijuana at Pitt and had been offered mushrooms a time or two (but always declined, not ready to take a trip to the psychedelic world, even if it was just temporary), but the idea of heroin had always frightened her, ever since she had seen someone injecting it into a vein in their foot at a party.

"Sorry, I just really need a drink," Hazel said, feigning a smile. "Is it possible for a girl to get a gimlet around here?"

"*Absolument,*" Guy said, half-bowing. "A gimlet and I'll get us the mescaline. You will love it. We will share the experience together."

The moment he started walking away, Hazel saw Vince coming towards her but not before the man from the front door was next to her, asking her again, "Want to smoke some opium?"

But then Vince was there and told him, "Sorry Grimes, not tonight. You'll find somebody else to smoke with, besides Puff isn't even here yet. But Hazel's with me." And with that, Vince took her hand in his and led her away from the man who still hadn't said anything else, or even given any indication he'd heard what Vince said. He just remained there, motionless.

Vince led her through the villa with both a swiftness and adeptness that suggested he had been here before. But then she figured he probably had, considering it was where *United Press* and

Time magazine put up their reporters and photographers and knowing that Vince played in the big leagues from both a professional and socializing regard.

Her hand still enveloped within his, Vince finally spoke and casually said, "Don't mind Grimes. He's a good guy, works for *Time.* But he got hooked on the stuff a year or so back," as they climbed a rather creaky grand staircase adorned with an Oriental runner that evoked a bygone era. Certainly not from one in which drunk and high American newsmen and women so carelessly trod upon it, oblivious to its prior significance and beauty. "And he just hates smoking alone."

"So who's Puff?" Hazel asked.

"What?" Vince asked, clearly confused by the question.

"You said to Grimes and I quote," Hazel said comically playing the part of reporter, 'Puff's not even here yet,' end quote. Clearly there has to be some good story there with a name like that," she said as she leaned against the wall, watching as Vince went to the windowed balcony and flung open the wrought iron door, the muffled sounds of outside life now intermingling with the interior sounds of the villa. The short staccato sounds of what Hazel now knew as gunfire were off in the distance.

"Puff," Vince began, stepping back into the room, "is the name of the finest opium purveyor in all of Saigon," which made Hazel laugh at his over-the-top theatrics. "Although it's only fair that you should know his real name."

"Which is?" she asked.

"Puff the Magic Dragon," at which point they both erupted in a fit of laughter. They laughed and laughed until it naturally subsided but never once did their eyes stray from the other's. He got up then from the bed where they had both been sitting, went to the door and locked it.

"Hey, Hazel said nervously, "what are you doing?"

"Nothing untoward, I swear," he said. "Scout's honor." And then did a rather feeble attempt at making the sign. "But if I don't lock this door your ardent and might I say too sleazy admirer who clearly wanted to see what's beneath those mocha-hosed legs will find his way in. He's a lech when he's not high or drunk; when he is those things, you truly don't want to be around him, trust me."

And in that moment her heart did. Her body, however, remained glued to the door. Kicking off his shoes then, Vince walked to the head of the bed, propped up two pillows against the rather ornate wooden headboard, a piece that seemed better suited for the likes of the Victoria and Albert Museum, she thought to herself, and then did the last thing she would have ever expected to see done from a bureau chief from one of America's largest and most prestigious newspapers. He jumped up onto it as if he were a 10-year boy, the ultimate act of misbehaving when mom and dad weren't looking, all the while grinning at her as slyly as the Cheshire Cat.

Her mouth agape, she said, "I don't know what's shocked me more—what I just saw you do or the fact that late 19th century bed is still intact."

"Trust me, in this villa, she's seen worse...a whole lot worse," Vince said, patting the mattress as if it were one of the guys. And then in the next moment he laughed, the blissful sounds of unadulterated laughter filling the room.

"Come here," Vince told her, patting the mattress once more but his tone now serious, all traces of gaiety completely gone, vanished just like that into the recesses of the room's French colonial past, much the same way that Charlie vanished into the night air. A part of her knew she should run, that she hadn't come here for this, let alone to be falling for a man who she aspired to be like one day. Twenty, thirty years from now, regardless of the outcome of the war, she professionally wanted to look back and say 'Vietnam was where my career in journalism began, where its foundations were rooted, where I became the writer I am today.' But more importantly, she wanted her coming here to matter, to not have been for naught. For it to have been worth it, to have defied her dad and in a sense abandoned the shell her mom had become after Milton's death. And Milton. She so desperately wanted to understand this war that had ended the life of her younger brother and thousands of others like him much too soon. Why in the words of President Johnson, American boys were being sent 'nine or ten thousand miles away from home to do what Asian boys ought to be doing for themselves.' And still being sent in droves, it seemed.

Staring at him from across the room, Hazel shrugged off her suede heels, ever so conscious of how much her mini skirt would ride up climbing onto the bed. But still she didn't move from her spot.

"If the Mountain won't go to Mohammed," Vince said, rising from the bed and coming towards her, "then Mohammed must come to the Mountain."

And then he was standing right before her, their eyes, hers an azure blue, his an onyx black, locked on each other. Neither spoke until a new song playing on the Sears Silvertone could be heard through the closed door.

Still not speaking, Vince took her right hand in his and then pulled her into his arms, every inch of her body seeming to perfectly fit into the contours of his.

They slow danced around the room as the muffled tones of Tommy James and the Shondells played in the background. And then he kissed her, hesitantly at first, perhaps unsure how she would respond, but then more passionately as her lips desperately sought his. Hazel had always thought moments like this were the stuff of cliches, best portrayed by the likes of Katherine Hepburn and Vivien

Leigh. But this wasn't some contrived script. This wasn't the latest Audrey Hepburn movie she'd see at the Penn Theater with Betty. No, this was real.

"I've never met anyone like you, Hazel Baxter," Vince said, murmuring into her hair, his voice warm on her skin. "You've bewitched me, as an old neighbor lady would say, when bewitching is exactly the absolute last thing I need in my life. I'm no good for any woman, I can't not be here, I don't feel alive back home. But I need to have you."

Have me? Hazel thought as he continued kissing the nape of her neck until she felt his mouth on her breasts. When, just tonight? Or always? Hazel had no idea if what he was saying was true. Or if he hadn't said those very same words to countless women before her. But she didn't care. She was neither high nor drunk and Hazel didn't think he was either; she just in that moment wanted to forget about everything else and be with him. And with that, his eyes alight with hunger for her, she started to undress until she stood completely naked before him, there in a room that reeked of pot and sweat, the sounds of psychedelic music reverberating through the 19th century French colonial villa. If only for that night.

When she awoke later, she was momentarily disoriented, unable to remember where she was. But looking around the richly furnished room, the early morning light already starting to filter in through the wooden shutters, it all came back to her, all that had happened the night before. And then it struck her that he wasn't there. That the other side of the bed was cold to the touch, that not even the impression of his body could be seen on the sheets. When had he gone? And how long had she been alone in the bed, in this room, in a house full of strangers?

Hazel started to dress then, a wave of both nausea and unease slowly rushing over her. As she opened the bedroom door, it creaked horribly loud, something she hadn't noticed from the previous night, but then of course the villa had been buzzing with the sounds of loud music and scores of people milling about. Now, in the dawn hours, the effects of heavy drinking and even heavier drug use had taken their toll on the party's revelers who were completely dead to the world, some passed out on sofas, others on the floor, a few even peacefully sleeping on the steps, but all completely oblivious to the young, naïve woman who crept past them as if she were a thief fleeing the crime scene.

But then she saw him. She started to rush towards where he sat in the garden. It was only when he turned to face her, somehow knowing that those were her footsteps and not someone else's, and the fact that he didn't speak, didn't come towards her, that she knew. His eyes took in the clothes she had been wearing the night before, now in a completely wrinkled and disheveled state that undoubtedly matched her hair and makeup. But it was the look in his eyes, one of a perhaps forlorn sadness, tinged with a side of regret that at that moment made Hazel regret what she had done too. She had opened a door she should have never opened and now the look in his face told her she needed to shut that door, because it would never be opened again.

Her intentions weren't honorable. In fact they were entirely selfish. But she hadn't wanted to be alone in her small, cramped apartment on Christmas day. Nor did she want to spend it with troops of any kind, lest she be reminded of Milton, reminded of the fact that this would be the first of Christmases for the rest of her life that she wouldn't have with him. So she decided to volunteer as a candy striper of sorts at the 3rd Field Hospital.

A nurse she was not but she didn't feel faint at the sight of blood, not that she had ever really come face to face with gross amounts of it. But Hazel figured being surrounded by injured and maimed soldiers and perhaps even civilians who had fled in the dead of night from their decimated villages to escape the ravages of death, well, that would undoubtedly be the best way to take her mind off everything, and by everything she was solely referring to him.

She had spent the first two hours at the hospital agreeably enough. Most of the men she encountered were in fair, even jovial spirits-some recovering from broken bones, others tropical diseases, and a few from artillery and shrapnel wounds. Hazel had written letters for those whose arms were in plaster casts, sang a few Christmas carols to men who simply wanted to "hear the voice of a pretty American girl" standing right there before them, and kissed the cheeks of two soldiers who were bold enough to ask.

But then one of the nurses on duty had asked Hazel to accompany her to one of the other wards. Upon entering the soundless and dark room, Hazel had drawn up short. For in front of her was row after row of metal beds, all filled with young men whose bodies and minds seemed trapped in the space that exists somewhere between life and death. And they all looked so young, most in their twenties and perhaps even younger, maybe even a recent high school graduate or two like Milton had been. Young men who should be just starting their lives but instead were being forced to begin saying their goodbyes. Hazel was reminded of the scene from *Gone with the Wind,* when Scarlett goes to the hospital to look for Dr. Meade to help her with Melanie's delivery and encounters all of the wounded soldiers from the recent Battle of Atlanta. Although these men were quiet, nary a sound being heard, no one begging for water, no one reaching for Hazel's arms as the Confederate soldiers had done to Scarlett in that infamous scene, she didn't feel overwhelmed or even frightened from the sight of the Black soldier whose jaw seemed to be partially missing or the one whose body was covered from head to toe in plaster or even seeing the blond-haired soldier who didn't have a single limb. No, Hazel felt nothing but shame for having been so selfish in her motives for coming here. When any one of those young men could have easily been her own brother.

"Smoke?"

Hazel had gone outside for some air, not that the air was ever that fresh in Saigon. It seemed that no matter where you were in the city, the air was always thick and heavy, and more often than not, nauseating from gas fumes and rotting garbage, not to mention the ever present fish sauce, nuoc cham, that Hazel had yet to acquire a taste for. All Hazel thought it smelled and tasted like was rotting fish, not a stretch in some Saigon establishments.

"Sure," Hazel answered, taking the proffered one from the petite brunette nurse. At five foot five Hazel felt as if she towered over the woman who seemed to only be around five feet tall. "Thanks," she told her as she bent down to the other woman's height so that she could light it.

"So what brings you here?" the nurse asked.

"Here as in the hospital? Or here as in Saigon?" Hazel said.

"Both, I guess," the other woman replied, smiling.

"I, um, I don't know many people and thought it might be nice to help out on Christmas. The boys are so far from home and I know my contributions aren't much of anything in the grand scheme of things but it seemed something at least."

"They're more than you think," the other woman said kindly. "And Saigon?" she asked.

"I'm a journalist," Hazel said proudly, this time without a hint of hesitation or doubt emanating from within her.

"No shit," the other woman said. "I don't think I've ever come across a female reporter over here. I thought Nam was strictly a man eat man's world, save for us nurses. But then again I haven't been here too terribly long. I only began my tour here last month."

"I arrived around the end of October," Hazel told her. "I'm Hazel, Hazel Baxter, by way of Butler, Pennsylvania," she said, officially extending her hand.

Taking it, the woman said, "Second Lieutenant Kathleen Marasini, but you can call me Kathy. Hailing all the way from you never heard of it, Galena, Illinois."

"So you volunteered to come here?" Hazel asked.

"You bet," Kathy said. "I had never wanted to stay a day more in little old Galena than I had to. And even after I finished nursing school, a big city like Chicago still didn't seem big enough for me. It just seemed, still seemed...-

"Too close to home?" Hazel added.

"Exactly."

"Was your family supportive of you? Coming to Vietnam I mean." Hazel asked, genuinely curious.

"My mom was," Kathy said, her eyes now clearly showing she was somewhere else, perhaps back in Galena of all places. "She was a sergeant in the Marines during World War II, stationed at Camp Pendleton, served as a field cook there. That's where she met my dad; he was a Marine too. Served in the Pacific during the war. Anyway, the war ended and he just wanted to get back to his boring, no-

nonsense life in Galena doing the same thing he had always done and his dad before him. My mom, well, she always wanted to see the world but dad always said, the second he set foot back on continental American soil, as he called it, in March of '46, he was never going to leave again."

"Well, the world's a different place now," Hazel offered, feeling bad she had somehow managed to upset this sweet girl who was clearly having a difficult time too in her own way on Christmas so far from home, even when it was boring small-town USA. "Who knows, maybe one day you'll travel the world with her, take her to countries you've visited."

"What about you?" Kathy asked, a look of steely resolve back on her face, the look she needed to keep perfectly maintained when you worked at the 3rd Field Hospital as a nurse.

"Well, in college I majored in French, and studied abroad in Paris one summer."

"Oh la la," Kathy cut in with a highly dramatic French accent which made Hazel laugh.

"I also majored in journalism and after I graduated I just thought that reporting on a war, a war that our men and boys were fighting in, well, it would be the best way to truly learn to become the best journalist I could be."

Not wanting to turn this into an interview, since it was the first genuine girl talk Hazel had had with a woman her age in months now, but she had to know. "I know you haven't been here that long but do you ever struggle with what you see here on a daily basis? Seeing the sight of death surrounding so many young boys?"

"I do," Kathy said, blowing a long stream of smoke over her shoulder. "I'd be a goddamn liar if I didn't say yes. But I knew what I was signing up for when I came here. Our boys need all the help we can give them and that's why I became a nurse."

"Will the boys in that ward make it?" Hazel asked. She didn't have to specify which ward she meant, she knew Kathy would know.

"Some will, some sadly won't. But here's the thing about this war," Kathy began. "We're saving more lives than we ever did in Korea or Europe because of the helicopter. We're getting them off the battlefields in record time. We're able to stabilize them at the front and then before they bleed out where they would have died alone and in pain, they're whisked off to hospitals here in Saigon and Da Nang where at least they have access to modern and advanced treatments to save them. The helicopter is helping to ensure that more American lives are not being lost here, more than already are."

Hazel could see the truth in that. The lessons of past mistakes are always learned from, arsenals of past wars are always built upon. And yet, she couldn't help but think what life would these men ever have if they survived and were able to return home? They were already fighting in a war that half of the American population saw as wrong and unjust, some even going so far as to call them horrible names like "baby killers." The helicopter saved them, but saved them from what? Now for the rest of their lives would they be forced to endure a horrific and perhaps never ending recovery amongst major handicaps and scars in a country that now looked down upon them.

In the weeks following the fateful party at Frankie's Villa and the lesson in humility she had received Christmas night when she spent it amongst the maimed and lost souls of the 3d Field Hospital, Hazel had kept busy, and more importantly, kept to herself. She had avoided going anywhere that she might possibly run into him, which meant no more meals or drinks at hotel rooftop bars (not that she could have afforded it on her own anyway) and no more live entertainment at the Five O'Clock Follies (not that she was missing out on anything worthwhile there from a professional regard). But the fact was she had never felt more alone in her life.

Since she had arrived in-country, Hazel had crossed paths with a few other female journalists, but none of these women would become her friends. Hazel knew that. She and they hadn't traveled this far, gone to such lengths to prove themselves worthy journalists just to gossip on the phone at night about their love life (not that she had a phone- the only way to reach her was at *Overseas Weekly* or Aterbea, the restaurant she lived above). But Hazel also got a sense that for the female reporters, Vietnam wasn't just about proving your professional merit to the men, it was also about constantly defending from the other women there the figurative territory you had acquired through your reporting and the respect you had garnered. For without that territory in a place like Vietnam, you truly were just a woman.

CHAPTER 8

HAZEL

January 1968

"Where ya headed to" Hazel shouted to the officer, struggling to make her voice heard over the whirring blades of the helicopter rotor. The officer looked up from the clipboard he had been inspecting, clearly surprised to see a woman standing before him, not that Hazel felt very feminine when wearing her black market fatigues, her hair a sweaty, frizzled mess under her boonie hat.

"Dong Ha, by way of Da Nang," the officer replied, not offering up anything else by way of useful information.

Well, Hazel thought to herself, this officer- officer what she wondered, trying her best to make out the name on his uniform's name tag without squinting and truly appearing helpless- clearly found her mere presence so off- putting she was deemed not worthy of an ounce of politeness. She didn't know why but she found this treatment, this behavior from some of the men here in Vietnam, to be worse than those who were more vocal in their beliefs that women didn't belong here. To Hazel, it felt that this Officer Szeged (that's it but my God, how did that name not escape the Ellis Island officials' cutting block like her own grandparents' name had with all those consonants together?) regarded her as not even existing.

"Have room for one more?" she asked, her voice steady, her racing heart clearly not.

He turned to her then, giving her his full attention, moving his clipboard to rest at his side, eyeing her not as a man does to a woman he finds attractive, but rather in a way that clearly said, "Go find someone else to bother with your childish prattle." But seeing the MACV ID hanging around her neck, this Officer Szeged knew she belonged here, well, at least in the sense that she was legally entitled to board any United States military aircraft in Vietnam (that had room, of course). And there was nothing he could do about it.

"Wheels up at 1400." And with that he walked away, not saying a single thing more nor giving her backwards glance, simply leaving Hazel to do nothing but wonder, where the heck was Dong Ha?

Dong Ha, Hazel realized after surreptitiously studying her now deeply creased map of South Vietnam lest Officer Szeged further cement his negative opinion of both her gender and her profession, was a name she already knew. It was in the far north of the country, almost directly below the infamous Demilitarized Zone. It was also in the Quang Tri province, the area where Milton had been stationed and where he had died.

She had drawn in a deep breath then, tears starting to form in her eyes when she remembered all those months ago the excitement she had felt upon receiving her brother's letters and looking up those foreign and bizarre sounding names he had written about on her Rand McNally map. And now, here she was herself, soon to see the same places and landscapes Milton saw.

As Hazel looked down at her watch and saw it was 13:50, she reminded herself that there was no room for sentimentality in journalism, let alone in a place like Vietnam. And she began walking towards the roaring Iroquois where a scowling Officer Szeged stood once more.

Scorched earth. Hazel had never seen anything like it before, an entire landscape utterly decimated, completely stripped raw of any natural beauty. She had a hard time imagining the burning embers, the gutted trees, the burnt and blackened ground as having once been pretty but clearly it must have been for the French to have come here, and then to have endured such a long and horrific fight to keep it.

Hazel had been told by various people- both military and press alike- that Agent Orange, the tactical herbicide being used to destroy crops and foliage as a means of exposing possible enemy hideouts was in essence a good thing, that it was helping to "root out Charlie," that it was yet another winning component of Westmoreland's war of attrition against the North Vietnamese. But how was it just, no, humane rather, to punish all simply by association? From the simple fact of not being able to distinguish between one Vietnamese and another? For too many Americans, everyone looked the same, everyone was Charlie. And looking back down at the darkened earth once more, there were clearly no exceptions.

Upon arriving at Dong Ha Combat Base, Hazel quickly felt like a fish out of water. From the air she could see that it was a sizable operation with many rows of white colored buildings that contrasted starkly against the red colored earth, the scourge for many of the men Hazel knew. Its fine sand and dust would penetrate everything, leaving an indelible red color in its wake.

"Head to the Mess Hall."

Hazel whipped her head around, surprised to see Officer Szeged speaking to her.

"You'll find men to speak with there. It has some of the best chow this side of the Pacific and when a soldier or a Marine has a belly full of hot cooked food, they're more than willing subjects. Especially when the person doing the interviewing could be a Natalie Wood stand-in."

Hazel was shocked. But even more shocked when he added, "And perhaps I'll find you there myself later on, although I don't want to talk about anything pertaining to the war." Before she could utter a semi-intelligent reply or even a thanks, he walked away from her a second time, although this time he was not scowling, but perhaps even smiling. And she thought she heard the faint sounds of whistling too, although she couldn't be entirely sure for Dong Ha Base, Hazel observed, was excessively loud. Just like the sounds of Saigon but undoubtedly a lot more orderly and efficient.

She put on her rucksack and started walking towards the buildings, but not having a clue as to which one was the mess hall.

"You a performer?"

Hazel looked to her left and saw a soldier wearing only a damp undershirt (wait, or was he a Marine? When they were out of uniform, she couldn't tell the difference) sitting in what was a barely shaded area smoking a cigarette. His hair was shaggy, a day's growth of beard adorning his face. He was young, Hazel could tell, perhaps even younger than her, but like so many of the men she had met so far, his eyes betrayed an age much older.

"Ha, quite the opposite," Hazel said, laughing. "I'm the world's worst singer and dancer for that matter so I'd be quite the disappointment to the men here. They'd ask for their money back if I were. I'm a journalist actually. And I'm hoping you could tell me where the mess hall is?"

"I'll take you," the younger man said, standing up, taking one last drag on his cigarette and then tossing it to the ground where he tamped it with his boot.

"Oh, I don't want to disturb you," Hazel rushed to say.

"You're not. You're also the first white woman's face I've seen in months, so in a place like Nam, this is a treat. Lance Corporal Napoli," he said, proffering Hazel his hand. "And the dragon-like army nurses don't really count," he said jokingly.

"Hazel Baxter," she replied, smiling warmly in return. "Marine?" she asked, hoping she was indeed right.

"Oorah," he boomed, his voice still no match for the cacophonous sounds of the base. "So you're really a journalist?" he asked her, adjusting his stride to match hers.

"Indeed I am," she said, astutely aware as they walked that every single pair of eyes were directly on her. A fish out of water indeed. And then she heard someone call out, "Hey Hemingway, who's the girl you're with?"

"Hemingway?" Hazel asked, dying now to hear the story behind the nickname.

"I'm a bit of a writer," Lance Corporal Napoli said shrugging. "And I brought with me a couple of his books. I've been here six months, seven to go, and have already re-read them two times each."

"I visited the apartment where he and his first wife Hadley lived when I was in Paris," she said, thinking perhaps this would what, impress him?

"No shit," he replied, but then quickly added, "Pardon my French

Miss Baxter." Okay, clearly not impressed if that was his response, Hazel thought.

"Oh, please call me Hazel," she told him, wanting desperately to establish a rapport with not just this Marine but any other man she encountered here.

"So where's home, Hazel?" he asked.

"Um, Butler, Pennsylvania. It's a small town north of-"

He cut her off then to add, "Pittsburgh." Smiling at her he said, "Which is home for me."

Upon arriving at the mess hall, Lance Corporal Napoli had introduced her to not just members of his platoon but also ones from his company. As Hazel sat there amongst the men, finding herself in a queen bee position for the first time in her life, the men simply hungry for the look and sound of a real American girl, enamored with everything she said, she simply enjoyed seeing the men consume their hot cooked meals with such relish. This was, of course, after she had been educated on the difference between A-rats (A-rations) and C-rats (C-rations) and the dreaded above all of the latter—ham and lima beans or as Private Claymore of Carson City, Nevada burst out, "ham and muthas." To which Lane Corporal Napoli smacked him on the back of his head and said, "watch your mouth."

"So when you're in the field, it's always C-rats?" Hazel asked, wanting to know every little to last detail of what these young men's lives were like. What Milton's life here had been like.

"Yeah, they look bad," Private Claymore began "but beans and baby di-"

This time Private Claymore was cut off by a Black soldier from Detroit named PFC Harrison Whitestone who everybody seemed to call Whitey as a joke since he was the blackest man Hazel had ever seen. "Man, what's wrong with you. If I had done speak like that in my momma's house I woulda been whopped from here to 1980," to which everybody laughed.

"It's okay, I'm pretty sure I know what you're referring to," Hazel said half-laughing, half-cringing inwardly that she was being treated as if this were the 1880s and she would need her smelling salts any moment from all the rough and unsavory "man talk."

"One time when we were on a dangerous mission in the field, for a longer stretch than usual, they actually choppered us in T-bone steaks and fresh and juicy nectarines, still in a crate that said the words 'Fresno, California' on it," Private Daniel Haggarty of Boston said. "I'll never forget that."

"Yeah," PFC John Bianco of Urbana, Illinois said. He then proceeded to cross himself and kiss the Virgin Mary medallion that hung around his neck.

"Hey, don't you remember how the next day Staff Sergeant O'Rourke destroyed all the leftover crates of them before we moved out?" Private Claymore said. "Hacking at it like it were Charlie himself hiding in one."

"Wait, why would he do that?" Hazel asked, not understanding.

"So Charlie couldn't eat them," Lance Corporal Napoli said. "Charlie's diet consists of nothing but small rations of dry fish and rice. Why should he benefit from the United States? Let them starve to death on their Communist ideals." And with that, he abruptly got up from the table and left the mess hall, the men quiet until Whitey whistled slowly and said, "damn."

"What are you most looking forward to about returning home?"

Hazel had struck up conversation with PFC Moser after noticing the numbers 3368 on the soldier's flak jacket but then also on the side of his helmet. He had laughed and said "sugar, that right there is my goddamned date of estimated return from overseas," pointing to the numbers which Hazel now realized were dates- 3368- March 3, 1968.

"I'm what you call a 'short timer' meaning I got less than 100 days left to serve on my tour of government paid hell."

PFC Moser was friendly and incredibly young. He told her he hailed from a small town in Mississippi called Alligator, that he had never been anywhere further before than the Arkansas state line, and that he had made his pawpaw proud with all the gooks he had killed in his almost 12 months here. "He had done killed a lot of kraut eaters during the First World War, well, I'm making the Moser family proud again."

"Working on my hot rod, seeing my girl Ruby Sue," he said laughing, taking a big swig from his glass Coke bottle. But then in a serious tone, his eyes taking on the "thousand-yard stare" that Hazel had heard so much about, he added, "Not wondering when I wake up each morning if today's gonna be the day the Good Lord takes me...by way of Charlie's hand of course."

Although Hazel had met with other groups of men, a combination of both soldiers and Marines, by the time evening had come around, she had found herself back in Lance Corporal Napoli's platoon once more. Maybe it was the hometown connection, or that he was a Marine, or maybe it was just the simple fact that in so many ways he reminded her of Milton. No, not in looks or the way he spoke but rather the way he seemed genuinely interested in what she had to say. Like Milton had always been even if it were a topic he had no interest in or more often, had no idea what she was talking about, her 18th century French literature course which she had struggled through always coming to mind.

"So how many of you are short-timers?" Hazel asked, thinking this could be a potential piece for *Overseas Weeekly*.

The men who had been laughing and talking so animatedly only seconds before suddenly grew quiet, a strange almost unexplained look passing over each of their faces. None of them answered and even Lance Corporal Napoli remained quiet which somewhat surprised Hazel, as she thought he would at least be the one to explain what was going on, what had just happened for the mood amongst them to change so abruptly. But he didn't.

After what seemed a painfully long amount of time, it was Private Claymore, the unabashed 18-year old from Nevada who Hazel's babushka would have said needed his mouth washed out with soap who answered, speaking as if he were reciting lines from a Greek tragedy, and yet wasn't it? The deaths of so many young American men.

"Up until last month there were two in our platoon," Private Claymore said, 'Reds' and 'Yuma.' It's kinda unheard of to have that."

From the grim looks on the men's faces, Hazel didn't have to ask to know what he meant. Death often came before you got to your final "wake up" in-country. 365 days and a wakeup was a tour of duty for a soldier in Vietnam, longer by a month for a Marine but as Hazel remembered Milton proudly telling her after enlisting, "no one's as tough as us," as if he had already made it through the 13 weeks of basic training at Parris Island when he had yet to board the Greyhound bus that would take him there.

"Reds was so happy to have made it to his 100 days. He was my first short time that I knew since I got here," Private Claymore continued. "We'd ask his opinion on something- stuff that had nothing to do with Charlie, and he'd always just say-"

Whitey broke in then finishing, "I'm too short to give a shit."

The men softly laughed then, remembering their fallen brother.

"You see ma'am," Whitey said solemnly, "being a short timer is in its own way like a badge of honor. Meaning, you've almost made it. You're almost back on the block."

"You're almost home," Private Claymore added in a reverent tone.

"Yeah, it's a better badge and more to be proud of than a CMH," PFC Bianco added.

At Hazel's blank look, he added, "casket with medal handles. Our name for the congressional medal of honor which no one really seems to receive unless you're flown home in a Glad bag."

Glad bags, the macabre nickname given to body bags, Hazel knew.

Whitey continued then. "When you have a short timer in your platoon, you guard them like they're precious cargo. You want to see them make it to the Freedom Bird just as much as they can't wait to get on it."

"How can you protect them out here in the boonies?" Hazel asked, wanting to know as much as possible.

"Namely, not letting them walk point." Lance Corporal Napoli finally spoke then and added by way of an explanation, "the man who walks in front on a combat patrol."

"Reds had 62 days to go," Private Claymore said.

"And Yuma?" Hazel asked, feeling as though she were being blasphemous by speaking the name of their fallen brother who she had never known.

"26 days."

And both the men and Hazel grew silent once more, the enormity of those two little words settling heavily over all of them.

"This here's Baxter. She's going to be accompanying us on today's country fair," Lieutenant Harris said to the platoon gathered before him, the night sky still a dark black as dawn hadn't yet arrived.

Hazel couldn't ignore the fact that she was nervous. Although she had left behind the familiar confines of her life in Saigon since arriving in Dong Ha the day before, it was still a combat base, and a combat base when you're surrounded by American life at every corner was hardly a taste of being "in the field." But today she would be. Today, she would encounter native Vietnamese peasants and see them in their native landscape against the backdrop of war. She would also witness American boys, boys like Milton, also against this same backdrop of war, far removed from the comfort and familiar scenes of base life like glass bottles of Coca Cola, meatloaf and mashed potatoes, and songs like *Light My Fire* and *Soul Man* playing in the background.

Having been to the Butler County Fair many times throughout her life, Hazel was familiar with what a country fair was and couldn't imagine anything remotely similar to it taking place in the Vietnamese countryside. She didn't quite imagine there being fair rides and games and funnel cake for sale.

"Why's it called a 'country fair'?" Hazel asked the corporal standing next to her, a Corporal Freemont, she noticed.

"You know," the corporal said. "We round up the folk, people instead of animals are on display, that kind of thing. All the while searching for Charlie, flushing him out. And we bring in our docs and medics too, treats for the kids. Get on good footing with the locals, help the locals to see the good in the South Vietnamese troops too. It's just them and us jarheads who go on 'em. A good time by all," he added almost sardonically and walked away.

The night before Hazel had bunked with the base's Army nurses, thankful to have had a cot to sleep on and a shower to wash away the sweat and grime from the day. She knew that once she was in the field, such a luxury probably wouldn't come again until she was back in her Saigon apartment. Not that she wanted to hurry back any time soon; she was keen to stay away for as long as she could or as long as the squads and platoons would have her so as to lessen the chances she'd run into him. Saigon was a huge city but also incredibly small if you were a Western English-speaking journalist there.

Within an hour of being on patrol, walking with the men from Sergeant Harris' unit, Hazel was already drenched in sweat. She was laden down with her rucksack but knew it was worse for the men who carried fully laden packs or rucks as they referred to them; Hazel remembered in one of Milton's letters that the weight of an average ruck was 60 pounds. Those 60 pounds they carried on their backs meant they were fully armed and yet they could never fully relax for fear of stepping on a landmine or being taken out by a VC sniper. Hazel knew Charlie always came out at night and yet the American boys still could never let their guard down, no matter the time of day or setting of the sun. And as Private Claymore had said the night before in an almost eerie way, "Charlie owns the night."

Hazel felt something on her scalp just then, desperately praying that it was nothing more than a mosquito or sweat trickling down. Just as she was about to take her helmet off, she felt it being forcefully put back onto her head, almost as if it were being jammed down.

"What the hell do you think you're doing?" a Marine yelled at her. "Never do you take your helmet off when on patrol. Got that?!" he asked, screaming the last part at her as he stomped off.

All the men had stopped including Lieutenant Harris, who looked at her then, his gaze impenetrable until he turned his back on her once more. Most of the men looked at her with vague indifference, nothing more than human curiosity. But no one said anything. No one apologized for the Marine's outburst but wasn't that what female reporters in Vietnam wanted, to be treated just like any man? She had made a mistake and knew she had been reprimanded accordingly for it. You make a quick and easy mistake like she had in the boonies of Vietnam, you could be a goner just like that. She could not cry. No, she simply would not cry no matter how much she wanted or needed to at that very moment.

The squad started to move again, although Hazel hung back, not wanting to be anywhere near the Marine who had reamed her out.

"It's mandatory that you have your helmet on at all times when on patrol. Well, this here's patrol, ma'am," a soft voice said to Hazel.

She looked to her right and saw that a boy who looked like he could be 15 or 16 was speaking to her.

"Other times, it isn't mandatory but you'd be sensible to wear it," he continued. "It won't stop one of Charlie's bullets but it could deflect it enough to save your life. But the moment you don't have it on, you're a prime target for a VC sniper. A head without a helmet is what we'd call a 'clean kill,' a 'guaranteed shot'. He was just trying to protect you, Larson I mean, even if he was a bit too brusque about it."

Hazel knew that this was as much of an apology as she'd ever get but also knew that she was in the wrong, completely. And so she was determined to put the incident behind her, vowing to never bring that kind of attention upon herself again.

As they passed through a thicket of burnt brush, Hazel asked the young Marine what it was.

"Bamboo, ma'am," he replied. Black felt marker graffiti on his ruck spelled out the words **too young to vote but not to die**. "Well, what once was."

"Bamboo ashes," Hazel murmured. This was the first time she had seen the exotic plant she had first read about in Pearl S. Buck's novel *A Living Reed,* now in a dead state. She remembered reading that it often grew 20 feet and higher, close-spaced and in clumps and yet here it was in ashes at her feet, the smell of burning embers still faintly in the air.

Hazel walked in silence after that,

As they approached the village, Hazel hung back slightly as she watched the men from the unit go into action. Some went deep into the village, their weapons at the ready, their faces now hardened with a steely reserve, while others stayed back at the perimeter. It was then that Hazel remembered a soldier telling her that during the "fair," no one was allowed to leave or enter. And what would happen if they did?

She saw the people coming out of their bamboo huts then, some on their own perhaps out of curiosity, but most at the urging and prodding of the Marines who were assembling them in a central spot. What Hazel saw was mostly women and children and old men, much older than her father. But then younger men whose hands were above their heads, guns fixed to their backs were being led out too, segregated from the women and children. As Hazel went deeper into the village she could see the Marines and ARVN soldiers tearing apart the huts, turning over pieces of sparse furniture inside them, shredding the mats with their bayonets. A baby started to cry and almost as if on cue, others followed.

Suddenly she started to smell smoke. She walked, wanting to discover the source of it, and saw bales of hay being lit on fire by Zippo lighters. The flames grew larger until they looked like mythical creatures dancing against the lifeless and desolate landscape, as if an Indian shaman were telling a ghost story.

"Don't lie to me you VC whore or I will *cat cai dau* you," Hazel heard Corporal Freemont yell at a Vietnamese woman who was prostrate on the ground until two ARVN soldiers who were each gripping an arm hauled her up again to face the corporal.

Hazel saw the woman looking at Corporal Freemont with sheer defiance, her silence acting as her tool of opposition and non-conformity. But then she saw the woman spit at him, her saliva hitting him squarely in the face. Hazel was stunned, Corporal Freemont was clearly taken aback as were the two ARVN soldiers who had been holding her. But in that brief moment of shock, the men's grip on the woman's arm had slackened enough for her to make a run for it. She only got a few dozen feet when the sound of a gun firing pierced the sound of the babies' crying and the destruction of the village and the woman's body falling hard to the ground, to the red clay earth.

"Guess she's not going to be competing on Charlie's Olympic team anytime soon, eh boys?" Corporal Freemont joked to the Marines who had come to gather around him. The two ARVN soldiers hurried over to the woman who was now screaming in pain, blood gushing from her right calf, and dragged her back into the village, indifferent to the trail of blood left behind in their wake.

Hazel was glad to see the woman was still alive, thinking perhaps a leg wound was not that bad after all, praying that she had been dragged away to receive medical attention and not further interrogation. But then she remembered what Kathy at the 3rd Field Hospital had told her about the helicopters making it possible to save more men than ever on the battlefields, to get them to hospitals before they would bleed out. But Hazel knew no Huey would be touching down to save this woman from imminent death if that's what it came to.

The corporal's eyes locked with Hazel's in a look that absolutely frightened her. In the days and months that followed that morning, Hazel often wondered that if she had said anything then, in the moments that followed the shooting, anything against the actions of the corporal, would he have shot her too? For in that brief moment, the corporal's eyes had no longer appeared human. He appeared someone else entirely, someone possessed almost demonically by the death and destruction of war.

After leaving the village, the men behaved as if nothing had happened, talking with each other, carrying on as if it were the lunch period at school. But this was daily life for them during their 12- or 13-months tour of duty in-country. She had gone hunting once with Milton when they were teenagers and she still remembers the numbness she felt upon seeing the deer fall, knowing that the animal's life had been snuffed out in a mere moment. She didn't know what had become of the Vietnamese woman from earlier. Had she lived? Had she bled out? Hazel didn't dare ask lest she be accused of being sympathetic towards the enemy. But the moment the woman's body had fallen it was as if she had gone in a time machine back to that cold December day in 1959 when Milton had gotten his first deer kill. Hazel knew she could never kill a living creature, let alone take another person's life. And yet she knew this was war. This was the war that her brother had been a part of. She knew from his letters that the VC and North Vietnamese often immersed themselves amongst the South Vietnamese because until 1954, the year that France had formally surrendered to Vietnam, forever relinquishing its hold on its prized colony, it had been just one people, the Vietnamese, with no designation separating the two.

Milton had once written that "North Vietnam is a Communist nation and as such, the women play just as much a role in its military as the men do. Their women soldiers wouldn't think twice about killing any of us Americans."

Had Corporal Freemont been justified in shooting her as he had?

Hazel believed he had aimed for her leg on purpose, to stop her from running, as opposed to outright killing her. Was she VC? Was she spying for the North, reporting back to the NVA about American military activity? Could she be why the short timers Reds and Yuma never made it home?

Hazel was near the back of the platoon, once more next to the quiet and much too youthful looking Marine whose graffitied helmet had said, "Too young to vote, but not to die." She was just about to ask him where he was from when she saw ahead one of the Marines drop to the road and another scream out, "SNIPER."

The young, quiet Marine rushed Hazel then, almost tackling her to the ground as if they were playing a game of football, his body remaining still on top of hers. Hazel's heart was racing then, wondering dear God, was she going to die out here too, less than a hundred miles from where Milton had been killed? She wondered how long they would have to stay down, lying on her stomach, the taste of the Halazone tablets she had taken earlier that morning to purify the water to drink now rushing to the back of her mouth in the form of bile.

She heard a gun fire then, and what seemed like an interminable amount of time later, someone yelled the words, "all clear." And the young Marine got off her and extended his hand to hers, pulling Hazel up.

"Oh, I lost my canteen," Hazel said, more to herself than anyone in particular. But the young Marine must have heard her because he said, "I see it ma'am, I'll go get it," trotting off to retrieve where it had landed in the chaos, just across the red clay road.

And then came the sound of an explosion, followed by a massive fire ball that looked straight out of a nightmare. Then the agonizing cries of a human being. Red clay ashes now.

The young Marine hadn't been killed instantly by the mine. Rather his body had been torn in two and for a couple of minutes he had still been alive even while separated from his lower half. His screaming had stopped then, his helmet graffiti indeed serving as a prophecy on his own much too short life.

When she had seen the young Marine's boot (it was not with the other), she noticed a dog tag tied with the bootlaces. Hazel was confused, thinking they were always worn around the neck.

"It's so if the body's ever fucked up beyond recognition, having it in the boot helps with the recovery of the remains," a listless Marine said, closing the eyes of his fallen brother, then gently placing his flak jacket over his upper half until a chopper could come to collect the remains.

Hazel had been in the field for barely a day and already she had personally witnessed someone dying right before her eyes. She had seen just how precariously brief a human life truly was, but especially so during times of war. How could anyone become desensitized to death when it was right in front of you like this? When what she had witnessed was happening dozens of times throughout this country each and every day.

In the time spent waiting for the helo that would take PFC Carlisle's remains back to Dong Ha and then onto the mortuary at Tan Son Nhut in Saigon before going home in a casket and not a 'Freedom Bird,' Hazel kept to herself. None of the men had said she was to blame for his death, that if it hadn't been for her he'd still be alive, not even the menacing Corporal Freemont. It was never anyone's turn to die, and yet death and Charlie's elusive and murderous hand seemed to go in tragic tandem.

When she saw the radio operator conferring with Lieutenant Harris over the area's coordinates to pass along to the pilot she knew then she was going to ask if she could get on the helo when it came and head back to Dong Ha. She had planned on being with them in the boonies for at least another few days, but Hazel couldn't do it, couldn't be out here anymore. And she knew none of the men would be sad to see her go. Perhaps they even saw her as a bad luck symbol as men often had of the presence of women on the battlefields throughout history.

As the helo took off, the men crouched down low on the red clay earth, appearing smaller and smaller the higher up it climbed, Hazel knew she could never be around the men of the 3rd Marine Division again. She didn't want to be the sole reminder of why their fallen brother had died. Of why the universe had decided that it was a Claymore mine that would end PFC Carlisle's life before it had ever really started, before he'd even have a chance to vote for his president.

"Hazel?"

Hazel froze at the sound of her name. She didn't turn around but she knew who had said it. She knew that voice without even seeing him.

Hazel didn't move, she just stayed still on the sandbag pile where she had been sitting for she didn't even know how long it had been anymore, physically and mentally exhausted over all that had transpired in the course of less than a day. She had just remained here motionless, looking out onto the landscape that was filled with nothing but the loathed red clay earth.

So he came to her and before she knew it, Vince Cerny was there standing in front of her.

"What are you doing here?" he asked, concern for her starting to appear on his face, not just because of her physical appearance but because he could tell she had been crying.

"What do you care?" she coldly said, looking away from him.

"Hey," he said, lightly taking her sweaty, dirt-stained chin in his large hands. "Talk to me," he added, almost imploringly.

"There's nothing to say to each other, Mr. Cerny," saying his last name with a tone of cold and intentional indifference. "You made that perfectly clear that morning at Frankie's Villa." What she didn't say was, "the morning after we slept together, the morning after you took me to bed and decided you'd had enough because you got what you wanted."

"That's not what I wanted," he snapped, which made Hazel's head immediately whip around to look at him.

"I mean yes, it was what I wanted," he began exasperatedly, "more than you could possibly know, but you can't expect to make long lasting friends in a place like Nam, let alone have a normal, healthy relationship. It just doesn't work that way here. Maybe the life expectancy of a journalist has better odds than that of a jarhead or soldier but that doesn't mean we're invincible either, that one day we won't just die in a chopper crash or detonate some mine when on a patrol with a platoon."

At the mention of a mine detonation, Hazel felt her heart constricting and turned her head around once more.

"Life's too short here. We all have to go sometime but that sometime is a lot sooner when you step off that plane at Tan Son Nhut," he said in a kinder and softer tone now. "I've been here since '65 and plan on staying till the end, whenever that is. I just can't have my head in any place but the war and reporting it."

"I never asked you for anything," Hazel said, still not looking at him.

"Yeah, but we can still be friends, can't we?" he asked, behaving now as if he were the young, naïve student and she the seasoned teacher. "Or at least be civil to each other?"

"I have nothing more to say to you, Vince." She jumped off the sand bags then and said, "Pretend we never met, because I have." She walked away from him, towards the mess hall, not once looking back. Because if she had, she might have broken and actually told him that she could never forget him, no matter how hard she tried, that she was lying. Because how can you possibly forget someone you've fallen in love with.

Man on the Street transcriptions-
January 13, 1968

Me: What's your name?

Interviewee: PFC Nelson, 11th Infantry Brigade

Me: Where's home PFC?

Interviewee: Flagstaff, Arizona

Me: How long have you been in country?

Interviewee: Five months, three weeks, and two days.

Me: And how many country fair operations have you gone on during that time?

Interviewee: Three

Me: And do you consider them to be a successful endeavor?

Interviewee: Yes and no. Yes, because on two of them we found huge stashes of weapons the VC was storing in the village's hay bales. No, because the Vietnamese people are liars. They lie and say they aren't VC or that they haven't seen any VC lately when in fact they have. Not to mention, our lives are doubly at risk. We go into these shitholes to help the people, we bring them food, doctors to help them, supplies, that kind of thing, all the while, they know Charlie's laid some kind of mines in the village and our boys end up stepping on one. That's how

JULIE TULBA

my buddy lost his leg. He wasn't bagged and tagged but he might as well have been with the miserable life he's gonna have now.

Me: Do you believe the United States Military should cease these operations?

Interviewee: Absolutely.

122

CHAPTER 9

HAZEL

January 29, 1968

After striking up a conversation with a Captain John Ryzmeric, general medical officer at the MACV Compound in nearby Hue, and learning that he was going to be returning there that afternoon, Hazel found herself on another chopper, her MACV ID once again serving as a type of emotional lifeboat. After her confrontation with Vince, she knew she needed to get out of Dong Ha as fast as possible and didn't want to risk the chance of being seated next to him on a chopper back to Saigon either.

Hue, Hazel would learn, was considered to be the cultural and religious center of Vietnam and because of this, had been mostly left untouched by the ravages of war by both sides. This made her immediately think of the southern city of Savannah, Georgia and even the Arno Bridge in Florence, Italy—places and things that human beings couldn't rightly bring themselves to destroy.

Vietnam's third largest city was the evocative capital of the Nguyen emperors, the showcase of the former dynasty's riches and glories, its charm made even more alluring by its location along the Perfume River. She had been told that the city was divided into two districts- the Citadel, or the Old City, which was north of the Perfume River and had been built in the 19th century, designed after the Forbidden City in Peking, whereas the modern city was south of the river, where the MACV compound was located and where Hazel hoped to secure lodging.

Hazel had been immensely curious upon hearing that the Citadel was walled-in and that half of the city's population lived within it in one or two story houses that were surrounded by stone walls, complete with a moat. She tried imagining what life would be like, living within an enclosure like that, living as if it were still 1868 and not 1968.

Since she had arrived in Vietnam, she had always been struck by the stark contrast between old and new. Mini-skirts and go-go boots were as prevalent a sight on the streets of Saigon as the traditional long gowns and palm-leaf conical hats that were worn by women. And it wasn't an old versus young person type of thing either, like what existed back in the States. Hazel had seen just as many young women wearing the traditional gown with trousers as she had older women. She took this to be more a case of the droves of refugees pouring in each month from the countryside into Saigon, rural young women where conservative values were still adhered to, including dress.

Captain Ryzmeric had told Hazel that in addition to Hue being revered by both sides, it had been at the center of the Buddhist Crisis of 1963 and the Buddhist Uprising of 1966. Other than the city's small number of Catholics, Buddhists and intellectuals were not generally supporters of the South Vietnamese government, especially following the 1963 coup and execution of the former South Vietnamese president, Ngo Dinh Diem, who himself had strongly favored the country's Roman Catholic population and discriminated against the Buddhists.

Besides being significantly smaller than Saigon, Hazel could tell it was a much more conservative city.

"We don't have a huge presence here," Captain Ryzmeric was saying. "The compound houses about 200 U.S. Army, Marine Corps, and Australian officers and men at any given time."

"So what's their role here?" Hazel asked, curious about such a small number of military personnel being based in the country's third largest city.

"We serve as advisors to the 1st ARVN Division."

When Hazel didn't say anything, he added, "We want to go home too, Miss, not be here a day longer than we need to. It's not just the doves and hippies on the college campuses who think that. But our mission isn't complete until the South Vietnamese soldiers and American forces are trained to complete the job themselves long-term. We leave prematurely, we pull out now, then what was the point of all our sweat and toil?"

And blood, Hazel thought to herself.

Hazel wasn't sure if she agreed with all that. What he just said sounded too much like a politician's speech, too much toeing the top brass line, but knew she was being somewhat unfair. He was a captain yes, but he also wasn't in the war room with Westmoreland and Johnson and McNamara. So instead she asked, "where's the nearest U.S. base then?"

"Phu Bai Marine base, about eight miles south down Route 1."

Hazel supposed she'd need to head there to hitch a ride back to Saigon when the time came.

The MACV compound, Hazel soon saw, was a compound in every sense of the word—ugly and heavily fortified and it seemed to her, almost purposely devoid of any of the charm that could be found in the Old City on the other side of the river. She had a hard time believing that it had once been a French hotel during colonial rule and that guests resembling Jay Gatsby and Daisy Buchanan (well, their French counterparts of course) would have once graced its halls. But it was nothing like the fleeting glance she caught of the Citadel, a scene straight out of a James Michener novel. If the people of Butler could see her now. See where forever precocious and curiosity seeking Hazel Baxter had gotten to.

"Any recommendations on where I could stay?" Hazel asked, once they had exited the chopper.

"Well, there's a little hotel just a few blocks away from here. It's small, used to be a private home back during colonial rule. Faces the Perfume River. But I've heard from some Western locals that it's nice and safe. Even has a bar too."

Hazel wanted to ask if he knew how much it cost a night, but she knew she'd not only look desperate but also inexperienced if she couldn't afford a hotel tab in a war-torn nation like Vietnam.

"How long are you planning on staying here?" Captain Ryzmeric asked.

Hazel wasn't sure how to respond. Was forever possible? She seemed safe here, had anonymity…at least from the journalist community…would be able to blend in more easily with her French. She had a good hunch that far fewer people spoke English here than in Saigon where it was commonplace. But she knew she couldn't hide out forever, that she would need to get back to Saigon sooner rather than later in order to transmit her copy to the *Eagle* on what a typical day in a Vietnam military hospital was like not just for its patients but also its medical personnel. And, of course, her interview with one of the priests at Notre-Dame Cathedral Basilica of Saigon and subsequent writeup on what it was like to experience midnight Mass on Christmas Eve to the *Pittsburgh Catholic*. Not to mention, she knew Ann wouldn't find cute her disappearing act considering she hadn't turned in any pieces in almost two weeks.

"A few days probably," Hazel answered, vague but legitimately honest too.

"Well, good luck. I can't say you'll find much to write about here in Hue that would be of interest to the folks back home. Just a lot of people that don't seem to want to join the modern world."

"Thanks," Hazel answered and with that took off in the direction of the river. Maybe the folks back home wouldn't be interested in Hue but she sure was. In many ways it reminded her of Colmar, a fairytale-like place in northeastern France she had visited whose old town seemed firmly rooted in the past with its cobblestone streets and medieval and early Renaissance buildings. Modernity had come to France, to Vietnam, and yet in places like Colmar and Hue, the old was embraced with a fervent and reverent passion.

But unlike in Colmar and even Saigon where white faces like hers were commonplace, here she quickly found she stood out, her black market military attire making her even more visible, more American and not some French expat. Some of the locals she passed eyed her curiously while more eyed her suspiciously. Maybe a few days would be a few days too long, she thought, as she approached the Hotel de l'Horloge, reading the sign over the door. Well, it looked promising enough as she caught sight of the slow flowing Perfume River it faced.

Opening the door, she stepped inside and said "*bonjour*" to a small older looking Vietnamese woman who was dressed in the traditional attire—an ivory colored silk long gown and black slacks.

The woman looked up, taking in Hazel's disheveled appearance and her military garb and said in heavily accented English, "I don't speak English," to which Hazel immediately replied in fluent and hopefully authentic enough French, "Not a problem. I just arrived and was hoping to book a room."

"*Américaine?*" a voice asked in French as a middle-aged white man emerged from the backroom. Entirely French, Hazel knew him to be, and knew she couldn't pass herself off as French now.

"*Oui,*" she replied. But then rattled off in French, "I'm here covering the war for a paper back home, the *Pittsburgh Post Gazette,*" not even stopping to think that this French man living in Vietnam wouldn't have the faintest idea where Pittsburgh was. But Hazel figured that was better than mentioning the even more geographically obscure *Butler Eagle.*

The woman still hadn't said anything else, just eyeing Hazel suspiciously. The man was studying her as well, but she thought it was more a combination of the fact that she was a woman, a young woman at that, and perhaps he didn't take her for a journalist, either. That, what, she was a spy? A CIA agent posing as a stewardess who worked for Air America, the CIA's clandestine airline?

The woman said something to the man in Vietnamese to which he immediately fired back in a sharp rebuke. She huffed off to the back where he had first emerged.

"*Bien,* and how long will you be staying with us?" he continued on as if the tiff with his what, wife? employee? hadn't just happened.

"Two nights," she said, figuring she'd start there and see what happened in sleepy Hue. If nothing else, she knew she could write her latest piece for *Overseas Weekly* about going on Operation Country Fair and its tragic conclusion without any distractions.

"Is it always this quiet"?" Hazel asked, realizing she hadn't seen or heard a single guest the whole time she had been inside.

"It's Tet, Vietnamese Lunar New Year, many Vietnamese are home with their families," he replied in a tone that was neither friendly nor inhospitable.

He became quiet then, so Hazel stopped trying to make further small talk as the Monsieur went about entering her details in beautiful script into his leather bound book that clearly looked as old and time forgotten as the city outside.

"Follow me," he spoke then. "I will show you to your room."

He led her down a long hallway that in many ways reminded Hazel of the interior of Frankie's Villa. But she supposed all French colonial villas resembled each other to some fashion. The room was small but cozy- a spare twin bed adorned with an elegant mahogany headboard with elaborately carved etchings of dragons. There was a matching mahogany armoire and when the Monsieur turned a switch on, an overhead rattan ceiling fan started to faintly whir.

But it was when the Monsieur opened the portico doors to her balcony overlooking the Perfume River that Hazel gasped. How could there be war when such beauty as the scene before her existed?

"I may never want to leave," she told him. He knowingly smiled as he stepped out onto the balcony behind her. They both stared at the slow and serene sight of the flowing river before them, a sampan, a traditional flat-bottomed wooden boat, floating by as if to further enhance this exotic fairy tale.

Hazel thought the Monsieur had left but then heard him say, "there's a small bar at the back of the hotel. Be sure to come down for an *aperitif*. I can also recommend a good French restaurant nearby."

Hazel had packed a casual yet plain periwinkle dress in her rucksack, just to have something in her possession other than her now sweat and mud caked military fatigues. She had also thrown in a pair of cheap sandals she had bought on Tu Do Street. The dress was incredibly wrinkly and in dire need of a pressing but it still felt glorious to put it on after her cold shower. She knew it was a lot shorter than what was appropriate here but she didn't have much choice in the matter. It was either standing out as a Westerner or standing out as U.S. military. She reasoned that in a place like conservative Hue, the former was preferable to the latter. She would ask the Monsieur if there was somewhere she could buy some cheap clothes too. The room was not as expensive as she had feared and figured she could splurge on some black-market goods too. Stuff was probably still cheaper here than in Saigon, if a lot less fashionable.

She found the Monsieur in the bar, a solitary creature who almost resembled Humphrey Bogart's character in *Casablanca*. She was reminded of the scene in Rick's Café when Sam finds Rick sitting alone, drunk and lost in his thoughts after Ilsa Lund makes a shocking reentry into his life one night. Except there was no Sam here in Hue to play "As Time Goes By."

The Monsieur turned towards her, almost as if he knew she was thinking about him. He immediately got up and pulled out one of the chairs. "Please, sit down."

"Vermouth?" he asked her as he went towards the bar.

"Yes, that would be great," she answered.

"How long has it been a hotel?" Hazel asked, curious why a Frenchman would have stayed after France's defeat in '54, knowing how much easier it would have been to return home. I mean, how many of those loyal to the British crown chose to stay in the newly minted America after Britain's surrender in the Revolutionary War?

"It was my family's villa originally. I was born here in 1921. My *père* built it in 1913, shortly after arriving here from Montpellier. His father had been a clockmaker back home." Hazel smiled upon hearing this, remembering the sign above the door she had seen, Hotel de l'Horloge, the clock hotel. "He owned a small rubber plantation in the A Shay Valley but my *mère* hated it, being so isolated and alone out there even though she was surrounded by my brothers and sisters."

"Is your family still here?" Hazel asked.

"My two oldest brothers were killed in France during the war. My middle and younger brothers were killed in the Indochina War. My sisters and mother returned to France after my father died of a heart attack in '53."

"*Je suis désolé*," Hazel told him although saying the words 'I'm sorry' to someone who had clearly suffered so much loss in his life sounded trite and devoid of any genuine meaning. "And yet you stayed?" she asked, curious as to why he would after all that.

"My wife, as you saw earlier, is Vietnamese. And France is not home to me. How can a place be called home when it's one I've never been, seen with my own eyes? Where I am looked upon as an outsider to my fellow Frenchman because I 'went native' in their opinion. When I chose not to fight for France during the world war, fight for a country I didn't even know."

"Did you fight for her here?" her, of course, being mother France, Hazel asked, curiosity getting the best of her, thinking how incredible an article she could write about a person like this.

"*Non*, and for this my family stopped speaking to me." A pause then before he added, "and for this I am a pariah on both sides. And as you saw earlier, even with my wife at times," he said half-joking to which Hazel smiled.

"Guillaume Blanchet," he said, extending his hand to hers.

"Hazel Baxter," she said putting her hand in his.

"Well, Hazel Baxter, Vietnam will always be my home. War keeps coming here but I'm not going anywhere. Be sure to tell your readers that," he added as if he had somehow again read her mind.

Monsieur Blanchet invited Hazel to dine with him and his wife, who was introduced to her as Chau. Out of respect, Hazel planned to address her as Madame Blanchet. She didn't speak to Hazel, nor to her husband but Hazel was appreciative of the fact that they didn't speak in Vietnamese in front of her either.

Hazel didn't know what to make of the Madame but she knew this— she was an incredible cook. The whole time she had been in-country, Hazel had tended to avoid the local fare, having learned her lesson after getting violently sick one night following a dinner of "meat" on a stick she had purchased from a vendor who had been cooking it on the street. She never knew what the meat was; she fervently hoped it wasn't cat or worse, rat. (She knew some Saigon rats were as big and plump as cats, who she often found to be mangey and almost emaciated.) But after feeling like her insides had come out of her, eating nothing but a half-stale baguette she had bought for the following two days, she had vowed to never try local street food again. But the smell of Madame Blanchet's home cooking was too much to resist.

Monsieur Blanchet told her one dish was called, 'com hen,' rice with baby clams. Hazel couldn't ever remember eating clams before except for that one time when she was a kid going to her friend Theresa's nonna's house. She had made them linguine with clam sauce, all the while telling them to "*mangia mangia*," even though they were two eight-year-old girls and not high school linebackers, unable to pack away the steaming bowl full of pasta before them. Then there was the 'bun bo,' a beef noodle soup accompanied by 'banh bot loc,' cassava with pork and a whole shrimp wrapped in a banana leaf. Everything was spicy, each bite tasting decidedly more exotic than the last. But she was loving it. Although she had flown halfway around the world on her own, come to a country where she didn't speak the language and where its people and land were in the throes of war, she hadn't felt different, she hadn't felt like she was truly on her own. But here, dining on local fare in a place she hadn't even known existed until her encounter with Captain Ryzmeric, she finally felt like she was the intrepid traveler, the fearless wanderer whose curiosity would never be sated by the confines of society's standards of home and convention.

Hazel didn't care if she ever married or had a family. She just knew at that moment in the Hotel de l'Horloge that she had always wanted this.

After dinner they all retired outside to the balcony, drinking a digestif that Monsieur Blanchet had poured for them, the slow moving Perfume River floating by before them.

"Do you think war will come here?" Hazel asked, not wanting to ruin the mood but genuinely curious to both the Madame and Monsieur's thoughts. Two people who straddled both sides, both cultures, and who had borne witness to more loss and heartache imaginable. The American War, as the Vietnamese called it, had already been going on for three years now with no end in sight. They had fought the French for ten. Hazel couldn't see how Hue, a city not far from the DMZ, could remain unscathed forever, no matter how much both sides revered it.

"*Non*," Monsieur Blanchet replied. "Both sides are many things, being *stupide* is one of them. But I think they are smart enough to know that no good will come from destroying a place so tied to their history, to their people and ancestors."

Madame Blanchet stayed silent. Hazel thought nothing of it of considering how quiet she had been the whole time since Hazel had arrived at the hotel. Except now she had a look as if she knew something they didn't. Like it was the most delicious secret ever.

Armed with a steno pad, Hazel spent most of the morning holed up at a local café working on her article on Operation Country Fair.

When the proprietor learned that not only was she a French speaker but also had spent time in France, he had proceeded to tell her a good deal of his life story. It involved time spent studying at a prestigious French *lycée* in Dalat (or so he claimed) as his father had been in the French government here. She presumed his mother had been Vietnamese although he didn't say. Hazel had seen some mixed Vietnamese in her time in the country so far, individuals of all ages. The most jarring, though, were those Vietnamese children that clearly had a Black father. Heartbreakingly, they were usually the ones she had seen roaming the streets, likely without a home or parents. Ann had told her that any mixed child in Vietnam was more or less a permanent stigma, but those that had Black GI blood in them were societal outcasts. Abandoned by the fathers who never knew or cared about them, and abandoned by their mother and her relatives for being a symbol of permanent shame. It would be difficult to write but Hazel could see the topic of the mixed Vietnamese children as perhaps something she could tackle. As for who would want to publish such a piece, she didn't know.

Hazel had eaten half of the most incredible French bread she'd ever consumed (even in France) and was on her third cup of coffee when a scruffy yet handsome white man walked in. She wasn't sure of his nationality but knew he wasn't an American. This was confirmed when the chatty proprietor rushed out from the back and proceeded to kiss the man on both cheeks.

Her face grew warm when she heard the handsome man asking the proprietor in French what the story was with the American dame, specifically if she was here with anyone. Before the proprietor could answer and inform him that the 'dame' spoke French, Hazel turned around her seat and surprised even herself by saying, "Well, this dame has a name and also knows French so maybe you can include me in the conversation you're having about me?"

The man stared at her, his face immobile until he broke into the loudest and richest laugh ever.

"My apologies," he said, offering Hazel his hand. "Vincent Moreau."

Jesus, Mary and Joseph, Hazel thought to herself, thinking she had to have heard wrong. But no, she hadn't. Only her luck would have her meet a handsome guy in Hue freaking Vietnam who naturally would have the same...exact...name of the guy she was trying so desperately to get over. Granted his thick and beautiful French accent hardly made Veen-sont sound like Vince, but still.

He was staring at her then, unsure if she was perhaps a little crazy so she quickly took his outstretched hand in hers, his fingers and palm warm to the touch and replied, "Hazel Baxter. *Américaine, évidemment.*"

"But of course," he answered, smiling wickedly as he did.

He proceeded to join her at her small bistro table, her steno pad filled with notes and ramblings pushed aside for the bottle of Beaujolais he had ordered.

Hazel wasn't sure if it was the wine (undoubtedly the wine) or the fact that Vincent was entirely charming (too charming perhaps, by the way he was plying her with alcohol) but she felt the most relaxed she had in a long time, her angst about her failed romance at least temporarily forgotten.

He told her he was a photographer for *Le Monde,* the national newspaper of France. Hazel wasn't the least bit surprised by this; every photographer she had come across in Vietnam so far, especially the non-American ones, were decidedly good looking.

When he suggested they walk along the river even though a light rain was falling, the low clouds hampering the picturesque views, Hazel readily agreed, not wanting to part with this utterly perfect distraction even if it was at the expense of her half-written article. When she stood up, she immediately felt lightheaded and started to wobble until he put an arm around her waist and pulled her closer to him.

"*Ça va?*" he asked her, his face mere inches from hers.

"I'm good," she replied, lost in the depths of his dark brown eyes.

When he kissed her in the sampan he had hired to take them on a ride down the river, soft raindrops falling upon them, she had eagerly met his lips. And when she laid back on him, nestled between his legs, the sights of the Old City, the walls of the imposing centuries' old citadel floating by them, Hazel thought again to herself, "how is there a war going when something like this exists? And I'm right in it?

Hazel wasn't sure on all that had transpired between the ride in the sampan and being back in her room at the Hotel de l'Horloge but somehow, she was there again, with Vincent and her slowly dancing to the sounds of silent music in-between intermittent kissing while taking swigs from a bottle of cheap red wine he had "bought" from a restaurant. They eventually made their way to the antique bed and collapsed upon it, kissing some more. When she reached to undo his zipper, he quickly but gently stopped her fumbling hands and whispered to her, his breath warm on her ear, "*Ma petite*, I think for now, you should sleep. There's time enough for that *demain*."

Tomorrow. Hazel didn't object, not in the least. Had she been reasonably sober, she would have felt rejected once more, that what was it about men in this sweat bath of a country who didn't want her? But considering her highly inebriated state, her head was already lying upon the pillow, her mind nearly in a sleeping slumber.

She first thought she was dreaming, her sleep induced state having taken her to the front lines although of course here in Vietnam there was no front, no goal other than to not die that night at the hands of the elusive enemy who appeared just as quickly and stealthily as they had disappeared once more. She dreamt the sound of rocket fire then, and maybe mortars too, loud deafening sounds that made her think what a vivid dream she was having, there was even a thudding sound too.

"*Ma petite*, wake up, wake up. I think we are under attack."

And then there was Vincent roughly shaking her awake, both of them still fully dressed. She fumbled for her Hamilton watch on the nightstand, knowing that it had to be the middle of the night and yet she could see through the portico doors that had been left open, light illuminating the night sky along with what sounded like a child's toy that made an annoying whistling sound.

"Hue is like Savannah," Hazel said, still half asleep, still half drunk from the night before. "They'll give it to General Adams like Sherman gave Savannah to Lincoln," she added before laying her head back down on the pillow.

"For fuck sake-" and before he could say more a rocket struck, followed by the sound of shrapnel flying, the ground shaking beneath them knocking Hazel clear out of bed. A sickening feeling rushed over her then when she realized how precariously close they had just been to being killed had the rocket not landed a couple of hundred feet away. Her watch had read 3:44. She was completely wide awake now, whatever alcohol buzz that had lulled her to sleep only hours earlier completely dissipated.

She threw her MACV-ID around her neck, grabbed her passport, and panicked when she didn't see her steno pad with all her notes she had jotted down from the night before.

"We need to get out of here, now," Vincent screamed at her. "And I need my fucking camera!"

"And I need my goddamned notes," she screamed back at him, about to say more when the door opened and the Monsieur was standing there, a whimpering Madame behind him, both clearly surprised to see Vincent in her room.

"We must go now," the Monsieur said to them, regaining his attention to the slightly more pressing matters at hand. "They are bombing the New City. Please come with us, there's a bunker to hide in."

Vincent said to the Monsieur, "I'm a photographer. I've got to get my camera. Please keep her safe."

He kissed her on the lips and hurried off down the darkened hallway to the hotel's front door.

"Come, we need to go now before another one falls on us," the Monsieur said distractedly, as he ushered Hazel and the whimpering Madame, who was talking frantically and Hazel thought almost nonsensically, in Vietnamese, towards the back of the hotel.

I'm a journalist. I'm bearing witness to something major, something unfolding before my very eyes, something none of the others back in Saigon are seeing, Hazel thought. I have to report on it. I have to bear witness. I have to get to the compound.

And before she knew what she was doing or had rationally considered what she was about to do, she said to the Monsieur as he opened up what she presumed were doors to the bunker, having already half-pushed/half ushered the Madame down the darkened steps, "I'm sorry I have to go. I can't hide," and took off away from the river, his shouts to her to come back, that she was a *"personne folle,"* a crazy person, were soon muffled by the sounds of mortar and rocket fire as she started running towards the front of the hotel, running towards what she hoped she remembered as being the direction towards the MACV compound.

In high school Milton had been a running back on Butler's JV football team. He had been good but not good enough to make varsity. He was fine with it; it was their dad who was more disappointed. But by his junior year of high school, he was already set on joining the Marines the moment he turned 18. As she ran towards the compound, the memory of her dead brother was with her once more. That night she was a running back, not running to avoid the other team's defense, but running to stay alive, running to make sure her story of what was taking place that night in sleepy, culturally rich and significant Hue was heard 'round the world.

The incoming rounds never seemed to end, a non-stop barrage of mortar that made a plopping sound when leaving the tubes followed by a few seconds of silence until they landed with a thud and explosion upon impact. Hazel soon learned to differentiate between a mortar and a rocket. The latter made a whistling sound coming in, the explosion even bigger and scarier than a mortar. And most frighteningly, the ground shook each time one landed, a vivid and stark reminder that life could end in the blink of an eye, with the detonation of just one mortar round, just like that.

Were she to survive the night, Hazel would always believe that it had been Milton who'd saved her.

Hazel saw the guard's booth just as she was about to round the corner and drew up short, bending over at the waist to catch her breath. It dawned on her then that the final steps she had to take to reach it, to make it to the compound, would be in the direct line of open fire. She felt like she was going to throw up then, the previous night's heavy drinking paired with not enough food to soak up all the booze paired with fear and her stomach cramping were making her wheeze as if she were an eighty-year old woman and not one in her 20s.

Running for it meant she had a 50 percent chance of survival. That is provided the compound hadn't been overtaken yet and the booth she was eyeing wasn't currently being manned by a North Vietnamese soldier, only too happy to take out the blond haired, blue eyed American she-devil.

And before her legs even started working together, Hazel screamed out the words, her hands up as if she were surrendering, "I'm an American citizen, don't shoot!!" as she rushed towards the booth, although her voice was no match for the deafening sounds of the mortar and rocket fire.

A bullet whizzed by her head then, or was it bullets? She just knew had her head been tilted half an inch to the right, it would have hit her. But then she heard the most beautiful words she had ever heard before in her life-

"Hold your fire, it's a goddamn white woman!"

And then hands were grabbing her, pulling her so hard and so fast she felt like she was being lifted.

Someone started to yell at her, "Stay the fuck down,"- and then that horrible whistling sound to which someone screamed, "Take cover!!!"

The ground violently shook then, shrapnel flying everywhere, the scene before her eyes a fiery orange color until Hazel felt a sudden searing pain in her leg. She couldn't see anything but when she placed her hand to her right thigh, she immediately felt a sticky gooey substance coating her fingers.

"Get her inside, NOW!," one of the men whose darkened faces Hazel couldn't see screamed towards the others.

She was pulled up then, a Marine on her side. The moment she stood, she cried out in pain and before she knew what was happening, one of the men threw her over his shoulder as if she were a 50-pound ruck. And then everything went dark.

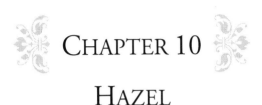

CHAPTER 10

HAZEL

January 31, 1968

When Hazel opened her eyes she thought she was dreaming for she didn't recognize anything that her eyes took in. A rough green army blanket covered her and when she moved it aside, she saw that she was dressed in a much too big Army utility shirt. When she pushed it up, she saw that her stomach was completely covered in a white bandage. A wave of confusion overtook her until the door opened and in stepped a man who looked to be about her father's age and who from his stripes she saw was a major.

"Miss Baxter," he said curtly, pulling up a chair besides the coy, "I'm Major Clarkson. How are you feeling?"

Hazel didn't answer, still not sure if this was a dream that she was going to wake up from any moment.

"You were hit by shrapnel almost two days ago, do you remember?"

And then it all came rushing back to her. Quiet and scenic Hue, kissing Vincent in the sampan on the Perfume River, the Monsieur and Madame, and then the attack.

"Is it over?" Hazel managed to croak out, thinking she hadn't heard any mortar or rocket fire since she'd awoken. She realized then it was the sound of faint small arms fire she was hearing.

"Not by a long shot. Hue is still very much under attack. The VC planned attacks all throughout South Vietnam, they're calling it the Tet Offensive. It's bad in Saigon too but nothing like here."

"But they didn't take the compound?" Hazel asked, still trying to wrap her head around everything like namely, how had she managed to survive the night before, or was it two nights ago now? How on earth was she not in a body bag, a telegram winding its way to Butler at this very moment? How was she, a civilian and a woman at that, still alive after all that had happened the night before when her brother, a trained Marine, was dead at 19.

"No, we've managed to keep control of the compound, and a few other buildings in the New City. But they took the Citadel. At this very moment, all of Hue south of the Perfume River is under North Vietnamese control."

At her blank look he added, "That's basically almost all of the city. That out there, just a few hundred yards from this here compound, well you might as well be in Hanoi, for how much Charlie and the rest of the gooks have control of things."

"Where am I?" Hazel asked, wanting to fill the silence that had descended upon the small, almost airless room.

Ignoring her question, Major Clarkson began, "Miss Baxter, I need to ask, why were you in Hue? You do realize you're at this very moment in one of the most dangerous, if not the most dangerous, places in all of South Vietnam? We're looking at days, maybe weeks of lethal urban warfare to retake the city, something our boys have never had any experience with."

Hazel looked at him then, noting the wedding band on his tanned and almost gnarly knuckles, wondering who was his wife back home waiting for him, wondering if he had kids that were her age, wondering if this military man had a son himself in the Army.

"To escape reality," she answered which was the truth but elicited a severe scowl from him in return as he thought she was being flippant.

"Well, you can't get any more real than an active urban war zone which is what sleepy Hue has become overnight," he answered, getting up to stalk towards the tiny window. "I don't approve of women being near or in the midst of war. Why the Pentagon ever allowed female reporters to come over here, I'll never know. They just get hurt and in the way." With his back still towards her he continued, "Staff Sergeant Higgins said your wound was superficial, that it just needs to heal. So you need to rest. Which is good since you can't go anywhere. Not that I want you here. But we held the compound during the worst of the assault, it's not about to fall now, so you can't get any safer than within these walls."

And as if the universe had been listening in on their conversation, something ricocheted off the roof. It wasn't a thundering sound like the mortars and rockets had been but considering what Major Clarkson had just said about them being smack in the middle of an active battle and how Hue was virtually under Communist control, an uneasy feeling descended upon Hazel's stomach.

"Sniper fire," the major said by way of explanation for the noise.

Hazel didn't dare ask could the same said sniper fire make its way through this hooch window to where she lay prostrate on the bed. Nor when would she be able to get out of here, get back to Saigon. She had been completely aghast at his stereotyping of not only her profession but also her gender. As if women only belonged in newsrooms serving as fact checkers and typists to the gallant men doing the reporting.

"Could I please have a notepad then?"

Hazel remained in bed for the rest of the day and then was given the okay by Captain Ryzmeric, whom she was happy to be reacquainted with and who she learned had been the one to examine and bandage her shrapnel wound, to be up and about. There was no water; someone told her the water supply had been cut off. Nor were the latrines functioning. Hazel had never felt so dirty before but kept any complaints to herself, knowing that the Marines who were doing the fighting on the streets outside the compound's walls had it infinitely worse.

After hearing that a female journalist was at the compound and worse, didn't have her camera with her, a Specialist Grady with a thick Boston accent had said she could have his Rangefinder camera. When Hazel had objected, saying she couldn't possibly accept it, he had just shrugged and said it was 'no big deal' since his tour was up soon, and that he didn't really want to 'take with him any memories' of a country that had killed so many of his friends. She didn't dare ask him if his DEROS, his date of estimated return from overseas, would be changed now due to the intense fighting taking place outside the compound's walls, a literal battle of life and death by the sounds of it.

Armed with her new Rangefinder, Hazel accompanied a Staff Sergeant Higgins, a giant of a man with flaming red hair, to the roof of the tallest building in the compound to see the fighting. She had scoffed when he insisted she don a flak jacket and helmet. But in an almost eerie tone he had asked, "do you have a death wish?" Hazel didn't protest anymore after that.

She had heard some of the men at the compound calling the fighting that was taking place on the streets of Hue "urban warfare," and how the United States military was grossly ignorant and completely unprepared for this type of fighting- close-quarters combat, room to room fighting, staying off the streets by moving forward and blasting through walls and buildings.

On the streets below, she watched through the lens of the camera as Marines fought house to house against the enemy. One moment there was a wall and in the next moment there wasn't, a tank having blown a round through it, the scenes of a life disrupted now on display for the entire world to see. *Click.*

She saw another group of Marines who were huddled beneath a massive tank and thought what a terrific photo this would be. The camera's shutter sounded then, audible only to her ears, permanently capturing the sight of the eight Marines, their rifles at the ready, a look of frightened yet determined fierceness on each of their faces. *Click.*

She drew back in horror when she saw a Marine cautiously walking on Route 1 and then the next moment, falling to the ground, blood seeping through his sweat stained shirt, fellow Marines instantly rushing to their fallen brother's side, shielding his body with their own as someone screamed out the word, 'Corpsman!' *Click.*

She saw a Marine break the window of an abandoned vehicle, watched him climb into it, and then mere moments later heard the sound of its engine revving, racing down the street as bullets ricocheted off its roof and shattered its back window. *Click.*

And then she saw the true meaning of modern warfare when she saw fire being sprayed onto the same building from a tank. To Hazel in that instant, it looked like Maleficent from *Sleeping Beauty* after she had turned into a dragon and was battling against Prince Phillip. Flames that were the stuff of nightmares. *Click.*

"That there is the M67 Zippo," Staff Sergeant Higgins said from behind her, momentarily startling her as she had forgotten he was still there.

"Isn't it a bit much?" Hazel asked, seriously. She was met with a look of disgust from him.

"Lady, clearly you've not been here very long if you think a flame thrower is 'a bit much.' Spend one month in the boonies on patrol, get caught in some of Charlie's punji booby traps, then you'll see that whatever it takes to take out the enemy's position is not 'a bit much.' You're what, some college educated flower child? I bet you also think we were wrong to use the atomic bomb on the Japs to win the war."

Hazel didn't say anything for she didn't want to further anger him, or worse, do anything that could possibly get her MACV-ID rescinded. She knew it had happened at least once to another female journalist before her.

"Why don't they stop?" Hazel asked, referring to the almost continuous sounds of sniper fire around them.

"Because a sniper knows that eventually he'll get one. Humans will always be more careless than the methodical nature of a sniper's marksmanship."

When the tank rolled on, Hazel took one last picture with her camera of the now desolate and war-torn street scene- cars abandoned by their drivers that were riddled with bullets, shrapnel the size of a human fist, and pieces of destroyed buildings littering the path where the people of Hue had walked in peace mere days earlier. And then just before she was ready to release the camera's shutter button, a stray dog wandered into her frame. *Click.*

On day 3 of what everyone at the compound had taken to calling the 'Tet Offensive,' Captain Ryzmeric came to see her at the hooch where she was staying and asked if she would assist at the compound dispensary and work at keeping an accurate count of Americans who had been wounded and killed in action.

Each and every one of the men who passed through the

compound's small dispensary building, reminded her of Milton. It didn't matter if they were white or Black, they were all so young, yet all maintained a sense of such bravery and stoicism that she knew men double their age didn't possess.

Some of the wounds of the men who came through the dispensary's doors weren't too serious. Their eyes seemed to alight at the sight of her, a female in the midst of this hellish setting. Hazel talked to them, asked if they had any girls back home waiting for them, although one was so brazen, he went so far as to say that Hazel was the prettiest girl he'd ever seen and that he was willing to end it with Martha back home in Butte if Hazel would be his girl. He was saying all this as the medical corpsman was stitching up a flesh wound on his right arm, and all without any painkiller having been administered. He told Hazel, "I'm anxious to get back out there and rejoin my brothers."

And then the small operating room which was only outfitted with four beds was suddenly filled all at once, each bed occupied by a gravely wounded Marine. Hazel had never been squeamish but the sight of one Marine whose blood effortlessly poured from his stomach made Hazel want to flee. But it was the image of the fourth Marine who was brought in and placed on the last open bed that made her stop dead. Even with his ashen face and gaping head wound, Hazel instantly knew who it was- Lance Corporal Napoli of Pittsburgh, the Marine who had been nothing but kind to her at Dong Ha the moment she had arrived there, the Marine who Hazel would have wanted to see make it home to Pittsburgh, back to seeing movies at the Warner and eating a plate of spaghetti topped with his nonna's mouth-watering homemade gravy, enjoying a Sunday dinner at his family's Bloomfield rowhouse.

Just then two doctors rushed in. She heard the word "tracheotomy" called out, then she heard someone say, "hold his legs down goddamnit," but it seemed that not even the strength of these two men could stop Lance Corporal Napoli's quivering body. And then she heard the exhausted and defeated words, "call it."

Tears welled in Hazel's eyes. It wasn't the first time she had been around death, but it was the first-time death had been so literally near to her, someone she had known, even it was a brief exchange.

She went outside then, shuddering as she tried to take a deep breath, the air laden with the scent of gunpowder. Tears fell onto the page when later that night, she updated her killed in action number.

On the fourth day, Hazel heard that some of the men from the compound would be accompanying a few Marines to a nearby house to save some civilians who were trapped there. Hazel asked if she could go. The sergeant naturally scowled at her request but when she told him that she spoke fluent French and perhaps could even be of assistance to the frightened civilians, he grudgingly conceded. He also looked immensely pleased when he roughly and rather unceremoniously plopped the "steel pot" helmet onto her head.

"I'm not being known as the asshole who had a lady killed on my goddamned watch," and with that headed back towards the compound's administrative office.

She stayed close to the tank, nestled between five of the soldiers who had been volunteered by a sergeant for this mission and the three Marines who were leading it,

The Marine leading point extended his arm suddenly, lowering it to his side which even Hazel instantly knew was to "take cover," for just then the sound of intermittent sniper fire erupted. At that moment it wasn't just diesel and sweat that Hazel was smelling. For the first time in her life she realized that it was possible to smell fear too.

"It's coming from the church!" someone yelled.

And a few minutes later, Hazel watched in disbelief or was it amazement, as the tank cannon was aimed at the steeple and after that came a sound that mimicked a monstrous clap of thunder, and the steeple, which had been there moments earlier, came crumbling down.

The all-clear signal was given then.

"The Carnage of Hue"
By Hazel Baxter

Urban warfare. It's a term that most of us are not familiar with, let alone your average Marine whose basic training at Parris Island readies him for combat against the Viet Cong in vast open spaces, not house to house or building to building fighting. But here in Hue, the sleepy, culturally rich city only 50 miles south of the DMZ, street-to-street, 11-blocks-wide and eight-to-nine blocks-deep fighting is what's been going on since the North Vietnamese and Viet Cong forces staged a series of surprise attacks throughout the country on January 31 that's become known as the Tet Offensive.

In the span of mere hours, the North Vietnamese and Viet Cong managed to capture almost all of Hue, a city divided by the Perfume River into old and new quarters. For this generation of young men who are fighting this war, it was the MACV Compound that became their Chosin Reservoir. It was Specialist Frank Dozema who became this generation's Mitchell Paige, a Marine with the rank of Platoon Sergeant, who fought off an entire Japanese regiment at Guadalcanal during the Second World War. In the early morning hours of January 31, the 804th North Vietnamese Battalion conducted a sapper-and-infantry assault in an effort to completely overrun the compound, home to a mere couple of hundred officers and men. Many of them serve as advisors to the Army of the Republic of Vietnam; the majority did not have combat experience. But it was these same men, men like Dozema, who sprayed machine gun-fire at the city's police station that the enemy, commonly known as "Charlie," had overrun and who ended up succumbing to his wounds, that staved off the enemy, that kept them from declaring complete victory in their malicious sneak attack.

It is not just the Marines of Task Force X-Ray who are without urban combat experience but also its leaders. Lieutenant Colonel Ernest C. Cheatham Jr., an experienced commanding officer of the 2d Battalion, Fifth Marines, a leader known for his innovative and brilliant tactical skills, had never fought in a city before. But Lt. Colonel Cheatham and his Marines are learning as they go, learning the painful lesson of how ground gained is measured in mere inches, and how every alley, street corner, and window is paid for in blood. Room to room fighting which lasts hours has now become the new norm in warfare. Here on the battlefield that is Hue, one no longer has the luxury of simply being able to shoot at the enemy to kill him. Rather, one has to blast his way through the building, and then room by room, wall by wall, advancing slowly inch by inch under the cover of tear gas which the enemy quickly became aware of. All the while eluding the ever-elusive enemy who has become extremely adept at digging spider holes in gardens and on streets, creating a constant stream of cross-fire between all buildings and streets at all times as the dead from both sides line the streets until it's safe to retrieve the bodies, which is almost never.

And like all wars but especially one in which the battlefield was one's school, one's church, one's home, it's the civilians here in Hue who are paying the steepest price, tragically caught in the crossfire of both sides. However, it's the enemy who seems utterly indifferent to the suffering of its own people, its sniper bullets and mortar shells meant for U.S. and ARVN forces instead ending the lives of South Vietnamese citizens. The Railroad Bridge and Truong Tien Bridge, connection points between the old and new city, have been destroyed by the enemy, thus rendering it dangerous and to some degree, almost precariously impossible to escape the fighting.

In this former imperial city that's revered for its religious and cultural status, Bazookas, M40 recoilless files, flamethrowers, C-4 explosives, tear gas and gas masks are not a sight you would expect to see. But overnight that's what Hue has experienced. Its people are no longer insulated from the war that has infiltrated almost every corner of their country.

Hue has gone from being a place neither mentioned nor heard of by the American people, a city of little importance to the Washington War Machine, to being a name in the hearts and minds and on the tongues of every American citizen as the brutal Battle for Hue continues today inside the Citadel, the city's Old City, the final bastion of the PAVN. It's clear that America and its fighting men won't rest until the flag of the Republic of Vietnam is flying above its buildings once more, its yellow and red colors blowing proudly in the wind even at an unimaginable cost in human life.

CHAPTER 11

HAZEL

"These are good."

The moment Hazel got back to Saigon, she had headed straight to the Associated Press office which was located in the Eden Building opposite the Continental Hotel and walked up the four flights of stairs with the demeanor of someone who knew where she was going. But in truth, she didn't. She had never been here before. But long ago Vince had told her that Horst Faas, the editor of photography for the Associated Press was a fair man and that he gave all photographers a fair shot, man or woman. He bought the image, he wasn't buying the person who took it. He said that the AP would even develop the film in the bureau's darkroom.

Although Hazel felt she was a far superior writer to photographer, she hoped that some of the photographs she had taken in Hue of the battle were good, good enough for the AP to want to buy, good enough for her name to finally get out there on a national, no maybe even a global scale. Not to mention, she had been in Hue from the moment the North Vietnamese attacked. She knew few American journalists could say that; no one had been on the ground like she had been. It was only now, days after the fighting had begun and the body counts had started accumulating that the networks themselves were sending people there to report, famous newscasters, seasoned vets like Walter Cronkite whose visits to Vietnam could best be described as glorified publicity stunts.

Hazel breathed a sigh of relief, followed by a silent prayer. "Please let him purchase at least one of my photographs, if not more."

"I'll take three."

Faas' gruff words interrupted Hazel's prayer followed by disbelief. Had she heard him correctly?

"Here, these three," jabbing his finger in the direction of the three images that Hazel still couldn't believe she had witnessed herself firsthand.

A photography legend like Faas thought her work was good enough for the AP. But when she looked up at the images on the clothesline in the hot and foul-smelling darkroom of the AP Bureau, which reeked of urine and the ubiquitous fish sauce odor that seemed to be everywhere, she startled a moment when she realized that these were images she could have just as easily idolized herself back home, picking up the *New York Times* or the *Pittsburgh Post Gazette* to read. Expressive didn't even begin to describe the scenes captured in each of them.

"The AP retains the copyright on all photos purchased. No discussion. You've got a good eye though. Who do you work for?"

"I'm a freelancer," Hazel replied, somewhat embarrassed, her freelance labeling still making her feel somehow inferior to any legitimate correspondent attached to a bigtime newspaper. "I've written pieces for my hometown paper, *The Butler Eagle*, *Pittsburgh Catholic*, and *Overseas Weekly*."

"Well, keep up what you're doing and you'll be working for the big leagues in no time. No more of that religious or small-town bullshit writing."

"So what happens next?" Hazel asked, genuinely curious how this particular process for a news outlet as major as the AP worked.

"I'll send these over the wire to New York for sale around the world," he told her matter of factly. "And we go from there."

The world, Hazel thought. My God.

"Here," he said, handing her a piece of paper. "Write your captions on it."

She took the paper he handed her, trying to think of the best words to describe the haunting and heartbreaking scenes before her in less than a sentence.

"Give 'em to me when you're done."

U.S. Marines wounded during the Battle of Hue-3 February

*

A U.S. Marine carries an injured Vietnamese child from Jeanne d'Arc High School

*

Vietnamese civilians escaping the fighting pass the Truong Tien Bridge that PAVN sappers destroyed on 7 February to make it to the American side

And then the unthinkable happened. Faas asked if she had written anything about Hue and she said she had, but was quick to add that it wasn't necessarily a play by play account. He skimmed it and then said, "I know someone at *Life*. Do you want me to see if they'd be interested?"

"As in *Life* magazine?" Hazel asked rather incongruously.

"Is there any other?" he replied, not really smiling but not scowling either, which she took as a good sign.

"Where can I reach you?" he asked, as if knowing her hovel of a Saigon apartment didn't have a phone.

"I live above a restaurant, Aterbea. They let me use their number as a way for people to reach me," she replied, jotting down the restaurant's number on a small piece of paper and handing it to him.

And then the very next day, she received a call from Faas saying that *Life* magazine wanted to buy HER story. She couldn't believe it. Likewise she knew that this lucky break, her lucky break, came at a huge cost- the lives of countless young American boys- lives like Lance Corporal Napoli, the men whose dead bodies lay entombed in body bags that she sat next to on the flight back to Saigon. Not to mention the innocents of Hue, people like the Monsieur and his wife. Were they okay? Had the North Vietnamese found their bunker? She had heard men at the compound say that foreigners were being rounded up and arrested by the North Vietnamese. She wondered what had happened to them in the days since the battle began.

WESTERN UNION

Class of service

This is a full-rate Telegram or Cablegram unless its deferred character is indicated by a suitable symbol above or preceding the address.

The filing time shown in the date line on the telegram and day letters is STANDARD TIME at point of origin.
Time of receipt is STANDARD TIME at point of destination.

DAJ26 10=WUX BUTLER PA FEB 17 825A
MRS. JOHN FAIRE
403 FRANKLIN STREET

XCD21=AUX SAIGON,
REPUBLIC OF VIETNAM
FEB 17 9:25P
HAZEL BAXTER
63 RUE PASTEUR

LIFE MAGAZINE? COULDN'T BELIEVE MY EYES WHEN I
OPENED THIS WEEK'S ISSUE AND SAW MY FRIEND'S NAME
IN PRINT. SO PROUD OF YOU
LOVE=
    BETTY
       925P

THE COMPANY WILL APPRECIATE SUGGESTIONS FROM ITS PATRONS
CONCERNING ITS SERVICE

"Lady, didn't you just come from there?"

How could she explain to this what, this teenager with a thick Texas accent, that she needed to get back to Hue. That not only was the fighting not finished, but neither was her reporting on the battle. Hazel didn't have an edge anymore, print but also television reporters had descended on Hue like bees to honey. This once sleepy Vietnamese city that was firmly rooted in its ancient imperial past, a city that had been of little importance to either the South Vietnamese or American military, had suddenly become the city that everyone was talking about, the city that American families back home would perhaps even be able to locate on a map, no longer obscure and foreign to them.

"Yes, but I need to get back. I'm not doing any good here in Saigon." Hazel wanted to add that she wouldn't get an ounce of truth from attending the 'Five O'Clock Follies' at the Rex either. Heaven knows what grossly exaggerated body count figures the officers were selling to the unconvinced or lazy and complacent reporters, depending on whom you were speaking to.

"If that's what you want. There's a supply plane leaving at 0700."

"Thanks."

Approaching the city, Hazel could still see the Viet Cong flag flying over the Citadel. She knew that ever since the Marines had taken back the New City, they had joined up with ARVN forces in the Citadel and had been battling it out against the Viet Cong and North Vietnamese army ever since. And from the air, Hazel could also see the horrific devastation that lay at their feet. Hue, a city once revered for its elegant beauty and impressive history, lay in ruins. The putrid smell of decomposing flesh and smoke from fire, rockets, and other modern weaponry filling the air, assaulted her nose the moment she stepped off the plane.

She had been paired with a military escort from the 1/1st Marines. During her brief respite back in Saigon, she had made the trek again to Cholon, Saigon's Chinatown, this time alone, where she spent money she didn't really have on black-market military apparel once more, her old duds a casualty to the siege, most likely burned or under dust and rubble at the Hotel de l'Horloge. But she knew without them, MACV ID or not, she wouldn't be allowed to accompany or be anywhere with the military.

It had rained for weeks in Hue, a rain almost as relentless as the indomitable might of the VC. Watching the Marines attempt the final assault on the citadel was the final piece of the puzzle that was the taking back of Hue, ridding it of a Communist presence. Thick heavy droplets of rain ran off of Hazel's poncho.

"Hey, don't you speak French?" someone called out.

All heads turned to Hazel, who herself had turned her head, looking around to see who the person was talking to when she realized he was talking to her.

"Yes, I do," she answered back.

"Come with me."

She followed the sergeant major out to a waiting jeep where an officer was seated in the back. He didn't look old enough to be a colonel, she thought, as she glanced at his rank. But he did look exhausted like all the other Marines she had encountered in Hue who had been on the frontlines for weeks now. The sergeant major opened the door and she got in. The colonel then got in the front passenger seat.

"Miss Baxter? I'm Colonel Roberts. I've been told you speak fluent French."

"Yes, Colonel I do."

"Good. I need a translator. I believe this local man has some good intel but he doesn't speak any English, and I course do not speak any Vietnamese or French."

"I'm happy to be of help, sir."

Moments later the jeep pulled up in front of a nondescript building whose front was entirely gone. A completely normal sight in Hue now. Hazel still couldn't believe she had been here and had seen what it once was. Would Hue ever be rebuilt like Germany had been after the war? Cities like Dresden and Cologne that had been almost obliterated by aerial bombs.

She followed behind the colonel and the other Marines and inside saw a middle-aged Vietnamese couple, the man holding a small child on his lap who was crying uncontrollably and almost hiccupping as a result, the woman wailing. On the table before them lay an 8 x 10 picture frame, the glass part of it shattered in the middle. Beneath it lay a black and white photograph of a beautiful young Vietnamese woman dressed in the traditional costume.

Hearing the tone of impatience coming from one of the men, undoubtedly the colonel who had better things to do, Hazel sprang into action. She turned to the man who seemed the most composed and asked him in French, "The colonel said you have something you wish for the Americans to know?"

The man looked at her blankly for a moment. Hazel feared that perhaps he was mentally worse off than the wailing woman. But then in quiet but elegant French he began, "Yes, my name is Ngo Dung. This my wife, Linh, and our granddaughter Anh. Five nights ago the VC came into our house. They saw a copy of an English language book, an American book, *The Old Man and the*

Sea. It was my daughter's book. She had been studying English at the university. She had returned to school after her husband died. She wanted to give a good life for her child. They shot her. They shot my Binh."

Hazel had heard rumors that the VC were doing this. Killing anyone on the spot with suspected ties to America, even with something as innocent as an Ernest Hemingway book. Killing a young woman, mother of a child, in cold blood.

She quickly translated for the colonel and his men.

"Please tell Mr. Dung, thank you. That we will relay what he's told us to the appropriate officials."

As they left the building, the colonel said to Hazel, his men perhaps already aware, "there are rumors of mass graves outside the city. We've been told that thousands of locals have been taken since the fighting began. Some immediately shot like that man's daughter, others taken away and who haven't been seen since. We just don't know. We won't know anything until we retake the Citadel. I'm telling you this out of courtesy, I don't want to see this printed in any newspaper, understood?"

"Of course. Colonel. If I may ask, have you heard anything on a local Frenchman, a Mr. Blanchet? I was staying at his hotel before the battle began. I left the hotel and ran to the MACV Compound the first night of the offensive. I don't know what happened to him or his wife. And also, a French photojournalist, Vincent..." Hazel trailed off, ashamed she couldn't recall his last name.

"Miss Baxter. May I remind you that our mission here is not complete, that at this very moment our boys are still battling it out against Charlie and his crew. When all of Hue is once again back in Allied hands, then we can investigate any claims of mass graves and premeditated civilian killings. But until then, we stay on course. We simply must if we are to win here."

And with that Hazel was summarily dismissed, almost as hastily as she had been summoned in the first place.

If we are to win here.

It was something about those words that gave Hazel pause. If we are to win here, not when we win here. He had deliberately used the word 'if' and not 'when' to describe the weeks' long battle as if he himself was still not certain of the outcome, even though by now it seemed that the Marines would be victorious. Although she had encountered many soldiers and Marines who felt the war to be a lost cause, this was the first time an officer had ever uttered such sentiment in front of her, even if he had said it more out of turn than anything else.

But did the stakes for the United States' victory in Vietnam go beyond just Hue? Was more resting on the outcome here than most people knew? She knew there was going to be a presidential election later this year back home and knew that the war was probably going to be the election's biggest issue but also its most divisive one. It had long been rumored that Bobby Kennedy, JFK's younger brother, would run, a natural fit many felt, the right man to carry on his brother's legacy and vision that was cut prematurely short. And then there was Senator Eugene McCarthy of Minnesota. Hazel had read that McCarthy planned to run on an anti-Vietnam war platform, college students being his biggest and most fervent fan base. Kennedy himself seemed to be against the war too. Johnson still seemed to be popular with the American people, but his war was anything but.

Hazel had never been remotely interested in domestic affairs, especially political ones, but she couldn't help but think 1968 was going to be a year to remember.

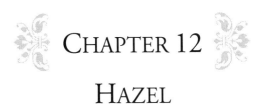

CHAPTER 12

HAZEL

February 24, 1968
Hue

"Hazel?"

Hazel stopped, stunned to hear that voice. But she didn't turn around. She couldn't.

"I'd ask what you're doing in the middle of a war zone but I saw your article in *Life*. Congratulations, Frenchie. I truly couldn't be any more proud and happy for you."

She knew he meant it, she knew he was being genuine. But it was the mention of the nickname he had bestowed upon her all those months ago, when she was so naïve and green that made her hesitate, unsure of exactly how to respond. She turned around to face him. American Vince, her Vince.

"Hello, Vince," giving him a faint smile. He looked awful she couldn't help but think. Like her, he was drenched, like her, he looked as exhausted and weary as she felt. "When did you arrive at the party?" she asked almost cynically, her experiences these past few weeks having made her a full-fledged seen it all wartime journalist, perhaps even on par with the likes of such greats as Martha Gelhorn and Dickey Chapelle.

"I was actually in Khe Sanh for a while. Westy thought the NVA was going to be doing something there, there was talk that the NVA would attack to try to seize South Vietnam's northernmost regions, give themselves an upper hand before any future peace negotiations. They moved a ton of men and ammunition and supplies there."

"All to divert U.S. troops and material to Vietnam's most remote areas, all to have that surprise element, Tet," Hazel said, suddenly feeling sick and depressed over the enormity of how it all could have happened. How it all could have gone so wrong.

"Maybe you should take Westmoreland's job," Vince said jokingly.

"So there was never any battle there?" Hazel asked, feeling completely ignorant on anything not having to do with Hue and the battle here.

"No, it's pretty bad there. The NVA launched a series of coordinated attacks at the end of January against American positions. Our boys were pinned down pretty bad for weeks. I mean the fighting's still going on. But sentiment and attention is- "

Hazel cut him off to say, "Is elsewhere. It's not exactly been a garden party here either."

Silence then entered the space between them, the sounds of gunfire and heavy artillery filling the void.

"Why are you here Vince? Why now?"

"Come get a coffee with me. Please."

Coffee was gotten from an open pot in the compound's courtyard that was then ladled into canteen cups. But it was hot and soothing against the relentless, almost chilling rain.

"When I heard that Cronkite was coming to Vietnam, I finagled my way into accompanying his team."

"Why?" Hazel asked, not understanding why someone like Vince, a journalist who didn't let celebrity names or fancy titles remotely distract him from his mission and purpose of always providing unbiased and accurate news, would be so quick to follow. "Besides, isn't he more or less best buds with Johnson?"

"Exactly. But him coming here I knew was big. Cronkite in every way is an old-school journalist, part of the 'boys club," the World War II generation, the voice of why the values of God and democracy must prevail against the evils of communism. I mean, the last time he was here was what, in '65 I think? When it's safe to say the war and Vietnam looked a hellava lot different then. Not to mention, the number of troops stationed here was quite small."

"And the number of KIAs," Hazel added, her heart constricting then, thinking of Milton who was still in high school, who still had his whole life ahead of him.

Vince looked at her curiously. He seemed about to say something but thought better of it. "Exactly," he added. "I had dinner with him and his team at the Caravelle some nights ago. He said that when the first pictures started emerging of the brutal street fighting in Saigon at the start of the Tet Offensive, pictures from all over South Vietnam, for the first time ever it wasn't just sadness and anger over the loss of our boys. It was the incredulity and doubt of the American people that the U.S. could really win this war. He said that he needed to come here himself to see first-hand what was actually going on, and not what Johnson and his cronies were spinning."

"Yeah, but Cronkite is CBS news, the face of America," Hazel countered, "the voice you hear each night on your television after dinner. He's not going to go on air and drop some huge bombshell to the Smiths and Joneses after they finish their dinner of meatloaf and peas."

"Hazel, don't you see? He didn't just come to Saigon and sit in on the daily briefings at the Rex and head back to New York with a stopover in Honolulu for a mai tai and some sun. He went to Hue where almost a month after fighting began, it's still going on. Where the American military might didn't kick the NVA or take back Hue in hours. He wanted to see for himself, the real truth of what this war is and has become. I think something big is coming."

Bee
New York City
2005

"Wait, you're telling me my mother, Hazel Czerny, ultimate recluse of Butler, Pennsylvania, was one of the first journalists to report on the Tet Offensive in what history books call one of the bloodiest battles of the war?" Bee asked Suzanne in utter disbelief.

"And that's exactly why I never wanted to have kids," Suzanne said, downing what was it now, her third whiskey soda? Or was it her fourth? She didn't appear the least bit woozy and looked like she could even at this very moment drink the biggest and toughest of men under the table. "They don't realize that their parents actually had lives before they decided to tie themselves to the whole ball and chain that is parenthood. And in many cases, a life that was a lot more exciting and adventurous than rearing babies."

Bee was about to protest but then stopped herself, realizing that at least some of what Suzanne said was true. Her mom hadn't always been a translator of French novels, hidden away in her hermit state in Butler. She had traveled to the other side of the world in search of adventure, in pursuit of making a name for herself in her field and had done just that. Her mom had gotten a byline at *Life* magazine, barely out of college. Bee felt so woefully inferior considering her career choice and more importantly, her woefully, nearly empty passport.

"Hey, don't compare yourself with your mom, at least in regards to career paths or successes," Suzanne said, wagging her meticulously hot pink manicured index finger at her. "I mean that's like comparing apples and oranges. You knew before becoming a librarian and working with dusty books and old maids that there was never going to be the thrill of the chase like you have when following a lead, or the fame and glory that comes when your story is picked up by a national or even global outfit."

"I know," Bee began, "and I know now that I barely knew my mom but that didn't necessarily seem her personality either. I can't believe she was ever driven by fame or power hungry."

"All right, women's rights lesson 101. All of us female journalists at that time were power hungry in the sense that we wanted absolutely and unequivocally to be considered just as good as any male journalist. We were sick and tired of having our gender, or the fact that we couldn't stand while taking a piss in the field, define us."

Bee could see why this woman would have gotten along swimmingly with the boys back in the day and probably even now.

"But you're right," Suzanne continued. "Your mom wasn't wanting fame like many of us were, the dream of one day winning the Pulitzer. She just wanted to be the best damn reporter she could be and at that time, wanted the truth about what was really going on in Vietnam making it back to the American living rooms, when every night the whole family sat in front of the tv set, eating their, pardon my French, shitty TV dinners of questionable meatloaf, mashed potatoes, and peas. She didn't want her brother's death and the deaths of all the other young boys to forever be tied to a lie, a damning and painful falsehood."

Seeing Bee's blank look, Suzanne said coldly, "the lie that we were winning the war, that we were stopping the wave of communism. But then everything changed the night 'Uncle Walter' dropped his bombshell on the American people."

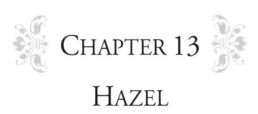

CHAPTER 13

HAZEL

March 2, 1968
Saigon, Vietnam

"[I]t seems now more certain than ever that the bloody experience of Vietnam is to end in a stalemate ... [I]t is increasingly clear to this reporter that the only rational way out then will be to negotiate, not as victors, but as an honorable people who lived up to their pledge to defend democracy, and did the best they could."

"This is Walter Cronkite. Good night."

It wasn't until Hazel had seen with her own eyes on camera, Walter Cronkite delivering those explosive and downright shocking words, that she actually believed what she had heard days earlier on the AP newswire, that she knew she hadn't dreamt it. On live television, on the evening of February 27 to homes all across America, in CBS News' "Report from Vietnam: Who, What, When, Where, Why?"

Cronkite had basically said the war was unwinnable. The war that had already cost more than 10,000 American lives, the war that was supposed to have been a "sure thing."

When word had gotten out that Channel 11would be airing the actual footage of Cronkite's CBS clip, Vince had sent her a message at *Overseas Weekly* inviting her to come to the *Washington Dispatch* main suite of offices at the Caravelle to watch it. Since they had returned to Saigon a few days earlier, Hazel hadn't seen or heard from him. Although they had spent basically the entire time they were in Hue exclusively together, almost to the point of tuning out everyone and everything else around them, even though for both of them it was non-stop work, they had made no promises about the future, spoken no words on anything else but them in the moment. And for the first time in a long time, Hazel was fine with that. Until she got Vince's message and didn't know quite how to take it. But she knew she needed to go. She needed to see the clip with her own eyes. It was 1968, not 1928; radio and printed words would no longer do for such an incendiary event.

The suite was filled with people. She knew some of the faces from her earliest weeks in Saigon but others were complete strangers. One thing was absolutely certain—Vince's face had lit up the moment he spotted her. And when her eyes locked with his and the smile on his face stayed there, Hazel felt like she could burst with happiness.

You could have heard a pin drop. Everyone in the room could probably recite the Cronkite clip verbatim by that point from all the coverage it had received, even on the other side of the world in a place like Saigon. Cronkite was the one person all Americans seemed to trust and revere, especially when it came to their news. For him to say the war that America had supposedly been winning all these years would end in a stalemate was as if every person in that room was hearing the truth for the first time. Just as television had changed the way the American people thought of political candidates after the Kennedy vs. Nixon presidential debate in 1960, the same could be said of this news clip that no one of the generation who lived it would ever forget.

"Stay the night."

Hazel hadn't asked and Vince hadn't offered to walk her back to her apartment, but after saying her goodbyes to the contingent of people in the *Washington Dispatch* suite who would momentarily be making their way to the Caravelle's rooftop bar where they planned on drinking themselves silly, Vince had fallen into step beside her, neither of them speaking. When they reached 63 Rue Pasteur, Hazel spoke.

She didn't entirely know what she was asking or rather flat-out stating. But she knew one thing. Life was too short to pine for the unknowns, to obsess about the one too many variables that didn't make sense in the equation. If Cronkite's clip had done anything for her personally, it showed her that events could change in the blink of an eye. Cronkite, who had once been a stalwart and ardent supporter of the war, of the American vision about bringing democracy to all corners of the world, had spoken the truth. His recent visit here, to ground zero, had changed all of that. He couldn't go back to the States and keep parroting what a bygone America was asking him to. And Hazel, well, she could no longer deny what her heart so painfully wanted.

Vince would give her nothing more than the promise of now- not tomorrow or the next day. Life was too fleeting to make promises that could be snuffed out just like that. But she would take it for it was enough, enough for now.

171

"Are you sure?" he asked, incredulity spreading across his all too familiar features but a faint glimpse of happiness.

"Let's have tonight," she answered. And before he could say anything else, she reached up to kiss him.

꽃

May 1968
Saigon

Hazel quickly settled into a routine with Vince. There was no set schedule of when they would see each other, no announcements of "honey, I'll be home for dinner." Neither had the luxury of the feeling of disappointment if they didn't see the other, and sometimes it ended up being days. It was war and each had a job to do. Ironically, they ended up spending more time at her small, basic apartment than his slightly plusher surroundings at the Caravelle. When she had asked him why, he had said, "because here I feel like it's just you and me, that everything else out there doesn't exist."

The only change he made to her apartment was buying a double bed, insisting after one too many painful and hot sleepless nights on her much too small army cot that it was desperately needed.

One night, they were lying together intertwined on the bed, sharing a Camel, each looking up at the ceiling, each lost in his and her own thoughts as the sounds of "My Girl" played in the background.

"I need to take you to Phnom Penh."

"Cambodia?" she asked in surprise, wondering where that had come from.

"Yeah," he said, taking a long drag on the Camel. "You'll love it, Frenchie. Absolutely beautiful. It's what Saigon used to be like. You'll really feel like you stepped back in time, like it's the '20s or something. It's just, it's completely untouched by everything going on here- no barbed wire, no barricades. Just a colonial paradise, even though the colonizers are long gone."

"Take me there for our honeymoon," she said jokingly.

"I will," he said, although to Hazel it didn't sound like he was joking.

They had never spoken about the future, not about engagement rings or weddings or anything of an official capacity. And although they tried to keep whatever it was discreet and private from the rest of the Western journalist contingent in Saigon, word had filtered out that they were a thing, that neither would be engaging in any drunken dalliances at Frankie's or some similar venue. It didn't matter much to Vince in the grand scheme of things, on how life was lived in Saigon. But Hazel, being a woman, a young, attractive woman at that, appreciated not having to constantly fend off the unwanted advances of the male journalists. She wasn't a fan of feeling like she had been appropriated by a man but in this case, she didn't mind it.

"So what's on your agenda for the next few days, Frenchie?"

Vince had been up at Khe Sanh for the last couple of weeks and so they'd had zero communication with each other. He had been there to report on Colonel Lownds, ground commander at the base, and the 26th Marines formally departed Khe Sanh in May. Vince had told her that the end was near in terms of U.S. troops remaining at the base, the same base that President Johnson had ordered be held "at all costs." Now Khe Sanh was on the verge of being abandoned just like Johnson had done to the American people when he'de announced months earlier that he wouldn't be running for reelection, throwing both the country and its people into a tailspin.

Rumor had it that Johnson, following the Cronkite bombshell said, "If I've lost Cronkite, I've lost Middle America." And then mere days later, Martin Luther King was assassinated in Memphis. Hazel knew she was entering a war zone when she came to Saigon. But she had no idea that she'd also be leaving one behind; that's how embattled and divided America had become. She had also read that anti-war protests on university campuses across the country were becoming more frequent and in some cases even turning violent, the protesters no match for the batons and hoses of the police. And yet the protesters would never back down and concede their cause. Not until every last American was gone from here and young men, boys really, were no longer drafted. And of course, the fact that one of the men vying for the Democratic party nomination to be president was basing his campaign on an anti-war platform, well, that only further cemented the anti-war cause. The fact that Eugene McCarthy, a senator from Minnesota whose name meant nothing to most of the American people and who had a pittance in his campaign coffers, had come precariously close to winning the New Hampshire Primary, upsetting LBJ, the sitting president, showed just how much the anti-war movement's momentum had picked up in recent months and that it wasn't going away anytime soon.

"I'm headed to Cu Chi tomorrow," she told him. "I'm going to try to farm out a piece to AP again. See if they pick it up."

Although Hazel would always be eternally grateful to all that Ann Bryan had done, not just by offering her a job when she desperately needed it, but also for her friendship, she knew that she had grown beyond *Overseas Weekly*. If a reporter was to make her mark on the world, being in the middle of a war was the place to do it.

"I-," Vince started to say something but then stopped himself.

"What?" she asked. "Say what you were going to say."

"It's not my place to," he said. "I don't have any right to."

"Would you just say it already," Hazel demanded, slightly exasperated over how cryptic he was being.

"Just be careful," he replied, taking her chin in his hand, forcing her to look at him squarely in the eyes. "The tunnels are dangerous. I mean, well, that's the understatement of the century. You know what the lifespan of a tunnel rat is?"

Tunnel rats were the men who performed underground search and destroy missions in the elaborate and extensive system of tunnels that ran the length of the Ho Chi Minh Trail. The tunnels had originally been created as a means of warfare against the French colonial forces but were now being used by the Viet Cong in the war against the Americans. It was said that between the sophisticated ventilation systems and structures like hospitals, barracks, and even kitchens, VC guerrillas could stay hidden underground for months at a time, making the already elusive Charlie that much harder to find.

But it wasn't just the VC combatants who were a threat to the tunnel rats. Everything from occasional cave-ins to booby traps of grenades and mines, to live booby traps like venomous snakes and scorpions, to poisonous gas was a potential cause of the untimely death of a tunnel rat.

"A month?" Hazel asked.

"Three seconds."

"You're joking," she said, sitting upright, pulling the already sweat dampened sheet over her.

"I mean it, babe, please be careful. I know you won't be going down in any that haven't been cleared yet, but this is Nam. Nothing is by the books here. And besides, I don't renege where promises are concerned," he said, slowly and teasingly placing light, delicate kisses on her bare skin, slowly tugging down more and more of the sheet as his mouth traversed the length of her arm.

Promises being that they'd honeymoon in Phnom Penh, which means they'd get married? Or just promises that he'd take her there anyway?

"I will," she solemnly told him, almost imagining that she was saying the words "I do" instead.

"Most of the dangers that we encounter aren't from below ground but actually above it. I mean, a lot of people automatically assume that it's the crawling through underground enemy bunkers when we're the most at risk in our job. But it's not. We sustain the most casualties when we're finding and disarming mines and booby traps."

Sergeant Nicholas Paine of the 25th Infantry Division was Hazel's "tunnel rat escort" today at Cu Chi. He had told her he had been in his role for five months. Considering what Vince had told her she was shocked to hear this. Her face must have conveyed this because he had cynically and almost sadly said, "Yeah, I'm a freak of nature, a lucky one to have lasted this long."

"What sort of equipment do you use in your missions?" Hazel asked.

"The only things we're given are a flashlight, a M1911 pistol or sometimes a M1917 revolver, a bayonet, flashlight and explosives. But most of the time, it's just a flashlight and a pistol."

"Why that firearm?" Hazel asked, completely ignorant on military weaponry, having assumed that all soldiers would want to have on them a bigger weapon like a rifle or machine gun.

"Because when we go down in a little bit, you'll see why below ground, fighting with the enemy in ultra-close quarters, it's golden. Sure, the blinding flash sucks and the muzzle blast makes you feel like you're gonna go deaf each and every time, but nothing is more powerful when fighting Charlie in ultra-close quarters. It also doesn't jam or run out of ammo like a rifle or machine gun does."

"So did you volunteer for this detail? Or were you assigned?"

Hazel asked, thinking no one could possibly want to do this job. Three second lifespan. Vince's words from two days ago kept echoing in her head.

"Well, for the most part, yes," he told her. "I knew I didn't want to be an infantry soldier. Marching all over, dealing with jungle rot, sleeping on the ground in the rain and all that shit. And I thought if I'd ever go to college, I'd like to study engineering. I thought this would be good experience. I just didn't know that there's no guarantee I'll get the chance to do that. But no one's assigned this detail. Everyone who does it has volunteered."

What wasn't said, of course, was that he'd have no guarantee of actually making it out alive to attend college back home.

Sergeant Paine's short and slight frame hadn't gone unnoticed by her. He had to be about five foot four inches as he was nearly the same height as Hazel.

"And you're short," Hazel added, then immediately blushing over how rude and emasculating she sounded.

He looked at her, all emotion vacant from his face. Hazel had no idea how he was going to react but then in the next moment the most wonderful sound emanated from deep within him— boisterous laughter deep in the heart of the Vietnamese jungle.

"Well, Miss Baxter. I know girls and all are clamoring to be treated equally back home but you really are one of the most abrasive and forward people, man or woman, that I've ever met. But yes, as my high school girlfriend was so fond of reminding me, I am without a doubt, short."

"You see, the gooks are short and skinny by nature. They've built their tunnels for their people, not for taller and bigger Americans to infiltrate and destroy."

"And there's enough of you?" Hazel asked, blushing once again over the rather insensitive nature of her words.

"You mean, with how many casualties we sustain on a monthly basis, there's enough of us 'short guys' to fill the void?"

He took her silence as confirmation that's exactly what she was asking.

"Yes, I realize GI Joe isn't five feet three inches but you know what, we come in all shapes and sizes and the U.S. military would be lost without us," he said almost proudly. Hazel greatly admired him for that. That, and his insane ability to have lasted this long in such a dangerous role.

"Are there any rules you have to take a blood oath to swear by?" Hazel asked, more jokingly than seriously.

But he answered her in a completely serious tone. "We're forbidden to ever fire off more than three shots in a row."

"But why?" Hazel asked, not understanding how that was a rule. What if the first three shots hadn't struck down the enemy? What if he was still moving and could potentially still kill you.

"Fire six and the enemy knows you're out of ammo."

The enormity of his words sunk in.

"You're done."

"Done doesn't even begin to describe what comes next," he told her grimly.

An hour later, Sergeant Paine had debriefed her on the official and unofficial rules that the tunnel rates swore by, as well as the many booby traps and beloved "tricks" of the Viet Cong. They loved to ensnare their catch by spearing the GI through the throat, impaling him in the small opening, the dead GI stuck up there, his buddies unable to get him down as they frantically tried to crawl out of the tunnels only to find more VC lying in wait for them. Hazel went white at this but the sergeant continued.

"I know back home the country thinks of us as baby killers," he said. "But you know something? The VC, they're pure fucking evil. And it's not just the men doing it. One of my buddies, a fellow rat, he was garroted a couple of months back. A fucking woman did it," he finished disgustedly.

Hazel said nothing. What could she say? She had been in-country now for more than half a year. And she had seen the evil on both sides. Neither military, Hazel felt, was inherently good or bad in how they acted and behaved. She knew most of it boiled down to the sheer psychological principle of survival, pure and simple. And in that moment, she said a silent prayer that Milton had never had to do this. No human being should ever have to do this.

Sergeant Paine seemed to recover then, remembering what his mission was, at least for today with Hazel there, manners and military civility returning once more.

"Ready to go below the earth?" he asked.

"As ready as I'll ever be," Hazel replied, feebly smiling back. Although close, tight spaces had never bothered her, she had also never been faced before with a situation such as this one. All she wanted was to not embarrass herself.

But Hazel had no idea that embarrassing herself would be the least of her worries.

The Lucy Show had just come on when the doorbell rang.

"Hazel, get the door," her dad said, not even bothering to look up from the newspaper he had been reading. As if Milton wasn't sitting on the sofa right next to her where they had been watching The Man from U.N.C.L.E. That is until The Lucy Show came on and then they had to

change the channel from NBC to CBS. Although their father catered to Milton at just about every turn, even more so now that Milton was older and his plans to join the Corps after graduation firmer than ever, when it came to television watching at night their mother was queen of the kingdom. That was the one thing their father didn't begrudgingly give their mother.

"Who could it be at this hour?" Hazel's mom asked, a look of concern passing across her face because the sound of a knock at the door at 8:30PM on a Monday night could only mean one thing, bad news.

Hazel untangled herself from the afghan she had been wrapped up in on the sofa and went to the door, peering through the plaid curtain that covered the glass. The man, because she could at least make out that, had his back to the door, but she could see he was dressed in a military uniform.

"It's a soldier," she said over her shoulder, as she unlocked the door, thinking that perhaps one of Milton's friends had joined up.

The moment she opened the door, the man turned and she gasped upon seeing who it was.

"Vince?" Hazel asked in shock. "What are you doing here? Why are you in Butler? How did you know where I live?" not understanding how Vince could be standing here at her family's front door. How could Vince be here and Milton still alive in there? She met Vince months after Milton's death. And he looked so young. So much younger than his 36 years. He looked like all of the other young men she had met so far, boys of no more than 20.

"And why are you in uniform?" Hazel blurted out, only then realizing that it wasn't an Army uniform he was in but rather a Marine's.

"I'm a Marine, Hazel," he said, giving her a look like she was crazy, that didn't she know he had always been one. "Aren't you going to invite me in?" he asked, slightly bemused that she was still out of sorts over his appearance.

"But-," Hazel stammered in a loss for words. "I don't understand how this is-"

"Hey, I'm Milton," Hazel's brother said, appearing from behind her, extending his hand to shake Vince's. "I don't always approve of the guys big sis brings home but if it's a jarhead, you're a-okay with me," Milton said jokingly.

"Good to know," Vince said, flashing Hazel a huge grin. "Because this one here," Vince said, pulling Hazel up against him, putting his arm tightly around her waist, "I want to marry her one day."

Marry her? Had she heard right?

"No complaints from me," Milton said, smiling at Hazel, giving her that wonderful Hollywood smile she had always loved, the smile that could melt her worries away, just like that. The smile that reassured her that stuff would be okay, even when their father drank too much and their mother cried at regular intervals, that with the two Baxter children, they'd always be okay.

"Dance with me, Frenchie," Vince commanded, extending his outreached hand to hers, until she took it and there on the rooftop bar of the Caravelle they danced to the sounds of The Association.

But it was only them as they danced; there was no one else around in a place that was always brimming with people, loud and chaotic. Nor were there the sounds of war. Only "Never My Love."

CHAPTER 14

"Hazel?"

Hazel thought she heard her name being called but she couldn't be entirely sure. Her mind felt as if it were in a dense fog. She could hear the sounds of activity all around her but had no idea if she was dreaming or if it was real.

"Hazel?"

Upon hearing her name a second time she opened her eyes which for some reason hurt to do so and saw what looked to be a man standing before her. But nothing was clear, everything looked so hazy. She started to lift her right arm and saw it was covered in white. And that it felt heavy.

But then she felt someone's touch on her, a rough hand starting to slowly caress her cheek. And then he was sitting down beside her, so close now she could clearly make out the dark hair, the small scar below his left eye, the faint smell of Brut Faberge cologne.

"Vince?" Hazel meekly chirped.

"Yes, Frenchie, it's me. I'm here," he told her, continuing to stroke her cheek.

"What happened?" she asked, not remotely understanding how she had ended up in a hospital bed. A hospital bed where? In Butler?

When had she returned home? And wouldn't she have remembered the long flight, the stopovers in Honolulu and Guam?

"You don't remember anything?" he asked, concern readily apparent in his dark onyx eyes that she could now see had deep bags underneath them.

"I was…" she trailed off, mentally stumbling over her words and her memories or lack thereof. "I was doing an interview…in the tunnels. I was interviewing a sergeant…and he took me down into one. He said it was cleared, that it was safe to do so. I just remember feeling so claustrophobic but then all of a sudden there was yelling…angry yelling but I couldn't understand what the person was saying, it must have been Vietnamese. And then I remember hearing the sergeant scream out the words, 'get down,' and then I heard a gunshot, and then a blast, and then I felt the sergeant's body on top of mine."

Hazel stopped then, everything that had transpired now emotionally catching up with her.

"You were wounded pretty bad, Frenchie," Vince said, picking up where she left off. "You got shrapnel wounds to your hand and your thigh and here," lightly touching an area on the right side of her neck that was covered by a thick bandage. "Thank God the sergeant covered you with his body, it could have been a lot worse."

"But Vince, he's okay, right? I mean he saved my life!" Hazel said, aghast at the thought that she was the cause of someone else dying.

"Hey, hey, shhh," Vince cooed to her, trying to calm her down, stroking her hair as if she were a small child. "He's alive, but he's probably going to be shipped home once he's stable enough for the flight. He took some shrapnel too, to his spine and feet. He uh…" Vince trailed off, clearly having been about to say something he now thought better of.

"Tell me," Hazel demanded.

More silence then until he said almost ashamedly, "They had to amputate both his feet."

Hazel fell back against the crisp if not cold, starched white sheets. "Hey," he said. "Look at me."

Hazel lifted her eyes to meet his. "Tunnel rats, they volunteer for those jobs as I'm sure you were told. But he didn't die out there. He's not going home in a body bag. There's no casket his parents will have to weep over, the sound of "Taps" is not going to be played, at least not now. Their son, their brother, or husband or boyfriend, he's still coming home to them."

Home as a cripple, Hazel thought. Home to a country that didn't want them for the job they hadn't wanted to do in the first place, from the country they had never wanted to go to.

Silence then until Hazel asked, "Where am I?"

"3rd Field Hospital. You were brought here by helo three days ago. They had you on morphine for a while so you were pretty out of it."

Hazel wondered if Kathy, the nurse she had met on Christmas while volunteering here, was still working. She must be, Hazel thought, remembering Kathy had only just started her tour then.

"How'd you know I was here?" Hazel asked, looking down at her bandaged hands now which resembled a badly wrapped boxer's hand. She wanted to add, because it's not as if we have a system where we check in nightly with each other, but didn't. He was here with her now, that's what mattered she told herself, and besides, the upsetting and worrisome nature of the last couple of days was readily apparent on his unshaved and anxious face.

"Word had gotten out that a female reporter had been injured in an explosion at Cu Chi. I knew immediately that it was you even before I had gotten confirmation from a good buddy of mine at MACV."

Hazel continued staring at her bandaged hands, not saying anything, so Vince went on.

"I wanted to send a telegram home to your family but then I realized that I don't even know their names. That I have no idea what your parents' names are except Mr. and Mrs. Baxter of Butler, Pennsylvania. And I know Butler's small but I can't imagine they're the only ones with that name."

"Sam and Anna," Hazel said quietly, still looking down.

"And Milton? Old boyfriend you're still pining for?" Vince added with some levity, clearly wanting to cheer Hazel up. "You said his name a tuuuuun," he added in a joking manner.

"My younger brother," Hazel answered, tears starting to well in the corners of her eyes. "He died here."

"Died where?" Vince asked confusedly, not understanding what she was saying.

"In Vietnam.

"You were both in my dream," Hazel told him, long after tears were shed and time spent recounting her brother's tragically premature death, her mother's mental decline and desire to stop living, and her father's emotional shutdown. "Only, it wasn't him in a Marine's uniform, but rather you. And you looked so very young too."

"Wait, hold on a second," Vince said, visibly agitated although Hazel didn't understand why he would be. It was just a dream and her dream at that. "You're telling me that in your dream I was in a Marine Corps uniform?"

"Yes, which was the strangest thing since you never were in the Corps but Milton had been."

"But I was, Hazel. I served in the Corps after I graduated from high school. I served in the war."

The war. Only Hazel realized he wasn't referring to the Vietnam

War but rather the Korean War. The last war fought to stem the Communist tide in which so many other young American lives were forever lost. And look at how well that turned out. But that would at least explain why he had looked so young in her dream. Because he still would have been a teenager.

"You were in Korea?" Hazel asked, dumbfounded now.

"But I never told you I was in the Corps," Vince spoke, ignoring Hazel's question. "How could you have dreamt that?"

"When were you there?" Hazel asked, now ignoring Vince's question, each of them deeply lost in their own swirling thoughts over the other's revelation.

"I went straight from Parris Island to Chosin, which on so many days felt like it was a one-way ticket, a one-way ticket straight to a frozen hell."

Battle of Chosin Reservoir. Hazel paused, trying to remember details on it. But Vince spoke now, although he was speaking from another time and place, one that wasn't 1968 Saigon.

"If you stopped, you froze. If you didn't want to move anymore, if all you wanted was just a little rest, you froze. I know Vietnam is its own type of hell, but Chosin," Vince shook his head before adding, "People have no idea what it was like for us there during those two weeks."

Hazel remembered as a child seeing newspaper headlines describing Chosin as a bloodbath.

"Every night the temperatures dropped well below zero, so many of the men got frostbite. The mountains just completely covered in snow, the icy roads almost always impassable. And the wind, the wind was so brutal and strong that it felt like you would just get picked up and thrown over the cliffs. Fighting a war is never easy, but fighting a war in those conditions, it was a nightmare that never ended. And the Chinese soldiers, they just kept coming and coming, blasting their bugles and shrieking whistles, and clashing cymbals, like it was their last hurrah and not ours. But they did this every night, every goddamned hellish night for two weeks straight."

His eyes were haunted now, the infamous "thousand-yard stare" having taken over them.

"We were surrounded and outnumbered and yet somehow we made it out of there, somehow we became the 'Chosin Few.' I survived when so many of my brothers didn't," he said his voice breaking now, a tear starting to roll down his unshaven cheek.

My God, Hazel thought as she looked at the man she loved, at the man she thought was emotionally impenetrable. But he wasn't, was he? No one really was. Everyone had their emotional demons that they carried within them.

"God, I'm sorry, Frenchie," he said, trying to wipe away at his tears in a way that only a man who didn't like showing emotion could. "Here I am crying like an old lady while you the patient are lying there like a true champ," cuffing her playfully on the chin.

"I want to know everything there is to know about you," Hazel said in a serious tone. "I love you, Vince Cerny. And I'm not afraid to say it anymore. Maybe you don't feel the same way about me, or maybe you do but you'll never say those same words back to me. But I do, that won't ever change. I don't want to lose you again so I'd rather have you in my life like this than not at all. You mean too much to me to not be a part of it. Just please don't ever push me from it again."

Silence then. Hazel had felt her heart racing when she said those words. Months ago she would have felt she'd said too much, gone too far with her impassioned speech but the Hazel of now, the Hazel who had survived Hue, who had almost died in a VC tunnel, was different. She was still just a woman of 22, the same age she had been when she walked down the steps onto the tarmac at Tan Son Nhut all those months ago, but deep down inside, she felt she'd aged 10 years. And a woman of an emotional age of 33 wasn't afraid to tell the man she was in love with that she truly loved him.

"Well, you know something Frenchie?" he answered, looking into her eyes with so much passion and intensity she had to blink.

"What?" she asked huskily.

"*Je t'aime aussi.*" I love you too.

They never spoke of how she had dreamt seeing Vince in his Marine Corps uniform, or seeing him and her brother standing there together, but secretly she knew that she had dreamt it for a reason. The dream that had the man she loved, with her dear brother in it together, that meant something, she knew it. And Hazel also knew that it was Milton's way of saying he would always be with her. And hopefully approved too.

Vince visited her every day at the 3rd Field Hospital for the week she was there. Frankly, she was a little surprised by this as she knew how much he hated staying in Saigon for a story. But he had told her "I was long overdue for some comedic relief," which he got by way of attending two days' worth of daily military briefings at the famed Five O'Clock Follies at the Rex.

And each day while sitting on her bed, their bodies always touching, he told her about his life before the war and she hers. Since being older and illustriously established, his was infinitely more interesting, which is why she was doing most of the asking.

"So what made you enlist in the Marines?" she asked one day.

"I didn't have anyone."

"I know that, but why enlist? And why the Marines?"

Vince gave Hazel a look that said, "you talk too much" but he just smiled at her.

"My dad was one. He was killed at Guadalcanal in '43. After that, my mom gave me up."

"What do you mean, gave you up?"

"Abandoned me, or the fancy way of saying, relinquished me to the state."

"And how old were you then?"

"Twelve. Old enough that no families wanted to adopt me. So I was in an orphanage until I graduated from high school, minus a few stints where I ran away or I should say, attempted to run away until they brought me back. And that very day I enlisted."

"There was no one else?"

"My mom was only 16 when she had me, my dad 18. They had run off together to get married after she got pregnant. My dad's folks were immigrants from the old country. My mom's folks, well, they didn't approve of him. Well, and I know his folks didn't want a daughter who didn't speak Czech or know how to make kolaches," he said, smiling now at what seemed to be a delicious memory.

"Where'd they end up?"

"They went to Chicago where they thought they could start a new life. But money was always tight, she lost two babies. And then after he enlisted in the Marines and he got sent away, well that just started a whole new slew of problems between them."

Hazel knew her home life growing up had been fractious but she had still had one, a family with not just her parents but also grandparents and aunts and uncles and cousins.

"I figured that by joining up, serving in the Marines, I'd make my old man proud, wherever he was. And I had always wanted to go to college. I knew I would never be able to do that without the GI bill."

"And your mom?" Hazel asked tentatively. "Did she ever try to find you?"

He didn't answer that last question and Hazel didn't push him to either. The emotional pain of being abandoned was obviously still a painful wound almost 25 years later.

And not until the day she was discharged and finally back at home, her once thick boxer style bandage on her right hand having been replaced by a slightly smaller and less cumbersome one, did Hazel learn that Vince had been married.

"The day I met you on the flight," he said, taking a long drag on his cigarette, "I was coming back from finalizing my divorce."

"Wait, what??" Hazel asked, shooting straight up in bed.

"I thought you'd like how I slipped that one in," he laughed, pulling her back down beside him, their naked bodies each glistening from the heat and sweat of the late afternoon, among other things.

"The beginning please," Hazel said primly.

"I met Lois at Northwestern. That's where I went. What's funny is that the whole time I was in Korea all I could think of was I never wanted to be cold again in my life, never live somewhere stuff could freeze. And I ended up right back in good old Chicago. But if Korea taught me anything it's that I yearned, no, I craved familiarity, normalcy, and Chicago was that. Cold and all. She was a student there too. But I think that's why I like it here so much. It reminds me nothing of Chicago and the memories I have of my parents or the orphanage I was in or especially Korea."

"A fellow journalism student?" Hazel asked, wanting to return to the story at hand, pangs of jealously now manifesting inside her over

191

this woman she didn't even know.

"Oh no, no Lo was an English literature major. But we met in the library one day. I had never really had a girl before, most girls didn't want to date a boy who was orphaned and lived at a home. So she was the first girl I ever really went steady with."

He paused then before continuing. "Looking back on it all now, I realize she was just in school to find a husband, I don't think she ever had any intention of graduating, nor do I think her dad ever had any intention of paying four years' worth of tuition. I proposed the spring semester of our sophomore year and the following year we were married. But she never returned to school after I proposed. She said she had too much to do in the way of wedding planning."

"Was she rich?" Hazel asked, a feeling of vast inferiority settling over her.

"Her family was definitely well off, although I guess you could call them a 'society family.' I think if I hadn't been a war hero, someone who had served his country, well, I don't think they would have gone for the GI orphan kid."

"And you loved her?" Hazel asked, afraid to hear his answer.

"I thought I did. But we were both so young. And I had no family models to know what true love, a good marriage should resemble."

"So what happened?"

"Being the wife of a low-level reporter didn't exactly appeal to Lo even though I got a job right out of school at the *San Francisco Chronicle*. But I was never home, just instead always wanting to break the next big story, and always yearning for more on a professional level. This Vince wanted to be the next Vincent Sheenan."

He was, of course, referring to an illustrious print journalist who had covered much of the world for more than forty years, someone who was on par with one of Hazel's journalist idols, Dorothy Parker.

"And I did, I worked my way up the ladder, paying my dues as I went. When the opportunity came up at the *Dispatch* I took it. I thought it would be a fresh start for Lo and me, thought she'd like DC more than she did San Francisco. But I was wrong. The new job had me traveling a ton, mainly internationally, and we grew even further apart. After Tonkin in '64, I started covering Vietnam full-time, coming over every couple of months, moving here in the fall of '65 and by the beginning of '66, they had promoted me to the role of Saigon bureau chief."

"You see," he said, turning away from her to peer out the small window which overlooked always bustling and noisy Rue Pasteur. "I never wanted to be home even if I could have. Everything here- the war, the people, the smells, it was a rush, a high even, that I could never get enough of. I could only get what my mind and body wanted by being here, even though simply by being here, I could die at any moment."

"So who initiated?"

"What, the divorce?"

"Yes."

"She did. She met someone, as the age-old story goes. Well, she might have met a lot of someones for how much I was gone but I guess this one was enough to make her want to be rid of her messed up in the head husband. He was a junior senator so needless to say, for Lo that was more along the lines of what she envisioned a married life being. So she went out to Reno, lived there for six weeks as the law requires and then she was able to file for divorce, just like that. I went back to sign everything and have it all wrapped up neatly, my wedding present to her, you could say."

"Do you miss her?"

"Not in the way you think. We had some good times, but mostly in the beginning, when, you know, everything's still new and endearing even. When I thought my life needed to resemble what societal standards have always said it should look like—wife, house, and 2.5 kids."

"And me?" Hazel asked, somewhat unsurely. "Where do I fit in all of this?"

"Getting attached to you was the last thing I wanted, let alone needed. I had just gotten disentangled from one wife and wasn't looking for a new one. But you know they also say that sometimes love finds you-"

Hazel cut in to finish- "when you least expect it."

"But I knew I loved you," he said "from the moment I saw you panic-stricken on the flight when the plane started to do its usual nosedive to the tarmac to avoid enemy fire," smiling broadly at her now. "And the more time we spent together, I knew I wouldn't be able to stay away."

"Then why did you—?" Hazel started to ask before Vince became the one interrupting her.

"Push you away after our night together at Frankie's?"

"Yes."

"Because I never gave much thought about me dying when I was still married. I figured if I was killed, Lo would be okay and no doubt would remarry just like that. With you," he said turning on his side now to directly face her, "it was different. I didn't feel I could do my job as a war reporter well if I was worried about getting killed in a mortar attack or put the lives of other soldiers and Marines at risk by not having my head be clear. I couldn't have any attachment that would impede my work, the sole reason I was here. But that day I saw you at Dong Ha, and you wanted nothing to do with me, that broke me on the inside more than any fragment from a grenade."

Hazel took a deep breath, remembering that painfully emotional day. And how running into him there was what led her to Hue, what led to her first big break in her career. Was the cliché saying, 'everything happens for a reason' actually true? Is this what the universe had wanted for her?

"I stayed away then," he continued, "knowing I couldn't have it both ways. And that day I also saw in you your grit and determination to stay here, to not leave after a meager two months like so many other journalists do. Then when I saw your story in *Life* and ran into you in Hue, I knew the universe had given me a second chance. A second chance with you, a second chance at actual love."

Love. Him telling her he loved her countless times a day were three words Hazel could still not get enough of.

"I know that what we have is the farthest thing from traditional, Hazel, but I love you and can't imagine my life without you now. I know you have in your blood the drive to be here, the same drive I have to always tell the truth about what's really going on here to the people back home."

She did. She was sure of this, just as sure of the fact that she loved Vincent Cerny. Nothing would ever bring Milton back, or the 20,000 other American boys who had died so far, whose lives would never play out in the way their moms and dads envisioned on the days they had been born. But she could at least tell the truth so their deaths meant more than a politician's lie.

And then reaching over to the decrepit rattan chair he had draped his pants over, he pulled out a small black box from one of the pockets.

Hazel gasped, seeing what he now held.

Opening up the box, Hazel saw an antique-looking pear cut diamond inside.

"Hazel Evelyn Baxter," he said, getting up from bed to kneel down and propose, "will you marry me?"

The Viet Cong's Subterranean Lair
By Hazel Baxter

Usually armed with nothing more than a flashlight, knives, and a pistol, down the 'tunnel rat' goes, down deep into the dark abyss that is the subterranean lair of the Viet Cong. It is here that the Viet Cong has built elaborate pathways, storehouses, arsenals, barracks, and in some cases, even a hospital and a kitchen. And it is here where one of the war's most dangerous jobs awaits our soldiers.

If you ask any man who made it home safely after his 12-month tour in-country (or the Marines who do 13) he'd tell you that all of Vietnam was dangerous—-the people, the land, even the insects. But ask any man who had been a tunnel rat and you'll soon learn how a tunnel rat assignment was like no other in Vietnam. That is, if you can find one who survived for the life expectancy of a tunnel rat is a mere three seconds.

From the beginning of the war, the Viet Cong has employed guerrilla warfare tactics against the enemy simply because it's always been the underdog when compared to the modern war technological might of the United States. And no tactic of the Viet Cong has proved to be more successful than its tunnels. Built during the First Indochina War against the French, these elaborate networks of tunnels and caves connected whole villages, districts, and in some cases even provinces. They snaked through as many as four separate levels for 200 miles, some even going as far as the Cambodian border. Hit-and-run raids have long been employed as a guerrilla war tactic throughout history, yet here it is not thick forest or jungle these unorthodox soldiers are escaping into but rather, disappearing into thin air, retreating deep into the earth. Entrances to the tunnels are almost always camouflaged and invisible.

It's because of how small the access holes to the tunnels are (2 feet wide by 3 feet deep) that the 'tunnel rat' needs to be thin and small of build. Your average GI or Marine of six feet, 180 pounds, would never be able to fit into the narrow, pitch-black passageways of the tunnels and once inside them, crawl through them in heat and stinking filth, intense feelings of claustrophobia setting in with every inch traversed. But you couldn't let your heightened sense of fear overtake you for once you entered a tunnel and started crawling through it, you might come out 10 or 15 miles away. There's no 'escape door' down there that will take you to safety.

And it's not just a matter of being able to fit into the tunnel and move at a fast pace when the need necessitates it; a tunnel rat also has to be highly skilled in hand-to-hand combat in case 'Charlie' drops a grenade in your lap in the dark, or disarming Charlie from his AK-47 which is always set to automatic. Ten thousand miles away from the Wild West of America, Vietnam's own version of the "quick draw" takes place, but here it is not on a dust filled open space but rather in frightening pitch black deep below the earth. Are you afraid of the dark has never taken a truer meaning than for these 'tunnel rats" who go in search of the ever-elusive enemy, only in a short time the hunter could become the hunted.

If you somehow survived the explosives which bounced off the red clay walls and the booby traps, the VC prove a resourceful and ingenious foe. They have a penchant for taking vipers tied in a shoot of bamboo with a piece of string and hanging them from the ceiling, waiting to strike an unknowing victim with almost instant death. Or setting boxes of scorpions with a trip wire that will open the box. You never know who is waiting for you there. But you can always smell him. While many American soldiers and Marines routinely engage in recreational drug use, 'tunnel rats' engage in nothing that will inhibit their senses. Just as vital as the pistol and knives they carry, it is their senses—their sense of smell, touch, and sound that aids them the most in their work. A tunnel rat will often sense a booby trap in the same way he can sense the enemy.

To their fellow GIs, tunnel rats are considered a cocky bunch, comprising men who keep to themselves, ridicule rank, and eschew drugs and self-doubts. But to the tunnel rats, the men who by all accounts sanely and lucidly volunteered for this job, it's these small actions, these mental traits that help in keeping them alive past the 'three second' mark.

CHAPTER 15

As Hazel placed the small wallet size black and white photograph into the envelope along with the note she had written to her mom, she still couldn't believe it. She was married. She was now Mrs. Vincent Cerny. But the plain gold wedding band on her left hand and the image of a radiant Vince and Hazel, he in a handsome suit and tie, she in a tea length white dress and accompanying fascinator, indeed confirmed it. She had tried calling home one day, Vince letting her use the phones in the *Washington Dispatch* office at the Caravelle but it had just rung, no one ever picking up. She hadn't received one letter from home, save for Betty of course, not even after she had sent a clipping of her *Life* magazine story. It was as if she no longer existed, was no longer the daughter of Sam and Anna.

Getting married in Vietnam had proved to be a lot more complicated than Hazel and even Vince had imagined it would be. But as they were told by numerous people, French and South Vietnamese officials alike, Vietnam had been ruled for nearly a century by French bureaucracy, and while France was no longer the ruling parent, red tape and paperwork were endless. This entailed a lot of waiting in lines at government agencies and countless translations, some of which even Hazel struggled over since the

French vernacular was from a much earlier era.

Hazel had wanted to wait until the wounds on her hands were completely healed but Vince had told her she would always have scars and she did. What had been an angry looking triangle on the palm of her right hand was now a faint scar, the three lines of the triangle only marginally visible.

The ceremony had been anything but memorable. It took place in the First Arrondissement in an old, decrepit building. The room itself looked like a classroom with a table covered by a mildewing baize cloth. The magistrate had stood behind the table with Hazel and Vince and their small bridal party seated in a row of a motley assortment of plywood and metal chairs.

Vince was an orphan, Hazel considered herself an unofficial one, so that day their eclectic group of friends from all over the world were their family. Hazel had invited Ann, of course. And Vince, who knew dozens of people in Saigon, ranging from journalists to cameramen to top military brass, had limited his side of the "guest list" as he called it, to just three people—Archie, a British reporter he had known for years from *The Times*; Billy, a fellow jarhead he had served with in Korea with and who had remained in the Corps all this time, having made a career of it. And who happened to be in Saigon as he was on his way to Hawaii for R & R. And then there was Jeanne, the lovely older French woman from Marseille whom Vince had introduced her to all those months ago at her restaurant and who Hazel had gotten to know well since she and Vince had officially gotten together.

The *Washington Dispatch* threw them a huge unofficial bash at the Caravelle's rooftop bar, copious amounts of wine and champagne having been somehow acquired, along with plates of duck, frogs' legs, French bread, and salad. There hadn't been a wedding cake but rather a platter stacked high with petit eclairs, one of Hazel's favorite things to order from the patisserie she had lived cattycorner from in Paris. It was not the wedding she had ever imagined having when she was a little girl, for Hazel never thought her wedding reception would include the sounds of bombs and gunfire and the smells of acrid smoke and fire, but she would not have changed one thing. It was to forever be her memory.

"Happy, Mrs. Cerny?"

"Deliriously so," she told him, wrapping her arms around his neck as he pulled her into a deep kiss.

And just then the faint sounds of a song that sounded familiar started to play. And he led her to an open space on the rooftop.

"Never my love," she whispered in disbelief, the song she and Vince had danced to in this same exact spot in her dream. And now here they were really dancing to it. "How did you know?"

"Always us," he whispered into her ear, his words hot against the nape of her neck. "Always and forever."

"Always and forever," she said back, knowing she would always remember this exact moment.

"How many nights are we going for again?" Hazel called out to Vince, who was shaving at the bathroom sink.

"Four," he called back. Appearing in the doorway, a small hand towel strewn over his shoulder, one cheek still covered in thick white shaving cream, he said, "Long enough for a wartime honeymoon?"

"Absolutely," Hazel replied, walking over to lightly kiss him on his clean shaven side.

They were headed to Phnom Penh just as Vince had promised they would. But that was back when Hazel wasn't completely sure about what her and Vince's future would bring. But look at her now, successful journalist and newly married and so deeply and madly in love. Maybe the women who fought for equal rights back home really could have it all- family and a job they loved. And she did love it. Even if Milton hadn't been killed, Hazel thought she would have still wanted to come here, to have dived right into the deep end that was wartime reporting. She had learned more in the past year than she'd had during her entire time at Pitt and the publications she had casually freelanced for. She was part of something that was a once in a lifetime opportunity, something only the Hemingways and Gelhorns and Parkers of the world knew about.

"What time is Archie getting here?" Hazel asked, returning to the bed where she was packing what she dubbed her "feminine ware," a slew of new dresses that Vince had treated her to. It was a welcome treat since she was either attired in her black-market military duds she was required to wear when she was in the field for a story, which was almost always the case, or not much of anything when she and Vince happened to be home together.

"T-minus 30, Frenchie," he said.

"And how long will it take to get there?"

"Hmm, maybe six hours?"

Hazel inwardly gulped. She had never particularly liked car trips; the longer they were, the more restless she got, not to mention car sick too sometimes. It was one reason she had grown to love getting around by Hueys. She never got car sick.

"Hey, don't worry Frenchie," he said coming to give her a hug, getting shaving cream on her bare shoulder as he did. "Archie even said he was cool if he plays the part of the chauffeur, with me sitting in the back seat with you," he told her smiling.

"Did I tell you I'm prone to motion sickness?"

"No," he said, playfully grimacing. "But I think you'll be okay."

And she was. She hadn't gotten sick once or even felt like she was going to. The trip had taken closer to seven hours with road blocks and traffic but the time had passed by easily enough- Hazel reading a French version of *A Farewell to Arms*, *L'adieu aux arms*, she'd bought at a junk shop in Cholon, sleeping some of the way, her head in Vince's lap, as she listened to Vince and Archie's non-stop talking and debating of matters, and also just looking out the window at the scenery.

Hazel was amazed that it seemed as soon as they crossed over the border into Cambodia, the scenery changed drastically. No longer was the land scorched earth, red clay ashes as it was in Vietnam. Here it was lush and verdant, endless rows of coconut trees lining the road for as far as the eye could see. But that's just what Vince had said it would be like. Cambodia was largely untouched by the ravages of war that had wrecked its neighbor for decades, first with the French and now the Americans. Here it was still an unspoilt paradise.

And it was the same in the capital. Hazel, who was so accustomed to seeing barbed wire and roadblocks everywhere, found what in many ways resembled a tropical Paris with the spires of Buddhist temples gracing the skyline and trees resplendent with leaves of a rich orangeish hue. You could almost forget there was a war going on.

"What kind of trees are they?" Hazel asked, pointing through the open window to the boulevard they were driving along.

"Flame trees," Archie called out from the driver's seat. "Beauties, aren't they?" as he pulled the car up in front of a yellow stucco building. The famed Hotel Royal.

"Gorgeous," she replied, alighting from the car where she placed her hand into the bellhop's outstretched one.

"*Bienvenue a Le Royal,*" he told them as Vince came around from the car to place his arm around Hazel's waist as she stared up at the building before them. She thought Saigon had gorgeous colonial architecture but Phnom Penh was something else entirely. The hotel's sloping tiled roofs featured both triangular dormer windows and wooden shuttered windows. It really was like walking a past of forty years earlier. The architecture was the same, the hem length for women drastically shorter.

"Did I tell you that the First Lady Jackie Kennedy stayed here once?" Vince said as they walked into the hotel.

"Really?" Hazel asked, thrilled to hear that she was staying in a place that one of her fashion and beauty idols had once stayed.

"Yeah, back in '67 when she visited Cambodia. They even served her a special cocktail they dubbed the femme fatale."

"I hardly think Jackie is a femme fatale," Hazel said laughing. Sure, the former president's widow was gorgeous but she hardly lured men into dangerous or compromising situations.

"That you know of," Vince said facetiously.

"Touché. Do you think it's still on the menu?" hoping she'd be able to write to Betty that she had drunk the specialty cocktail that had been created exclusively for Jackie Kennedy.

"I'm sure if it's not we can ask," Vince replied in an indulgent tone. "So since it's our honeymoon and all I reserved one of the bungalows."

"Yes, apparently your husband thought I'd be a third wheel,"

Archie joked, joining to stand next to them in the queue to check in. "Just as well. I don't want to be kept up all hours of the night," he added, making Vince laugh uproariously and Hazel blush a deep crimson red.

Hazel took a moment then to just listen to everything going on around her. It dawned on her that excluding their conversation, she didn't hear a single word of English being spoken. Vince had told her it would be like this, that the French community was still very large here, that unlike in neighboring Vietnam where a brutal and decades long fight had driven most of the French out, here the French were officially gone from a ruling standpoint but many remained because just as the Monsieur had told her in Hue, it was still home for them. The only home they had ever known. Hazel wasn't entirely sure how she felt about this bubble she now found herself in-literally and geographically removed from the intense war that was taking place next door in Vietnam and yet certainly not figuratively removed. No one who had spent time here could ever entirely remove what they had seen and experienced, this much she knew.

The interior of the hotel was just as stunning as the outside had been, albeit more like a "grand dame" past her prime. Although the main grand dark teak staircase which led upstairs to the guest rooms had seen better days, she could only imagine what it must have looked like at the hotel's grand opening in 1929.

"Meet you lovebirds by the pool in shall we say, thirty minutes?" Archie asked.

"Yes," Hazel immediately replied, answering for both of them before Vince could object. He no doubt wanted to stay immersed in their bungalow for as long as humanly possible and not hang with Archie the whole time. But Hazel was eager to explore her new surroundings. And besides, that was what being an intrepid traveler, a first-rate journalist was all about.

Vince playfully groaned but then took Hazel's hand as they walked off in the direction of their bungalow.

"Wait, you got married? In Vietnam? But why? When did flings become so passé?"

They had met Suzanne Quaglio, or Suzy Q as she told them to call her, at the pool, or Archie had met her first when he tried rather unsuccessfully to pick her up. But in no time, they had all gotten talking and soon discovered that she herself was a reporter. This wasn't really any sort of a surprise since one didn't travel to this corner of Southeast Asia these days for a vacation, although by the look and feel of Phnom Penh, one couldn't help but feel it was. Suzy had been the *Boston Globe's* D.C. bureau chief but somehow had pressured her bosses to send her to Vietnam. All of them had been vehemently opposed to sending a woman to cover a war but somehow she had prevailed. Spend five minutes alone with the woman and it was easy to see why she had been victorious. In a strange way, after listening to Suzy speak, Hazel couldn't help but feel glad she had started out as a stringer, a freelance reporter. She hadn't had to convince anyone, but especially a group of outdated and even sexist men, that she was good enough, that she could handle "it," handle war. She'd only had to convince herself.

Suzy looked to be somewhere between her and Vince's age. Although she was stunning in a Lana Turner kind of way (huge breasts that were dangerously on the edge of spilling out over her navy-blue polka dot bikini top…thick full scarlet lips that could only be described as sultry, and a beauty mark beneath her right eye that Hazel couldn't determine was real or drawn on) Hazel could tell that Suzy was smart. Sure, her looks had undoubtedly come in handy along the way when playing the game in the "boys' club," but she also had a look that clearly conveyed that no one, man or woman, remotely threatened or intimidated her.

Hazel must have looked surprised because Suzy then broke into a husky laugh saying, "darling, I'm kidding. If Vietnam of all places is where you found your prince charming, then mazel tov."

Hazel, Vince and Archie must have looked confused because Suzy then said, "What, a Jew couldn't have fallen in love with an Italian?" to which they all laughed.

"To love," Suzy said, raising her gin and tonic in the air with Hazel, along with Vince and Archie with their bottles of Bayon beer.

ॐ

"So since you're married now, you plan on packing it all in, exchanging the reporter's notepad for an apron? Taking us back what, another fifty years?"

Hazel was taken aback by Suzy's question, not just the stinging words but also the implication that Hazel was somehow solely responsible for the matter of women's rights. That if she had the audacity to "pack it all in" for the role preassigned to women since the beginning of time, she would be hurting her gender, regardless of the fact it's what she wanted. But she absolutely didn't.

"What gave you that idea?" Hazel asked, taking another sip of her gin and tonic. These she could get used to, thinking this is how a French colonialist wife must have felt back in the day, languishing about while wetting her palate with a never-ending supply of g & ts, and napping, or if you actually were enamored of your significant other, making love too.

"I don't know," Suzy answered nonchalantly.

Perhaps it had been the booze talking, Hazel thought, the other woman clearly not having anything of substance to back up her claim.

"You just, you're so young, you're both gorgeous so you're undoubtedly going to have a slew of gorgeous babies to match. And besides, you've already seen and done more than most women, or even some men for that matter, have in a whole lifetime," Suzy said, sounding decidedly sober and wiser now.

"Yeah, but I actually finished my degree," Hazel said, defensiveness starting to slowly creep into her tone. "So many girls don't. They merely go to college for the sole purpose of finding—"

Suzy interrupted her, "Mr. Right."

"Well, I was going to say husband but yeah, same difference, although probably for the majority of them, it is just 'a husband' and not at all close to 'Mr. Right.' And besides, how old are you anyway? You don't look that much older than me!"

Ignoring Hazel's question about her age, Suzy asked, "And what category does Vince fall in? The former or the latter?"

Hazel didn't even hesitate before answering. "The latter," which made both women smile.

"Will he support you if you want to keep working" Suzy asked after a moment.

"Well, of course, he didn't send me back to the States after we got hitched," Hazel said laughing. "And besides, I'm not exactly a 'Martha Gelhorn' for him to feel threatened professionally by me." She was referring to Ernest Hemingway's third wife, female journalist trailblazer Martha Gelhorn, who Hemingway couldn't stand when she got more of the spotlight than him. Needless to say their union didn't last and neither did Hemingway, who had been gone for seven years now after taking his own life.

"No, this is Vietnam, well, you know what I mean," waving her flawlessly manicured red hand around to indicate that they weren't actually in Vietnam at the moment.

And Hazel did. It was the bubble she had found herself immersed in from the moment she had arrived. It was the mental high that Vince had described so many times to her.

"No, I do," Hazel answered. "It's just that we've never really discussed it." Never discussed what life would be for them, consist of, after Nam. Vince obviously had a great job at *The Dispatch* but his official title was Saigon bureau chief. What about when the war was over, when there was no longer any need for American media outlets to have such a person, when Vietnam went back to being a country that few Americans could locate on a map? Would they return to D.C. or would he, would they be based elsewhere in Asia?

"I wouldn't worry too much," Suzy said, patting Hazel's knee, before leaning back in her chair, stretching her long limbs out before her, her taut and tanned body on display in her very revealing itsy bitsy teenie weenie yellow polka dot bikini. "I think the war's going to go on for a very long time. And I sure as hell don't think this place is always going to be Eden either. War's gonna come a knockin' here sooner or later."

That night at Le Cyrene, over dinner of crayfish and lobster, the hotel restaurant's specialty, Hazel came right out and asked.

"What are our plans for after the war?"

"What do you mean, Frenchie?" giving her a bemused look, as if the war's end was in sight.

"When we go home, or I mean, when we leave here? Well, what I really mean to say, where will home be?"

"I hadn't really given it much thought," Vince said in that languid manner of his. This usually didn't bother Hazel but tonight she found it highly irritating. "I can only see me, see us, here."

She wanted to say it more clearly. But not wanting to start a fight of which she would be the initiator, she merely said, "I know babe, but shouldn't we have some idea? I mean, no war lasts forever, especially one that with each passing month grows more and more unpopular. And now with Johnson not running and all the other candidates making pledges to end American involvement here, I think we need to start seriously discussing it."

Hazel felt bad. She didn't want to harp on the matter, not on their honeymoon in such a breathtaking locale. And she also knew that it was also a matter of their difference in age, their drastically different life experiences until now, until Nam. He had already been married, he had fought in a war when at that age, she was going off to college and taking classes on French literature and philosophy. And he was also 13 years older than her. Although Hazel had stopped looking at the world through rose-colored glasses as the Frank Sinatra song had gone, she still believed she had her entire life ahead of her, a life she wanted to build from the ground up with Vince. Then collecting her senses and calming herself, she felt that maybe that wasn't entirely possible since he already had a couple if not more floors on her. And that there wasn't anything bad about that either.

"Hazel, my plan is you," he said in a serious tone, taking her small hand between his two much larger ones which he then kissed. Looking into her eyes with a penetrating stare, he continued on. "My plan is always being with you, my plan is loving you till the day I die. I know you might not believe me, but my life has always happened, has always played out the way the universe wanted it and that includes you being brought into it, in Vietnam on an airplane of all things. Our life began here and wherever we end up after here, as long as you're by my side, I can make a home anywhere."

"Well, Mr. Cerny," Hazel said, becoming emotional now, "you took the words right out of my mouth."

But later that night, lying in bed in their darkened villa, the creaking ceiling fan making a quiet 'thump thump thump' every time it went round, the occasional groan of a pipe from the hotel's French era plumbing, it dawned on Hazel that she hadn't asked Vince about the most pressing matter. Kids. Were they going to have kids one day? And how many would they have? She knew after hearing Vince's story about his difficult childhood, the loss of his father, his abandonment by his mother, that it was a sore subject. And what about her? Did she want them? She had always said that no one or nothing was going to stand in the way of her career and she knew that Vince never would. And growing up, it wasn't as if she'd had great role models to go by- her mom had done the best she could considering her station and societal role and expectations for a woman of her time. And her dad, well, she and Milton had never gone hungry, had never lacked clothes, had even gotten the occasional toy on days that weren't Christmas or their birthdays. But his drinking had only increased as they got older. Maybe it was their childhood innocence that hadn't allowed them to see it when they were younger. But his lack of support for her drive and ambition to be something more than just a wife and mother had wounded her deeply, more than she would ever have admitted.

And then there was Milton, the whole tragic and incomprehensible matter of losing one's own child. At Milton's funeral, countless people had said, both to her parents and in whispered conversations at the funeral luncheon, that a parent should never have to bury a child, that a father should never outlive a son, that it wasn't how it was "supposed" to be. Hazel was so quick to judge her parents for how they behaved, what they became after Milton was killed. But had she judged them too quickly, too unfairly?

"Vince," she said, gently shaking him on his darkened bare shoulder which stood out in stark contrast to the whiteness of the bed's sheets, a faint sliver of moonlight filtering in from the top of the villa's wooden shutters.

"Hmm?" he answered groggily into his pillow.

"I need to ask you something," she whispered, although she wasn't sure why she still was, considering it was just them in the room and it wasn't as if they'd be disturbing anyone.

"What is it?" he said, his voice still lost in the depths of sleep and conveying a tone that his mind wasn't cognizant either.

"Do you want to have kids?"

"Yeah," he said, still speaking into the pillow, his back to her. "A whole gaggle of them. Although I'm not entirely sure how many constitutes a gaggle."

"Hey, I'm serious," she said poking him perhaps a bit too roughly in the ribs, that now seemed to awaken him.

"Ouch," he said, rubbing the area on his stomach where she had poked him after rolling over onto his back.

"Where's all this coming from, Frenchie?" he asked, then reached out to grab his watch from the night table to look at the time. "And at 2:33 AM too?"

"I want to know. We got married and I just want to make sure—"

He cut off her before she could say what could have potentially hurt one or both of them.

"When you had the type of childhood that I had, having your own set of kids or kid singular, is just not something you ever think about or dreamt about at any point. You're still too scarred from how your own parents messed you up to think about one day doing the same to a new human being."

Oh. Hazel's heart felt as if it had just plummeted five levels down a deep, dark elevator shaft.

"But," he said, putting an arm around her and dragging her to him so that now she was draped over his body, looking down into his eyes. "When you love someone as much as I love you, I wouldn't be opposed to it, at all. In fact, I think I might even want it."

"Do you mean it?"

"I do, Frenchie. I think we should just keep living our lives, being the best damn reporters, and making the most incredible love in the meantime."

"And if it happens..." she said.

"Then it happens," he answered effusively. "We'll just let nature take its course."

On their last night in Cambodia they dined at a French café called Les Pyrenees over a dinner of couscous and duck a l'orange, a place that Vince was familiar with from earlier visits to the capital. The owner, a French-Moroccan expat, had been delighted when he learned that Hazel spoke fluent French. If only Sam Baxter could see her now, see how useful "that useless" degree actually was. However, Hazel had to stop herself from turning on the "reporter switch," the one where she automatically gravitated to wanting to hear the other person's life story when speaking to him. It never got old to her, learning the reasons behind why someone would travel halfway around the world to a place he had never been, all because ever since he was a small child, he had been ingrained with the sentiment that this too was "home."

"Suzy thinks Cambodia isn't going to stay like this forever."

Vince's fork, filled with a heaping amount of couscous, paused in midair. "Stay like what?"

"This blissful insulated bubble."

"I'd hardly call it that," he answered wryly. "Go out into the countryside and you'll see the locals still living as harsh an existence as in the 1860s." And then lowering his voice he added, "No matter how much the King wants to modernize, bring Cambodia and its people fully into the 20th century, they still have a long way to go. It's not been a 'golden age' for everyone here, no matter how much the Western press claims it to be. Of course, all of this said and done at the behest of the King."

"Yeah, but look at how the war's stayed out of Cambodia," Hazel said. "He spurned us but has helped to save his people, save them from the same fate that's befallen so many of the Vietnamese."

She was referring to 1965, when Cambodia had officially cut ties with the United States. Prince Sihanouk's reasoning had been he wanted to "maintain the country's neutrality regarding the war in Vietnam." But his policies had still allowed Vietnamese communists to use the Cambodian border areas and the port of Sihanoukville.

"That's like saying Spain was actually neutral during the Second World War as it claimed itself to be when everyone knew Franco was actively helping Hitler," Vince countered. "There's too many people that not only admire the VC and the North, but support it too. And there's too many people here that didn't want an oppressive colonial government in charge of them and they sure as hell don't want a monarchy either. Their idea of a modern Cambodia is one where the people lead, and by people I don't mean a Western-inspired monarch or people whose skin color doesn't resemble theirs. I think one way or another, war will make its long-winded way here, thanks in part to the Ho Chi Minh Trail."

CHAPTER 16

"Hey babe, where was the Montagnard village you visited?" Vince asked her after getting home that day and kissing her. Was that worried concern, apprehension she detected in his tone?

"Hmm," Hazel furrowed her brow, trying to remember its name. "Dak, um, Dak Son, yes, that's it. Why?"

"It's not been officially confirmed yet but reports are coming out about a massacre there."

"Wait, what?" Hazel asked, not understanding what he was saying. "Americans were killed?"

"No, hundreds of Montagnards, they're saying."

Four months earlier

"It was the French who gave us the name you Americans now call us by. Montagnard, 'mountain dweller.' But we are 30 different tribes, all with our own languages and cultures. So how can one name apply to all of us?"

Jarai was a Montagnard, an indigenous person from the Dak Son in the country's Central Highlands. It was a priest at Notre Dame

Cathedral in the South Vietnamese capital who had put Hazel into contact with Jarai; the priest's mother was a Montagnard, although she had long since assimilated into mainstream Vietnamese society after converting to Catholicism as a young girl. Jarai also spoke fluent French, a fact which had greatly surprised her since she hadn't considered a nomadic people would be fluent in the language of their colonial occupier. But fluent he was. Never did a day go by here where she wasn't surprised about some facet of the country. She had traveled with him and a Green Beret lieutenant who had just arrived in country.

"Do the Vietnamese call you that too?" Hazel asked, pen and reporter notebook at the ready.

"No, to the Vietnamese we are *moi* to them. Savages," he added bitterly. "Because many of us practice, how do you say, animistic religion, and do slash and burn farming, that makes us animals to them, not worthy of their respect and more importantly, the respect of our own languages and cultures. Did you know that Diem banned the teaching of the Montagnard language, burned our books?"

Ngo Dinh Diem, the infamous South Vietnamese president who many regarded as a corrupt and unjust dictator, heavily discriminated against the Buddhist population and now Hazel learned, the Montagnard people too. It also hadn't come as any surprise when he was assassinated back in '63.

My God, it's just like America's history with its Indian populations, Hazel thought.

"They say they want us as 'one people,' united in the fight against the North, but I don't see it that way. They simply want there to be only the Vietnamese people in Vietnam's borders, and no one else, no other languages spoken, no other religions practiced, nothing that isn't 'Vietnamese.' We don't comply, we are erased."

"Then why are so many of the Montagnards fighting on the side of the South? Helping out the Americans?" Hazel asked.

"We are not fighting on the side of the South Vietnamese," Jarai said emphatically. "We are helping the Americans who have helped us build dams, and roads, bridges, schools, wells. They even give medical care to our sick. They are not looking to erase us."

This was true. As part of its Village Defense Program that America's Special Forces had established, Montagnard men that the Green Berets had helped train, fought alongside the Americans, helping to protect the forested homeland of the Montagnard which ran along the Cambodian and Laotian borders, areas that were heavily trafficked by the VC to not only move men and supplies but also when needing to disappear into thin air.

Hazel had only been successful in finding one Green Beret who was willing to be interviewed but it had been evident by the way he spoke that he clearly admired the Montagnard people, crossbows and all, which she learned was their preferred choice of weapon when given the choice. He had even gone so far as to call them 'excellent soldiers.' Coming from a career soldier, Hazel knew no greater compliment could have been bestowed upon Jarai's people.

Red clay ashes. That's what the land here had been reduced to. Homes had been burned to the ground, its residents incinerated inside. Those who had been able to escape into foxholes in their homes died of smoke inhalation. Bodies lay everywhere, a few corpses having been riddled with bullets, as if the one needed to kill them wasn't enough. Those that had survived the massacre, many by playing dead for hours, said the VC took even more hostages with them on their retreat, forced conscription. More than two hundred were dead, some U.S. officials were saying. All because they were supporting the enemy, the South Vietnamese, the same people who called them "moi."

Hazel considered herself tough, tougher than she had ever been since arriving here, since surviving Hue, since surviving the tunnels, since seeing the sheer horrors that man was capable of inflicting upon his fellow man. But it was the sight of the charred female corpse clutching a charred baby's corpse inside one of the burned out remains of a hut that completely undid her. This wasn't war. This was pure evil and at that moment, the image of the burned baby perhaps permanently etched in her mind, Hazel wished nothing but unimaginable hell to come to the VC who had done this. Done this to their fellow countrymen because that's what they still were.

CHAPTER 17

HUE

July 1968

Hazel didn't know what she was expecting. Hue, the cultural and historically rich city long revered by both sides, still lay in ruins. But she needn't have been surprised. The siege had happened less than six months ago while war still continued in all corners of the country. "Westy" was gone, recalled to Washington back in June, his request for an additional 200,000 American troops in the aftermath of Hue having been denied. It was, some say, the straw that broke the camel's back. And yet the American military presence here, more than half a million troops currently in-country, was the highest it had been since the war began.

She had come here after unofficial reports started filtering out about the discovery of mass graves, hastily dug pits that were said to contain hundreds of civilian bodies. When Hazel heard this she had immediately thought of the French Vincent she had met there who she had been so carefree with before the attacks and of course, the Monsieur and Madame. All this time she had often wondered as to their whereabouts, if they were safe, and most importantly, if they had survived the siege. She had asked around, and had even asked Vince to inquire since he knew so many more people than her. He hadn't asked her why she was interested in knowing about this particular French photographer, just said he would find out what he could. Which ended up being nothing. He was apparently a stringer and also in the country illegally. As he was not registered with MACV, that would make finding him all the more difficult if no employer knew he was missing. She often wondered how many foreigners had met a fate such as this—foreigners in a land embroiled in war—how would a loved one back home ever know what had happened to them. But Hazel knew they most likely never would. She realized now that such a move was selfish. Yes, at the time she first came to Vietnam, she told herself she was coming for her career, for her life to mean something. But she hadn't really taken into account what her actions would mean for her family and friends back home had she been killed or just gone missing.

They had agreed a long time ago that Vince would never block her from a potential story. She had conceded that he was permitted to voice his opinion, his concern, but it ultimately was her call if she went after it or not. Going to Hue was one of those instances- he didn't want her to go but he wouldn't stop her either.

"It can't be any more dangerous than being there in the midst of the actual siege," she said as she threw a spare reporter's notepad and an extra shirt and beanie hat into her rucksack.

"That's not what I was referring to," he said, concern appearing on his face.

"What, you think I'll flinch at the sight of dead bodies?" she said, half-joking but also half-serious. "I'm not a Victorian era lady, no smelling salts required."

"Mass graves, Hazel. Do you get what that means? Like really understand? Because a part of me thinks you don't with how cavalier you're being about the whole thing."

She paused then, remembering the first time she'd heard the term, 'mass grave.' It had been in an old issue of *Time* magazine she had found in the high school library, an article about the 10th anniversary of the liberation of a concentration camp in Germany. The pictures of the emaciated corpses, stacked high atop one another, as if they were pieces of trash you'd throw out.

"I knew guys, some of the biggest, toughest men you'd ever meet, men who maybe even wouldn't shed a tear at their own wife's funeral, and them telling me years later, how haunted they were by what they saw when they liberated the camps. When they found the mass graves of all the Jews." He took a breath before adding, "Once you see that, you can never erase it, Hazel."

The point of no return, she grimly thought.

"Someone had to document the horrors and atrocities of the camps in '45," she said. "Well, someone needs to do the same for the innocent people here. The American people back home thinks it's just us doing the killing of the civilians. We must let the world know the Vietnamese people are killing their own."

In cities destroyed by war, she knew that it took years, sometimes decades to rebuild. London and Tokyo had over time, and so had Berlin. Well, West Berlin that is. But of course, those cities' future destinies had been tied to the triumphant hand of the victors, the side that had won. Look at East Berlin—a quarter of a century after Allied bombs had rained down there, its leaders had been concerned with erecting a wall to keep its own citizens inside, trapped in a world of oppressive and restrictive laws. There were no principles to rebuild for a prominent and hopeful future. And what about the once former imperial city? Would a similar fate befall it?

She saw house after house whose fronts were missing or didn't have a roof or for some miraculous reason, were missing the first floor, but whose second floor remained intact. Even at a fast speed, she caught glimpses of life that was still going on inside those bombed out and destroyed homes, the smells of fish sauce and cooking oil still filtering through the open air. But life had to go on, didn't it? A soldier could lay down his gun and say he was done with war, done with fighting, but civilians in any war, any conflict, never have that luxury. War continues around them whether they want it to or not.

"How many people are still homeless?" Hazel called out, her voice no match for the roar of the Army jeep's motor.

It had stopped to let a ragtag looking family, an old man, a young couple and their three small children, cross the street, each laden with countless possessions, even the little boy who looked to be no more than five who stared at Hazel the entire time he was crossing. She smiled at him, hoping to elicit a smile from his little face, but he just stared at her, his face devoid of any emotion, a life so young who had known nothing but the ravages and pain of war. When they finished crossing the street, his older sister had to pull him along to keep going, for he seemed to be rooted in place, not once breaking his stare at Hazel.

"Not my pay grade to know that, lady," the young driver said, as he kept his eyes on the road, darting in and out of the potholes and other pieces of debris that made the streets undrivable.

No, but it's called being a human being with empathy she wanted to say but didn't. He was taking her out to the mass grave and she needed him, period. No benefit to getting annoyed at him.

As they left the city, the buildings becoming fewer and fewer, or she thought, the rubble of debris and ruins becoming less and less, it was the smell that hit her first. Although she detested the fish sauce that the Vietnamese people cooked with for everything, what she was smelling now she had no word for. It smelled like rancid meat, only worse. And it only got more intense, more malodorous the farther the corporal kept driving.

He stopped the jeep then, and tossed her something. "Here, you're gonna need this."

She reached out and saw that it was a bandanna.

"Don't worry, it's clean," he said laughing as he hopped out of the jeep.

She got out and found herself being attacked by what were they, flies? Gnats?

She held the cloth up to her nose and tried breathing in long, deep breaths.

"Badge," a stern looking Army man barked at her.

She fiddled with her ID that was around her neck while keeping a death grip on the piece of cloth over her nose and mouth.

"Lower it so I can see you," barking again this new order at her.

Lowering it, her skin all of a sudden feeling clammy and damp, sweat dripping down her face and back, bile forming at the back of her throat, it was then that she saw them. Saw the bodies. Saw dozens of bodies of all different sizes, men and women, laid out in what could only be described as three neat, straight rows. She saw individuals hunched over them, the sounds of crying and desperate wailing piercing the air. She saw one woman even prostrate herself in the dirt by one of the bodies.

Once she was given the okay to go closer, she crept along cautiously, quietly at the back, feeling that as an outsider, she was somehow intruding on this very raw and heartbreaking scene of fresh grief. But she was also searching for people she had known, however briefly it had been.

And then she saw him. Saw the Monsieur's decomposing body, saw the bullet that had entered his forehead, saw his blood-stained shirt that had been riddled with bullet holes. But she knew it was him. In the rows of Vietnamese bodies that lay before her, she knew it was him, the kind gentleman who had given her a fleeting emotional raft when she had so desperately needed one.

She heard Vince's words then, "Once you see that, you can never erase it, Hazel."

And then everything went black.

"Ma'am, can you hear me?"

Hazel slowly opened her eyes, coming to at the sound of this strange voice.

"Good," the stranger said. "Now I want your eyes to follow the light," he commanded as he moved a small flashlight directly in front of her eyes. She obeyed, her eyes following the light.

"Good," he said again. "Now I want you to try sitting up, but slowly." He moved aside from her then as Hazel sat up.

"Now can you tell me what year it is? And where you are?"

"It's 1968, and I'm in Hue," she croaked out. "What happened?"

"You fainted. I think it was just too much for you. Now, I saw your press badge but female journalist or not, I don't think any women should be here," he said in a tone that perfectly conveyed what he thought of the opposite sex and more specifically, what he thought its role should be.

The graves. The Monsieur's body, riddled with bullets. And then there was Vincent's body. One lone bullet right through his temple.

He handed her a Coca Cola, the glass bottle ice cold in her bare hands. "Down it, worry about the stomach indigestion later. You need to get your blood sugar back up."

She took it, placing it beside her, then extended her right hand and said, "Hazel Cerny."

He regarded her then, a look of momentary confusion passing across his face as in, were they really doing this now, here, next to a site of mass graves? But he accepted her hand and replied, "Sergeant Bines, Army Medic."

"Your husband can't be military," he said, looking down at the simple gold band on her left hand's ring finger. Hazel wasn't sure if he was asking, or saying this as a fact.

"Why do you say that? Today's man can't 'man' the fort back home?" she asked wryly. "Excuse the pun," she added as she took a huge swig of the Coca Cola.

"Well, I've no doubt that we have entirely different opinions and definitions on what a woman's place and role is, but I can't think of a single military man in any branch who would let his wife come to a war zone, female journalist or not."

There it was again, Hazel thought sadly. Having to attach our gender before our profession. Not once had she ever heard Vince or Archie be referred to as a "male journalist."

"You're right, he's not," Hazel said, swinging her legs back around from the cot, and then finishing off the bottle of Coke. "He's a fellow journalist like me. And for the record, we're all just 'journalists.' No need to call me or any other woman a lady journalist. Our female anatomy doesn't define us or produce the copy that makes our editors preen with pride. Our brains and intellectual curiosity do that."

And with that, she started to storm off, only halting a moment later as she realized that she had no idea where the driver who had brought her here was. Feeling a tap on her shoulder, she slowly turned to see Sergeant Bines standing there.

"You really need to take it easy- the heat, the smells- it's not unusual for anyone to faint- myself included," he said, a trace of a smile perhaps serving as his peace offering to her.

Hazel knew he wasn't the enemy. She knew that his opinion of her and her profession was not the only negative one, not the only outdated, even archaic one. He didn't wish her ill or even to fail in what she was doing, she knew that. And then she remembered him, she remembered seeing Vincent's body. And knew she had to tell the authorities about him.

"Have all the bodies been identified yet? Claimed?" she asked.

"Not even close."

"One of the dead, a white man, I know who he is. Well, I don't know his last name, but I assume it could be tracked down at least."

So Sergeant Bines took her to the South Vietnamese authorities who were registering the dead. She told them his name was Vincent and that he was a French citizen, a photojournalist, but still a stringer, no home base to immediately call. It wouldn't be easy, repatriating his remains, but it would be a start. He wouldn't just be a nameless John Doe found in the ravaged and bloodied remains of a war-torn Vietnamese city. The French Embassy would now know that one of their own had been killed during the Offensive. Although she knew he couldn't be the only one, not by far. And the fate of the Madame, Hazel wondered?

It was Sergeant Bines who drove her back into the city. He had actually proven to be a really good man. It wasn't that he thought less of the female sex, Hazel acknowledged, but more had a sense of wanting to keep them safe. Not modern enough of a mindset for Hazel but one that she couldn't be entirely critical of either.

As he accompanied her to the MACV Compound grounds where she was spending the night in one of the huts, he reiterated to her what he'd said earlier, about "taking it easy." And then almost as an afterthought, a joke really, he said, "especially if you might be in the family way," before walking off into the thick black night air.

And those words, 'the family way,' kept Hazel up all night. It wasn't just the sounds of human activity on the compound, or the ever present musical rhythms of the cicadas and other nocturnal creatures. Family way.

Hazel tried thinking back to the last time she'd had her period but knew it had to have been months. Her period had been rather irregular ever since she had arrived in Vietnam- a combination she attributed to the intense heat, the food, and just everything about her new life that was so utterly different from her old one. And after Cu Chi and then the wedding which had come about so suddenly, she just hadn't given it any thought. And the majority of the time, she and Vince never used any protection when they made love, too preoccupied were they on other matters that consumed their everyday lives. Such was life for a journalist in war-torn South Vietnam.

But then a more worrying thought crossed her mind. What if Vince made her go home, made her leave Vietnam to have the baby? What if she had to give all this up? Hand in all that she had literally risked life and limb for these past months? He was pragmatic, she reasoned to herself. He knew how much her career meant to her, how much time and energy she had invested in it. But that same pragmatism she so loved and admired about him could also stand to hurt her—she knew he wouldn't relish the idea of going to a Vietnamese hospital to give birth since she highly doubted she could do so in one of the first-rate American military hospitals here. Or could she? Vince was a vet after all (would that matter at all she wondered, during an active war?), and certainly knew enough high-ranking officials at MACV to perhaps pull some sway. But even she had to admit that the idea of giving birth in a dingy Vietnamese hospital, one that lacked many of modern medicine's technological innovations that were prevalent in American hospitals, frightened her. The sheer fact of what if something went wrong, with either her or the baby? The Vietnamese people were used to such primitive conditions. She certainly wasn't.

But first things first. She needed to tell Vince. And before doing that, actually find out if she was pregnant or not. She somehow sensed she was.

CHAPTER 18

Hazel had never been one for religion. If she were, then perhaps she would have been better able to grasp the whole biblical adage of "and with life comes death." In the days and months following Milton's death she had watched her mother give up on life except to attend Mass each morning at St. Paul's. But what exactly had religion given back in return? Her mother's outlook on life hadn't changed, she hadn't woken up one morning and decided to start living once more, remembering that she still had another child, one who still craved a mother's love even as an adult. But none of that had mattered.

So on the day she had gotten confirmation that she was indeed pregnant (this three days after taking a pregnancy test at a military hospital back in Saigon), she rushed home, knowing that Vince would be there waiting for her, as he had been up in Khe Sahn again for most of the month. Although the now infamous base had been closed on July 5, Marines had remained around one of the hills where fighting in the area had continued for another week until they were finally withdrawn, thus bringing the battle to a close, almost five months after it had started.

But as she frantically put her key in the decrepit lock and excitedly rushed in, she pulled up short upon seeing Vince's ashen face, his fingers clutching what appeared to be a telegram.

"What is it?" she asked, fear and bile rising to the back of her throat.

"It's for you, babe," he said, slowly walking towards her as if he was approaching his executioner. "It's from home…from Butler."

She took it from him then and walked towards the small table where she sat down.

"You read it?" she asked him.

"Yes."

"Then tell me what it says."

He looked as if he wanted to object, but changed his mind for he took it back from her and read in a faltering voice.

"Parents killed in auto accident. Bodies buried in Calvary. Couldn't wait for you. I'm so sorry. Betty."

He looked at her expectantly, clearly wanting to take his cues from her. But still Hazel said nothing. Her face, her eyes, emotionless. She just looked down at the simple gold wedding band that she wore. And still not looking at him, she finally said, "I'm pregnant."

And then those two simple words, words that should have brought her so much joy and happiness, were what finally broke her. She laid her head down on the dingy table and cried, deep wrenching sobs. Tears for the family that had never been the same after they heard about Milton and now tears for the family that was truly no more.

Hazel considered her life to be dichotomous now- there was the life she led and had before Vietnam and the people that constituted it, and then there was now, everything else that would follow.

As a child she had been enamored by stories featuring orphans as the protagonists- Mary Lennox in *The Secret Garden,* Sarah Crewe in *A Little Princess,* even Pollyanna Whittier. But now at age 23, soon to be a mom herself, could she call herself an orphan especially since she had no 'Jimmy Beans' or 'Martha and Dickon' in her life. Her life was real, it was not a children's story she could escape into. She was truly an orphan and yet so were the thousands of Vietnamese children who had been unwillingly inducted into a club no one wanted to belong to.

But she had Vince, who was worth all the Jimmy Beans and Martha and Dickons put together, she knew that. And she had the little baby growing inside her, one that she thought to herself she wanted to call Beatrice or Bee if it was a girl, for how much it seemed to buzz about inside her at all hours of the night.

Through it all, but especially in the first few weeks after getting Betty's telegram, Vince had been amazing. It was hard to celebrate the prospect of new life with unexpected death, but they did and for that Hazel was grateful. Neither were strangers to the institution of grief now, albeit in different circumstances surrounding their losses. But grief was grief, and it pierced the heart in ways that only those who had suffered great losses would know.

She had considered going home, returning to Butler temporarily, but Vince had asked her not to, that it would be too much for her, both physically and emotionally. It had been the one time he had ever asked her not to do something. She concurred after talking with Betty once on the phone in the Dispatch's offices and learning that a cousin of her father's and his wife, relations Hazel had never been around too often but who lived nearby, had been the ones to take care of the burials and funeral. The house had long been paid for, so dealing with the aftermath of it all, the tying up of loose ends, the disposing of the earthly possessions of the two lost lives could wait.

Her condition was that she was not going home to have the baby, that she was not doing it alone. And his immediate response had been, "I would never ask you to."

He did, however, ask her to accompany him to Honolulu. He was on his way back to Chicago to cover the Democratic National Convention which was taking place at the end of August. Although he had covered two political conventions before in his career, he told her he wanted to be there for this one considering the state of both the war and the country and the fact that it was taking place in his hometown. His plane would stop in Honolulu on the way to San Francisco and he wanted them to enjoy a break together, before it would be impossible for them to go anywhere, let alone on a plane thousands of miles away.

He booked them a beach view room at the Royal Hawaiian, which Hazel dubbed the Pink Lady owing to its bright pink façade. It was located right on the legendary Waikiki Beach and Hazel was in awe when she and Vince, both having been adorned with the flower necklaces the native Hawaiians called leis the moment they alighted from the taxi, walked out through the hotel's door and saw the breathtaking azure waters of the Pacific Ocean before them.

Hazel had only seen the ocean a couple of times in her life before then. The Atlantic had always reminded her of a poem by Poe or Byron, one teeming with dark and stormy undertones and meaning. But at that moment, the Pacific looked so vibrant, so alive, so utterly full of life. She wondered then if it were possible to ever be unhappy in a place so utterly beautiful.

As much as she had loved their honeymoon in Phnom Penh, it was Hawaii that left its blissful and beautiful mark on her. It was just what she had needed, giving her the emotional fortitude to look ahead, and not back, to come to terms for good with the unexpected deaths of her parents. And Vince had known this, had known it would have healing and restorative powers for her.

When word had first reached Vietnam about the chaos that was erupting on the streets of Chicago, battles between the city's police force and anti-war protesters Hazel couldn't believe it. It wasn't until Vince was home again in early September and told her what he had seen with his own eyes and what she had read in the initial copy he had written- police officers savagely beating protesters with their clubs even after they were lying motionless in the streets, tear gas sprayed on the crowds that wouldn't disperse, Molotov cocktails thrown with little regard to those caught in the crossfires, chants of "the whole world is watching." For it was, as all eyes and cameras were trained on the city of Chicago on those final days of August. Only then did Hazel comprehend the enormity of what the war was doing to the country, to the American people.

"I didn't recognize it, babe. I didn't recognize my own country," he told her the night he got home. Even though he was physically exhausted from the two days of travel, he was too wired up to attempt sleep. "It was as if America had become some despot nation in a dystopian novel, ruled by an evil tyrant in the high castle. The cops, they just beat the people, most of them having done nothing wrong except for the mere fact that they were there."

"And they all participated?" Hazel asked incredulously. "None of them protested, spoke out against what was happening?"

"What, the cops?" to which Hazel nodded her head affirmatively. "Yes. I mean, I even spoke to some of the McCarthy workers after and they told me they had organized a party in the Hilton, where the convention was, and they said the cops just beat them. And that all the telephones had been disconnected shortly before so they didn't even have a way to call for help."

Hazel couldn't understand it. Everyone knew before the convention even happened that Hubert Humphrey was going to get the nomination, was going to be the man who would go up against Nixon that fall. It wasn't as if the mere presence of McCarthy supporters there on the streets of Chicago would change anything. And wasn't that what America's boys were fighting for here in Vietnam, all these years now, all these senseless deaths later, the ability to exercise the right to free speech. And yet Mayor Daley and his Chicago police force had stripped those Americans of that Constitutional right.

"The only thing Daley did," Vince said, yawning now, his eyes closed, "was further cement the fact that we can't ever win this war if we can't win this new war at home, the war of a divided and fractured nation."

Hazel's pregnancy was undoubtedly not like any other American woman's. It was at the 3rd Field Hospital where her pregnancy had been initially confirmed and where she had gone a couple of times for brief examinations, primarily to make sure that all was well and baby was growing as it should be. But prenatal care was not something in ready supply or high demand in Saigon's American military hospitals. Hazel was just happy to have an American doctor see her and who before joining the army, had actually done a stint in obstetrics in his life as a civie.

When her protruding stomach finally became readily visible, Hazel stopped flying around the country on choppers. He wouldn't say so but she knew Vince was glad when this time came. So she started writing more human feature stories, namely about the long suffering Vietnamese people but specifically its children. She was particularly proud when a piece she wrote on the country's mixed race children, or *bui doi,* children born to a Vietnamese mother and an American father, was picked up by the *Christian Science Monitor.* But writing it had been heartbreaking, after learning of the cruel and harsh stigmas the children, most of them babies and toddlers, faced because of their parentage, not wanted by either parent- one because the conception was nothing more than a result of a wartime fling, the other because it brought shame upon the family. And she learned that it was even worse for those children born to a Black GI.

"And yet, there were countless mixed children of French and Vietnamese heritage," Hazel had said to Sister Lisette, "and who were accepted by Vietnamese society."

"Yes, that is somewhat true," the Sister had replied in her lovely old-world French. "And yet, France still makes up the cultural blood of the country today. To the North, France was the occupier, the cruel tyrant who robbed the country of its culture and language and patrimony for far too long. But France is still in the people's blood, runs through its veins. America, on the other hand, is the newest occupier, but here solely because of imperialistic pursuits. America is not tied to the Vietnamese culture and its people in the same way that France is. And that is why the Ameriasian children will always be outcasts, be rejected by their mothers' people."

Hazel didn't want to argue for the truth was, there was no need to. The Sister and her fellow nuns here at St. Benedictine's Orphanage took care of all children and each month brought in greater numbers of children as more and more refugees poured in from the destroyed and scarred countryside; the sisters didn't discriminate in their actions.

"My only fear is that when the North wins," the sister began, "it is those same innocent children who will suffer the most. For it will no longer just be a case of society rejecting them. Rather their sole crime will be looking like the enemy who invaded their land, killed their people. That is the true price they will pay for springing from a union that was never sanctioned by God and that should have never been."

His ear was pressed to her large, rounded belly as he gingerly massaged it with his hand. The darkened room was stifling, not an ounce of fresh air from the streets of Saigon reached inside the apartment. Hazel suddenly asked, "If something happened to me, where would you go?"

Vince looked up at her then, not grasping what she was saying.

Seeing his confused look, she added, "I mean, if I died in childbirth, or fell out of a cyclo and hit my head."

"Well, for starters, you're not going to die in childbirth," he said, raining light feathery kisses on her sweaty belly. "And two, you never ride in a cyclo so I think we're good there," he added as his mouth ran his way up to her neck.

"I'm serious, Vince. This war is going to eventually end. Where would you raise our child if I'm not here?"

"A big city. I grew up in one and spent so much of my adult life living in various big cities here and there. I couldn't imagine any other sort of life for my kid. I want him or her to be exposed to just about everything. Maybe San Francisco or LA, a taste of Nam but without the daily threat of death." A pause then before he added, "What about you, Frenchie?"

"I'm the opposite," she said. "I'd never want to do a big city without you."

"But I thought you hated where you grew up? Or at least hated its small-town feel, the people unwilling to explore beyond their borders."

Hazel wished at that moment her belly wasn't huge so that she could turn away and not face him. But sleeping, or more aptly, resting on her back was the only way she felt semi-comfortable in bed this far along in her pregnancy. "Because any big city, no matter where it was in the world, would always remind me of you," she said, looking up at the ceiling, at the half-functional ceiling fan that just went round and round, with each rotation getting louder and louder.

"I'd return to Butler," she said. "A place you never were, a place we were never together in, a place devoid of any memories of you."

"So you're saying you'd want even the memory of me to not exist?" he said, an air of defensiveness tinged with sadness now readily apparent in his tone. "If I was dead?"

"No, I don't mean it as harshly as that", annoyed that he wasn't getting what she was trying to say. Hazel felt so miserable—the baby seemed to never stop moving around anymore, her feet were so swollen, and she just ached from head to toe, made worse by the oppressively hot weather in Saigon.

"You die, I have to keep going," she began in her attempt to clarify her remarks. "I would have to be the sole parent for our child, be the beacon of strength, be our baby's everything, be not just one parent but both parents to him and her. I couldn't do that if I felt like I was drowning emotionally, if I stopped and fixated on every little thing that brought back memories of you. I wouldn't have the luxury of giving up, of wanting to stop living like my mom did after Milton was killed." Hazel wanted to add, or give up our baby like your mom did with you after your own dad was killed during the war, but she didn't. She knew that would be too hurtful a thing to say. "But I'd always have to keep going and that's the only way I would know how," and with those last few words she started to cry, the heat, her physical discomfort, her all over the place hormones, all catching up to her.

Vince sat up in bed then and semi-awkwardly drew her back up against his outstretched and extended legs so that she fit in-between them. Reaching over to the night stand, he poured water onto a washcloth and started to gently dab her, the feel of even the tepid water on her body a welcome relief.

"I get it," he whispered as he continued patting her with the moistened washcloth all over her body. "Who am I to judge or have an opinion over what you would do if I wasn't here? You do what you need to do if that time would ever come."

Hazel felt a bit better then, her body and mind starting to finally relax and feel at ease. Closing her eyes, she finally felt sleep starting to come.

"But that's not something you'll ever have to worry about because I'm not going anywhere," he added. But Hazel didn't hear him for she was finally asleep.

"Lady, you my numba one lady," the little Vietnamese boy said to Hazel with an impish smile. He looked to be no more than six or seven, yet his eyes had a haunted look to them. A grown man in a child's body, or rather, a child who had never had a childhood. "Give me dolla?" he begged.

"How about I get you a meal instead?" Hazel replied. And then noticing his bare feet she added, "And maybe some shoes too."

Hazel had yet to meet a Vietnamese child who hadn't tugged at her heartstrings, although since she had become pregnant, the heartbreaking sight of these street children, known here as *bui doi*- 'dust children' because they lived in the dust of the streets'- had gotten even worse. Vince often joked that his pay from the *Dispatch* wasn't large enough to feed and house the thousands of orphaned children here. But she knew their plight bothered him too- the sight of the maimed little girl who routinely begged for food and handouts near their apartment, the small boy of 10 who acted as the parent to his two defenseless little brothers who clutched at him as if he were their only lifeline- all of it undoubtedly brought back memories of his own childhood. Yet a home in a country not torn apart by war must have seemed like a paradise in comparison to what childhood here in Vietnam was like.

"What's your name?" Hazel asked as the little boy slurped down the bowl of hot noodle soup she had gotten for him. It was pho, a food that Vietnamese people seemed to eat all the time.

"Kevin," he replied. "I go to America soon, become a cowboy and fight the Indians, pow pow," he said raising his two skinny hands to imitate firing a gun as if he were in some gun slingin' battle with John Wayne himself.

"Where's your parents, Kevin?" Hazel asked, already knowing the answer but curious as to what he would tell her.

"Don't know numba one lady," he answered. "Always just been me. No brudders or sisters."

"Where did you learn to speak such good English?"

"GIs taught me," he said proudly. "I find them good bang bang girls over at Tu Do Street, they give me food and teach me English when I say I wan learn."

Hazel felt ill hearing this. What he had just told her was the perfect summation of how the Americans here were doing more harm than good, at least in regards to the hundreds of mixed-race babies being born each year, the sad and tragic result of nothing more than a casual fling.

"Let's get you some shoes," Hazel said as she took notice of the blackened soles of his little feet, the sight of them making her feel nauseous along with the fetid smell of his unwashed body.

"What do you think's going to happen to all the mixed-race children once the war's over?"

"You mean when the decadent sounds and sights of American

capitalism are no more here? When big bad Washington finally admits the unthinkable, that it lost and was never going to be victorious here?"

Hazel was enjoying a coffee with Suzy at one of her favorite cafes. She hadn't seen the other woman in weeks and Suzy's first reaction upon seeing Hazel was exclaiming in mock horror, "your figure!" which made both women erupt in laughter. Suzy had been up in the Quang Ngai province for the last week or so, covering a security operation that was being called Operation Champaign Grove. Although the VC and the PAVN had supposedly incurred hundreds of losses (or so the MACV war machine claimed, their penchant for inflating body counts growing more egregious each month), the U.S. still suffered dozens themselves. It was dubbed an 'operational success' but tell that to the wives and mothers and fathers and children of the 41 men who weren't.

Suzy had been in-country for a couple of months now and while she still seemed to act like the same tough, ball busting, no nonsense woman she had been when Hazel first met her at Le Royal in Phnom Penh, she also seemed shaken too, battle weary even. She had taken to chain smoking cigarettes, while at times her hands would shake. Hazel wanted to ask if she was okay but what could she say? This was war. This is what they had come to see, to report on, to be taken seriously, to gain acceptance once and for all in the boys' club of their field. Male reporters had gone home for less- tired and fed up with everything that Vietnam threw at them- craving the first world and materialistic comforts of home. This, of course, after they had gotten the lion's share of non-stop access to illicit drugs, raucous parties that even Bacchus would have blushed at, and cheap girls for hire.

And Hazel could see then that Suzy had finally entered the jaded stage of life in 'Nam- the war and the country no longer entirely intoxicating and alluring. The layers had started to peel back revealing a place and a people that you knew were FUBARRED, like looking at an accident on the road, one you couldn't look away from no matter how much you wanted to. A country that became a parasite wreaking havoc on your body, one you can never fully rid yourself of.

Not waiting for Hazel to answer, Suzy said frightenedly, almost prophetically, "I think those children will wish they had never been born. Even more than the mothers who bore them and abandoned them, all the while cursing the GIs who knocked them up. I think for these kids, if they think their lives are hellish now, they have no idea what's coming for them."

"What was your dad's name?"

"Steve, well, it was really Stepan, but he wanted nothing to do with the old country. So everyone called him Steve."

"If it's a boy, do you want to name him Steven?"

Vince said nothing at first, making Hazel regret having said it. The only times he had spoken of his mother had been with derision, but his father had always just been the figure who had died in war thousands of miles away when he was a kid. He had never spoken negatively or bitterly of him.

"I'd thought you'd want to name him Milton."

Now it was Hazel's turn to pause, to feel a tugging at her emotions which were all over the place these days. Hormones, Suzy had said sardonically one day after Hazel had burst into tears following her getting splashed from head to toe by a motorbike that happened to hit a deep muddy puddle at the exact moment Hazel had approached the curb.

"I'd like that for a middle name if you're amenable. But I want the first name if it's a boy to be significant for you," Hazel said.

"Oh, so you're telling me you've already claimed rights on a girl's name?" he said smilingly.

"If it's a girl," Hazel began, taking a deep breath, not entirely sure why she was nervous over telling him her name choice, "I'd like to name her Beatrice, although maybe we'll call her Bee since she's like a bumble bee buzzing around inside me anymore."

Vince's face looked pained then, making Hazel feel as if she had said or done something wrong. "What is it?" Hazel asked, alarmed, not getting where this show of deep emotion was stemming from.

"My mom was never much of a mom to me," he said. "But when I was little each night she'd read me *The Tale of Peter Rabbit.*"

By Beatrix Potter.

"I'd love to name our little girl that if we have one," Vince said pulling her to him and gently kissing her.

New Year's Eve 1968
Independence Palace

"It's all this right here, why I think most of the South Vietnamese will always be distrustful of their own government," Vince said as he twirled her around the dance floor or at least attempted to as Hazel's stomach was enormous at this stage of her pregnancy; less than two months to go until Operation Baby, as he had taken to calling it.

Hazel looked around, more closely appraising the opulent surroundings of the room they were in- the high vaulted ceilings, the grandiose chandeliers that some might call gauche, the guests of President Thieu and First Lady Madame Thieu, who were feasting on Western delicacies like caviar, foie gras, and imported Tuscan truffles, along with flowing glasses of Cristal Champagne. It was a lesson in out of touch reality, perhaps taken unintentionally from the pages of French history textbooks. But it was there, the glaringly stark and ever increasing divide between South Vietnam's elite and the rest of its population, most of whom lived in abject poverty.

"They may not agree with the principles and ideologies of communism but this government isn't here for them, isn't looking out for their best interests. They're out to make themselves richer," Vince commented.

"The rich get richer and the poor get poorer," Hazel added, saddened now over the true reality of it all. "But I thought Thieu was a lot better than his predecessor, Diem. And anyone has to be better than a person dubbed the dragon lady."

Hazel had said this jokingly but Madame Nhu, wife of Diem's younger brother who served as the president's chief adviser, also had fulfilled the role of first lady since Diem himself had never been married. She was by all accounts just that, a modern-day Lucretia Borgia, which was another nickname for her. Diem had long favored the country's Catholic population, often putting himself at odds with the country's Buddhist majority who were persecuted by his regime. Things came to a head in 1963 in what became known as the "Buddhist Crisis" when violent crackdowns began against Buddhist population, prohibiting them from publicly marking Buddhist celebrations, pagodas sacred to the Buddhist people desecrated and destroyed, and monks beaten. A few even themselves on fire to protest the shooting of Buddhists by Diem's regime. Madame Nhu called it a "barbecue" and stated, "Let them burn and we shall clap our hands" and also "if they (the Buddhists) wanted to have another barbecue, I will be glad to supply the gasoline." Literally, her Marie Antoinette cake moment. It was whispered that those comments were the final nails in the coffin for

Diem and his brother, who were assassinated in a coup d'état some months later in early November of that year. Considering she was also extremely vocal about her anti-American feelings, loathing the strong U.S. influence and presence in her country, and the strong influence she had on both her husband and brother-in-law, it's safe to say the U.S. government undoubtedly breathed a huge sigh of relief when the Diem clan was gone. This was particularly true of LBJ when he became the commander in chief and ultimate decision maker when JFK was assassinated just weeks later.

"That's not saying much," Vince told her, shaking his head. "Diem was a straight up dictator, arresting and killing anyone in opposition to him, trying to erase not just the Buddhists but all the Montagnards too with their so-called 'assimilation' policies,' that there's just one Vietnam," saying this last part disgustedly. "For years the U.S. has been holding up this country and their president, and we just can't keep doing this forever. Tens of thousands of ours dead with no end in sight. A war with no end if we never get out."

"Do you regret coming here tonight?" Hazel asked, wishing she had not pestered him to come after he, well, the *Dispatch*, had secured an invitation for the coveted Independence Palace New Year's Eve soirée.

"No, babe. I know how much you wanted to come, and to have a night out on the town with my beautiful wife? Priceless," he said, gently kissing the nape of her neck.

"Shamu and all?" she asked, stepping back so she could point to her grossly extended belly, which even under the exquisitely fitted empire silk bodice was very noticeable.

"Favorite mammal," he said, pulling her back into a bear-like embrace. "You are by far the prettiest woman here tonight," he whispered into her ear, the couple of tendrils that had escaped her fancy updo tickling her ear as he spoke.

"Hey, you two. Enough of that hanky panky," Suzy said, coming towards them. She looked positively striking and could have passed for Twiggy's twin. "A toast," she said, giving them the two glasses of champagne she had somehow managed to hold in her left hand without spilling, her right hand holding her own glass. "To the new year, to 1969, may it be the best year yet," she said, clinking each of their glasses. "And to baby Cerny," she added in a sweet tone.

"To 1969," Vince said, staring deeply into Hazel's eyes.

"To 1969," she said, clinking his glass for a toast that was just for them.

PART II

You can kill ten of my men for every one I kill of yours. But even at those odds, you will lose and I will win.—**Ho Chi Minh**

.

CHAPTER 19

Saigon
April 1, 1970

"I don't understand why they're sending you."

Vince was bouncing one-year-old Bee on his lap, who was giggling animatedly with each skyward bounce and by the silly faces her daddy was making at her. He replied exasperatedly at Hazel, "Because I'm the friggin' Southeast Asian bureau chief and we're in goddamn Southeast Asia."

They had been at it all morning and the previous evening when he had come home and announced that he was going to Phnom Penh the next day. Lack of patience and rising tempers were showing now.

"I know that, I just meant you have two correspondents who work for you who—"

Cutting her off he started to raise his voice. "What, because I get the bigger paycheck and delegate that means I shouldn't ever cover a story anymore? Just follow in the steps of all the big wigs who come here for a week or two, never go further than the Rex and then say to the folks back home that they were there, parrot what the MACV tells them to say?" Even the cooing and usually adorable antics of Bee weren't helping anymore. She had become quiet when she noticed her parents' unhappy faces.

"No, because you're a father now," Hazel replied, trying with every last effort to maintain her composure and maturity instead of succumbing to tears. She was precariously close to the latter. She wanted to add, "And because we need you. I need you," but didn't. She had vowed to herself before Bee was born that she was never going to be THAT wife.

Judging by how his face contorted when she'd said that, she wondered in that moment if he'd regretted having a kid, wished she'd never gotten pregnant because it looked like he was going to say something back to her, undoubtedly mean spirited and nasty judging by the way he had stopped himself, his inner voice perhaps having caught up with him and reminding him there was no going back when you said something you could never take back. But no surprise to her, he had been a wonderful father. Of course it didn't hurt either that Bee had been the most laid back newborn baby ever. No amount of artillery fire or explosions off in the distance would keep her from going down for a nap or wake her up prematurely. She was utterly impervious to the dangers around her, not when a bat had decided to nest in the mosquito netting of her bassinet or even when a rat the size of a small dog climbed over her as she sat on the floor of the tiny kitchen as Hazel cooked dinner one night. Hazel had been especially hysterical following the bat incident since she knew that bats here were often rabid. And while there was no shortage of American doctors that Hazel could ask a question of or take Bee to see when she came down with an incredibly high fever that lasted more than a day, or diarrhea so bad she wanted to throw up at the sight of its endless cascade and the smell, God, the smell of that mixed in with the heat of 'Nam, none of them were pediatricians. She often wondered if she was doing the right thing by not returning to

America, by choosing to raise baby Bee in the middle of a war zone. And although Vince hadn't entirely approved, Hazel had even adopted the Vietnamese way of diaper application—Bee didn't wear any since disposable diapers were basically nonexistent here and she had tired early on with constantly having to wash the cloth ones she'd had made. But he was a natural with his Bee—the rare times she fussed all it took was listening to the sound of her daddy's melodic timbre to sooth her. Hazel had to work a bit harder for her audience. Daddy's girl, she supposed, a closeness she'd never had with her own father.

But Hazel knew something was bothering him. There had been an air of restlessness about him for weeks now. He had been nominated for a Pulitzer for his reporting on Khe Sanh, which Hazel had possibly been more excited about than he was. He still routinely went out into the field, usually twice a month, at times for more than a week's stretch, embedding himself with whatever platoon or regiment he was with. One time he had returned home particularly quiet, not even bothering to gaze down at a sleeping Bee as he always did when he was gone for more than a week. Instead he had taken down the bottle of Wild Turkey he kept on top of their tiny fridge, poured himself a finger of it into the one chipped highball glass they'd acquired, downed it, then immediately poured himself a second.

Hazel wanted to ask him what was wrong, what had happened but she didn't. She surmised he was getting to that, judging by the third finger of whiskey he was pouring himself. Liquid fortitude, as the saying went.

"Rookie mistake 101," he said, downing the third. "And I made it. As if I haven't been living here for five years, been here since the start of all this."

She knew what drunk was, and he was just about there.

"I went out with the same platoon from two weeks ago. I wanted to, there were a lot of Midwest guys in it, even four from Chicago. It felt like home being around them."

"I don't understand," she replied, not grasping what he was getting at.

"You wouldn't," he replied meanly as he downed the fourth. "But it's safe to say the gang wasn't all there this time."

Hazel understood now. Who Vince had seen, spoken to, done formal interviews with—the platoon must have suffered bad losses in the last two weeks. It happened. Platoons, squads, units- from one battle, one engagement, one campaign, their numbers could easily be reduced by a quarter and often more. This was a sobering and tragic fact of life in any war but in Vietnam it seemed more frequent, even common.

"I'm sorry," Hazel said, walking over to him to place a comforting hand on his shoulder but he shrugged it off and said, "don't." He took a still quiet Bee, who he was still holding, and laid her down on the floor where a blanket was spread out along with an old Babar stuffed animal that Jeanne had given Bee shortly after she was born and which Bee faithfully slept with each night. Hazel had even found old copies of two of the Babar books in a shop and she read them to Bee each night, in French of course. Hazel hoped that Bee would become bilingual like she was.

Vince went into their small bedroom then and a few minutes later returned with his rucksack.

"There's a limo leaving from the Caravelle at 14:00 today," he said, not looking at her as he spoke, just starting down at a sleeping Bee.

Then softening he added, "I'll be back as soon as I can. But I have to go, you know this," he said, taking her into his arms to hold her. "They had a coup, Prince Sihanouk is out. The man who had long tolerated VC and North Vietnamese activity within his country's borders, opened up ports for weapons shipments to the VC, is no more. The fact that the man who's replacing him is a staunch anti-communist, anti-Vietnamese, this is huge babe. Lon Nol's on record having issued an ultimatum that all North Vietnamese forces need to leave the country. I mean, all of that on top of the rumors that have long existed about the U.S. carrying out illegal bombing raids on communist bases there. The coup could be this war's Sarajevo powder keg. You can quote me on that," he added, pulling back to study her while adding a wry smile.

"How's it even safe to go then?" Hazel said, unconvinced.

"What do you mean? You're living in Vietnam, probably one of the least safe places on earth," he replied laughingly. "And raising a baby too."

"It was a coup d'état, Vince. They don't ever happen from friendly faces and talks of peace."

"Yeah, but it was between the Cambodians, nothing to do with Western journalists and to my knowledge not even Archie is a closet commie."

"Yeah, and you know as well as I do, that the U.S. has a vested interest in Vietnam's neighbors and the fact that this has happened, it could all blow up very fast. And you could be right in the thick of it all."

"Bob would definitely be my uncle then if I got that story."

"Vince, I'm not—"

"I need to go Hazel, I can't do this anymore." Stooping down, he placed a kiss on top of Bee's head, gave her a hurried peck on her cheek and walked out, shutting the door behind him, not bothering to look back even once.

Saigon
April 7, 1970

"Suzy? Archie? What on earth are you guys doing here?"

When the knock had sounded at the door, Hazel checked her watch, alarmed that someone was at the door after 11 at night. At first she thought it was Vince but then reminded herself he wouldn't be knocking, unless of course he had lost his keys. But when she opened the door to find her two friends standing there and took in their grim faces, Hazel grew doubly alarmed.

"What is it?" Hazel asked, her voice catching, a horrible feeling of nausea rising to the back of her throat. "What's happened, is it Vince? Did something happen to him?"

Suzy still hadn't said anything but now came towards Hazel and lightly taking her arm said, "Let's go sit down." She led Hazel to the small wicker settee where they both sat. Archie came towards her now and lowering himself on his haunches, he took Hazel's shaking clammy hand within his.

"I was with Vince in Phnom Penh," he began, slowly and shakily. "He had bought himself a motorcycle there. You see the limo we took to get there, there were problems with the engine, we were having to stop a lot, it was always overheating. Vince said he wanted to get back to you as soon as he could, didn't want to be bothered and delayed by the limo." He paused then, looking as if he didn't want to continue or rather couldn't continue. "He was ahead of us, but then the limo caught up and we all stopped, because you see there was some sort of makeshift checkpoint on the road, on Highway 1, I mean. But none of us went towards it, just something about it didn't look right. Someone said it was the same car that several missing journalists had been traveling in a few weeks earlier."

Journalists being kidnapped and worse was becoming a more

common occurrence in Vietnam now.

"You could see there was a platoon of NVA soldiers in a nearby tree line, see they were taking up defensive positions in a line perpendicular to the road. After an hour of this waiting game, Vince just declared, 'Screw this, I'm going. It's Cambodia and I'm an American journalist.' We all called out to him, to wait, to not go, we had no idea who they were, if they were friendly or not, but he just kept walking towards the checkpoint."

"And they shot him?" Hazel croaked out, all of a sudden feeling dizzy, the room spinning.

"No," Archie quickly replied. "I mean, I didn't see that, see him get shot or anything. They took his motorcycle and then marched him off into the tree line. But I called the *Dispatch* as soon as I got back to Saigon. I wanted to be the one to tell you, I didn't want you getting some call or telegram from a stranger."

"I'm going to be sick," Hazel said, sitting up, running to the kitchen sink which she just reached before emptying her stomach of everything she had consumed that day.

For the first two weeks following news of Vince's disappearance, Hazel had been paralyzed with every tangible emotion her body could come up with. Grief that he was potentially, no probably dead, anger that he had acted with such recklessness by going up to the checkpoint alone, heartache that her daughter would never know her father. And just a profound sense of emptiness, devoid of direction, of purpose. She was emotionally lost. In a way she hadn't felt after hearing that Milton had been killed or even receiving Betty's telegram about her parents' death. Vince was the person she thought she would spend the next, what, 40 years with? Have another baby or two, raise their family together? Be the type of unit neither had had when they were growing up. And now here, he was gone. Just like that. She hadn't signed up to do life alone but now she was.

Both Archie and Suzy had told her to not give up hope, that he hadn't been confirmed killed, that perhaps he was just being held as a POW. There were reports now and then of journalists who had been taken by NVA soldiers only to be released weeks later. But now it was weeks later, and still no word.

The Dispatch had reached out as well to her in both the form of a 30 minute telephone call with some of the big wigs back in Washington who vowed that they would offer all the resources they could muster to keep searching for Vince. Also a telegram from the publisher himself who offered his sincere condolences, as if Vince was confirmed dead, his body in a bag back on a plane to the U.S. But none of that made Hazel feel remotely any better, any more confident that Vince would come back to her.

Archie and Suzy had both been great though, providing the emotional support she so desperately needed. Suzy stayed with her at the apartment, tending to Bee, which at any other time would have been comical considering Suzy's lack of affinity towards babies and anything small child related. But she took to it with a great knack. Archie too, although he ended up proving especially invaluable with contacting the American embassy both in Saigon and Phnom Penh and also bombarding MACV nonstop to look into Vince's disappearance. They always said they would, whoever Archie and sometimes Hazel would speak with. They made no promises, but maybe that was a good thing Hazel had thought; the prospect of a false promise was entirely disheartening. But all that changed after April 28. That date President Richard Nixon, the same man who had vowed in a campaign promise to end American involvement in Vietnam, authorized U.S. combat troops to cross the border from

South Vietnam into Cambodia. And of course the previously illegal bombing raids that the U.S. had been carrying out for months were now approved and in full public awareness and scope. Nixon had hoped that bombing the supply routes in Cambodia would weaken America's enemies but if anything, it further emboldened them in ways that would become apparent down the road.

April 28 happened, and just like that, the country that had been in its own time-warped and insulated bubble for so long, was now a war zone too. A war zone where finding credible information regarding a missing person would prove to be near impossible.

"Have you thought about going home?"

The question jarred Hazel even though she knew Suzy hadn't meant anything upsetting by it.

"And where's that exactly?" she answered defensively. "My childhood home is forever broken, no more, and now the home I thought I had built here against the backdrop of war, is broken now too."

Hazel knew what Suzy wanted to say but didn't have the resolve to. That Vince was dead. That he wasn't coming back and now with the war having spilled over the border, it seemed highly unlikely that America would be existing stage left of the Southeast Asian theater anytime soon.

And what Hazel thought about herself. Did she really have it in her to be a wartime journalist anymore with all that had happened, with how everything currently stood, in a painful emotional limbo.

"Then I think you need to get back out there. Start writing again, start chasing after stories. Your daughter needs you to, and Vince would want you to."

"You know what the most messed up thing out of all of this is?" Hazel asked. She took Suzy's silence as her answer. "Before Bee was born, we actually discussed where the other would go, would raise

Bee if something happened to one of us. Did I somehow foresee his death?" Hazel asked, her voice now breaking.

"Of course not," Suzy said, coming over to Hazel where she took the other woman in her arms as she let out wracked sobs. "You just both knew that this was war and with war comes risk."

"But it's like an evil prophecy that came true," Hazel said, her sobs now quickly quieting down to little hiccups that sounded like the ones Bee made when she was upset.

"No," Suzy said, still rubbing the small of Hazel's back to comfort her. "You knew that you were going to be a parent, knew that you were going to be responsible for another human being and were thinking ahead. Because that's what a good parent does, even if the kid was still baking in the oven at the time. Bee needs you, and she's going to need you for a very long time. You have to always live for her if nothing else."

CHAPTER 20

New York City
2005

"My mom was never affectionate with me growing up, but now it all makes sense," Bee said.

"What does?" Suzy asked.

"Why she was never loving with me, kind towards me. She blamed me for what happened to my dad, because I was the reason she badgered him to hurry back to Saigon, to her, to me."

"No, that's not at all how it was."

"How would you know?" Bee fired back defensively. "I mean, when was the last time you saw her? In '75 when the war was ending? You have no idea at all what she was like when I was growing up. She regarded me as her duty, her duty to my dead dad. And she fulfilled it by raising me, by not sending me to a group home like his own mom had after his dad was killed. But she never gave me an ounce of anything else," Bee said.

"You're right, I don't know, and I wasn't there. I wanted to visit you many times, I even offered on more than one occasion to come myself to your Butler, even though I know the restaurants and entertainment would have been sorely lacking," Suzy said jokingly. "I invited her to come to San Francisco, London when I was living there for a time, and New York. But she never did. Not even once. We shared so much and her reply was always the same, that she just 'couldn't.' I never pushed her and to this day, I do indeed regret it. She retreated into a hole she never came out of again for the rest of her life. But I do mean this. I don't for an instant feel or think she blamed you for what happened to your dad. I think if anything, she blamed herself, and that guilt was something she could ever absolve herself of."

Saigon
1970

For her first story back, her first attempt at writing something other than slop since Vince had gone missing, words on a page she hadn't dared submit anywhere, Hazel wanted it to be good, needed it to be good. She couldn't wait, nor did she want another Tet Offensive to happen. She'd never want to see that again in her life, here or anywhere.

Hazel had never heard mention of it directly, but Vince had, among the café elite, the contingent of Western expats here in Saigon. There were rumors of tiger cages at the Con Son prison, an infamous penal institution off the coast of Vietnam. She first thought the name was a joke, that Vince was joking. But he had never once smiled. He went on to tell her that these special cells had been built by the French after a student uprising around the turn of the century. They were said to be hidden deep within the prison complex, so inhumane and nightmarish that the government didn't want anyone knowing about them, let alone nosey Western journalists who would undoubtedly view human rights, even for prisoners, in a dramatically different light than their South Vietnamese counterparts. But wasn't that just the claims of North Vietnam and every other country that had ever fought against a colonial force, an occupying outsider- that they shouldn't be told how to run their country?

And the most disturbing thing of all- the prisoners said to be kept in the tiger cages were rumored to be nothing more dangerous than political prisoners, not murderers and rapists. But in a country like South Vietnam, in which democracy was laughably preached while autocracy reigned, political prisoners were indeed the greatest foe.

Hazel knew a congressional delegation would be coming to Vietnam soon, a "fact finding mission" as politicians and their junior staff referred to them. For Hazel and her colleagues, it was more of a "truth unfurling mission," since the truths had long been there. Nothing at this point needed to be "found out" but rather openly shared with the American people.

If she could get United States congressmen to go with her to Con Son, anything she would potentially write would have much more substance, and even more importantly, credence. There were too many people back home who still believed that the journalists here were nothing more than non-God fearing, Communist lovin' hippies. The American people at this point needed to hear the truth from their elected officials, people whose political future and legacy were tied to this war just as Johnson's was.

Saigon
July 1970

"I got it, Suzy!" Hazel said over the phone, her voice sounding alive for the first time in months. "A pass to accompany the congressional delegation that's going to be visiting Con Son Island. I mean, I was the one to get the idea for the visit into motion but I'm going to be able to go WITH them," she enthused.

"That's wonderful, darling! Who's all coming?"

"Montrose of New Jersey and White of Texas I think."

"That's all?" Suzy asked, surprise in her tone.

"I know, I would have thought there'd be more going."

"Well, you'll certainly have the insider angle for sure. I'll check in when I'm back, give that baby girl a huge kiss for me," and with that she hung up the phone.

For the last two months, Suzy had been going into Cambodia non-stop. Civil war had broken out there between Lon Nol's anti-communist forces which were supported by both the United States and South Vietnam, and the Communist Party of Kampuchea, known colloquially as the Khmer Rouge, who in turn had the support and backing of both the Viet Cong and the North Vietnamese army. When Lon Nol's pro-American government had ordered the PAVN to leave Cambodia immediately, the latter had to no one's surprise refused, and then at the request of the Khmer Rouge, promptly invaded the country in full-force. And just as Vince had predicted, Cambodia, a country that just like Vietnam years earlier, few in the West had heard of let alone could find on a map, was on everyone's tongue, it being the latest pawn in the war between countries, land holdings, and of course, political ideologies. The U.S. didn't want yet another country to fall to the evils of communism or see its ally South Vietnam overrun, while the PAVN wanted to protect the base areas and sanctuaries it had established in eastern Cambodia, without which its guerrilla warfare in South Vietnam would have been undoubtedly harder. No one was giving up easily without a fight to the death, the phrase that would forever epitomize this corner of the world.

Hazel had never said this outright but she never planned to step foot in Cambodia again. The more time went by, the more certain Hazel felt that Vince was dead, most likely killed on the day he was marched into the tree line on Highway 1. Yes, she was still a journalist, and yes, Cambodia was exploding before the world that was watching it and there was and would be so many stories there, but she couldn't do anything that would remotely put her life at risk, anything that would truly leave her Bee, her baby daughter, an orphan. She would not see history repeat itself as it had with Vince's parents, plus the fact that she too was all alone in this world. Her daughter would not grow up as an orphan. She even had put away the photographs she had taken from their honeymoon for they were too painful to look at. When Bee was older, when they were no longer here, with the wounds so fresh and deep, she would one day take them out again and show her.

Archie had been back to Cambodia too a couple of times and although he never said, undoubtedly to not give her false hope, Hazel knew some of this was to search for Vince. She knew Vince's disappearance had affected him too, just in different ways.

Since he was still considered missing and not dead, the *Dispatch* provided Hazel with a small monthly stipend. It wasn't a lot but without a formal declaration of death, Hazel wasn't entitled to his pension. It was enough to have hired a Vietnamese teenage refugee girl from the countryside, Lin, to look after Bee and do light housework (what little there was in the small apartment). But the girl was grateful, an orphan herself who had been living on the streets, begging for handouts. Like so many young women her age, Hazel knew it would have only been a matter of time before she would have ended up as a girl for hire in one of the many notorious bars and clubs on Tu Do Street; selling your body to American GIs was often the only way out other than death for these young girls if they wanted to live another day. Lin didn't speak fluent French and only a few words of English but having her there helped with Hazel's loneliness, helped keep the depression at bay. And Bee seemed to adore the young woman, which is what mattered the most to Hazel. But she saw so many Lins every week, most of whom didn't have an American to save them.

From the air it looked beautiful, this island off the southern coast of the country. Shimmering turquoise waters framed by white sand beaches. But she knew looks could be deceiving, for this island paradise was also home to a notorious prison that had been in existence for more than 100 years, first established by the French to house Vietnamese prisoners who had committed especially severe crimes. When the French left, it was turned over to the South Vietnamese government which continued to use it as a prison.

"I often think this would be the cruelest fate." Hazel turned to see Representative White speaking to her.

"What would?" Hazel asked.

"Being imprisoned, but being imprisoned in a place like this," he said, waving his arm to indicate the tropical island. "I mean sure, we've got Alcatraz back home, but San Francisco is a lot of things but it sure ain't tropical. Not to mention the water there is much too violent to swim to shore," he added in a faint Texas drawl.

"But if one never sees the outside, then you don't really know what you're missing," Hazel replied, having read that many of the former French colonial prisons contained what were called *cachots,* or dungeons. Once prisoners were in, they never came out.

"No, I suppose you're right," he said after a pause. "My aide tells me your husband was killed in where, Cambodia earlier this year?"

Hazel took a deep intake of breath, feeling like she had been hit by a bus. "Missing. Not dead," she said almost curtly.

"My apologies, ma'am, I didn't mean to be insensitive."

"No need to, it's easy to think that way when there's no confirmed death. But just like all the wives and mothers who get that dreaded telegram telling them that their son or husband has been listed as missing in action, one can simply not give up hope." God, she sounded like Suzy and Anne right now, parroting what they had said to her all these months, over and over.

"You're absolutely right. And I will pray he comes home to you too."

"Thank you, Representative."

Hell hath no bounds. That is the only way Hazel could describe the prison. The smell is what hit her first- the putrid odor of rotting flesh, human waste, unwashed bodies, all mixed in with the backdrop of unbearably hot temperatures and humidity.

Before today, Hazel had met privately with Representative White's congressional aide who was going to be coming with them. Although the visit itself had all been done "by the books," in terms of arranging it with the South Vietnamese officials, it was the tiger cages that the South Vietnamese couldn't know about. Especially after through several contacts, Hazel had been given a rough hand drawn map from a former prisoner on the island on how to find them. She knew she would need to let the congressmen know her plans in advance, but let nothing be recorded about them either. What she was attempting to do could potentially get her MACV ID revoked and even cause her to be sent home. And when she learned that this aide spoke a modicum of Vietnamese, she reasoned it truly had a high chance of working, with him serving as the distraction when the time came. Didn't the American people have a right to know who their allies were, the country and people it was sacrificing the lives of its own young men for?

The map led to the door of a building which was opened from the inside by a guard when he heard their group talking. By this point, Congressman White's aide was already chattering away to the two guards who had been leading them around the prison grounds, spaces that looked like a "model prison." Hazel couldn't help but think of the Nazi concentration camp in Czechoslovakia that had been dubbed a "show camp" to pretend to the world that all was well inside, that the prisoners had been relocated there for "their" safety, that they weren't being mistreated at all, that in fact they were leading a wonderful existence. That's who the South Vietnamese were modeling their actions after? The Nazis? Hazel felt an intense wave of disgust at this thought.

Inside, Hazel saw the stuff of nightmares, a scene that looked like it could have belonged in the Middle Ages. The tiger cages really did exist as Hazel looked down on the scene before her in horror. Small concrete trenches with bars on top. They appeared to be five feet wide, six feet long, and six feet deep.

All at once when the prisoners spotted the visitors they began crying out in whimpered tones, "water", some even saying it in French, "*l'eau.*" They were filthy, covered in their own waste, their bodies marked with sores and bruises; some even had mutilating marks on them. A few stood, hunched as they were, as they feebly fanned the many more prisoners lying prostrate on the filthy darkened ground. Many were women, some men, and then to her shock and disbelief, she saw what appeared to be a young girl of about 12.

Hazel was repulsed in a way she never imagined she could be. And she felt intense shame at this for no human being, white, Black, Vietnamese or American, deserved a fate such as this. Representative White looked like he wanted to vomit. Ever the Southern gentleman, he offered her his handkerchief which she gladly took and covered her mouth and nose. She took photo after photo of the scene before her.

And then telling herself it was now or never, she called out in French, "Why are you here? Why have they put you in such a place? Tell me, I am a journalist, I want the world to know about Con Son, I want the American people to know that the American government is letting this go on, go on during their watch."

Silence and then a weakened female voice called back in French, "We are not the hardened criminals they say we are. We are not murderers as they tell our families when they arrest us. We simply have spoken out against injustice, the unfairness against the Buddhist people."

And then another voice, this time in broken French, "I Buddhist monk. I still speak for peace."

And then more voices crying out almost simultaneously, each one trying to be heard over the other—

"We steal grass to eat when the guards aren't looking"
"We catch bugs and lizards for food"
"I can't stand up anymore, I've been kept in shackles for too long"
"I've been here for years, I no longer know how long"

At first Hazel had frantically tried to write down everything she was hearing, to record the voices that were trying so desperately to be heard. But she abruptly stopped for she knew these voices, these images, would forever haunt her. She would forget nothing.

"Hey, Frenchie, I've got a gift for you," Vince said, smiling broadly as he walked through the door. He kept one hand behind his back which Hazel could see was clutching something, as he kissed her on the lips and then gently kissed the top of Bee's darkened head as she slept in Hazel's arms. Any traces of the earlier fussing that had kept her from going down to nap for the last hour, not noticeable.

Hazel got up then and laid a sleeping Bee into the bassinet that she was getting a bit too big for these days. Vince then handed her a small parcel wrapped in brown parchment paper.

Unwrapping it, she saw that it was a book, a French language book called *Papillon*.

"I was passing by this bookseller and went in to browse. When he heard that I had a wife who speaks French, he said you should read it, that it was a huge bestseller in France for weeks. The bookseller said it's like Con Son Prison here."

Turning the book over, Hazel read the synopsis on the back-

Henri Charriere, called Papillon for the butterfly tattoo on his chest, was convicted in Paris in 1931 for a murder he did not commit. When he was sentenced to life imprisonment in the penal colony of French Guiana, one thought obsessed him: escape. After planning and executing a series of treacherous yet failed attempts over many years, Papillon was eventually sent to the notorious prison, Devil's Island, a place from which no one had ever escaped — that was, until Papillon. His escape, described in breathless detail, was one of the most incredible tests of human cunning, will, and endurance.

In French she uttered out loud the words- *le chemin de la pourriture.*

"What's that mean, babe?" Vince asked, always a look on pride on his face when she spoke in French. As he'd said many times before, this "bedazzled" him.

"The path of rot."

CHAPTER 21

New York City
2005

"Your mom never got credit," Suzy said, seeming to finally be winding down, the night catching up with her after she had knocked back what, six glasses of whiskey?

"What, of Con Son? The pictures you mean from *Life*?" Bee asked.

"Yeah, you see Horst Faas of the AP, he wanted to publish them but knew that if MACV got wind of it, that some American journalist who they had given clearance and authority to be there with a press badge, had snuck into some off-limits South Vietnamese prison, all in such a way that not only would the South Vietnamese look bad, but it would look even worse for the American officials, that person's badge would be revoked and they'd be kicked out of the country. So he left it up to your mom. She passed on the credit and recognition it would bring—"

Bee interjected to finish, "So she could stay in the country and keep looking for my dad. So nothing would remotely jeopardize that."

"More or less," Suzy said.

"And the man with the credit?" Bee asked.

"Representative White's congressional aide. Who after those pictures were published was blacklisted from Washington for not surrendering the film, for failing to keep it all 'hush hush' as Washington wanted him to. You see Washington's party line on Con Son was that it was a model prison, very much akin to a Boy Scout's camp away. Many were irate that there were some Americans who had the nerve to concern themselves with Vietnamese affairs, never mind the fact that wasn't that what we had been doing all those years? Concerning ourselves with a country on the other side of the world, all so that Johnny Red wouldn't take up shop there? Didn't we concern ourselves when we more or less assisted with the coup and assassination of Diem and his brother in '63? But that's American hypocrisy for you," Suzy finished, lighting up a cigarette. Taking a puff, she added, "But the aide got his sweet revenge years later when he became the party whip and made prison reform one of his party's top issues."

"But everyone, well, I mean everyone in the journalist community, knew it was my mom who had taken those photos, written the copy?" Bee asked.

"Everyone and their brother," Suzy replied. "Once Saigon fell and Vietnam was a firmly rooted Communist nation, America wanted nothing to do with its shame and disgrace. That same aide tried to tell the true story of the photos, of Con Son, but by that point your mom was nowhere to be found."

"Or didn't want to be found," Bee added sadly, her thoughts mixed on the immensely troubled woman who had been her mother, compounded even more with everything Suzy had told her.

"And that right there," Suzy said, slapping her manicured hand down on top of the ornate cherry oak coffee table, "is absolutely the truth."

It wasn't cruel enough that Hazel had dreams, almost nightly, about Vince. Now she saw him everywhere she went, or at least she thought she did. There had been the man she had followed through all of Ben Thanh Market, narrowly missing chopped up animal parts and fish heads being thrown into slop buckets, the market vendors indifferent to who they might assault with their flinging of bloodied bits. When Hazel finally caught up to the man, she had grabbed at him to face her. When she saw that it wasn't Vince, she offered an apology but the man responded angrily back in a language she didn't recognize. And then there was the time she had been having a drink with Suzy and Archie at the Continental Shelf and saw a man who looked just like Vince walk in. He was in Army fatigues like he had just come in from the field, and hadn't bothered to remove his cap either. Although she could hear both Suzy and Archie ask her where she was going when she got up from the table, she kept walking to who she thought was Vince. When she was standing in front of him, she noticed the stripes on his sleeve, noticed they weren't American ones. She was fixated on those stripes and didn't even hear him speaking to her in what was clearly an Australian accent. It was only when she felt Archie leading her away did she mumble "I'm sorry."

"You've got to stop this," Suzy said to Hazel while exchanging a worried look with Archie. "You can't keep going up to every person on the street you think is Vince. If he was alive—"

Hazel interjected to say, "Yes, if he was alive, he'd come home to me, come home to his wife and daughter. I know that. I know that he wouldn't be wandering through Ben Thanh or having a beer with his buddies. I just don't know how not to."

What, not to care? To obsess? Give up?

"There's no body, no confirmed death. How am I supposed to possibly give up when there's a chance he could still be out there, still be alive?" Hazel asked imploringly. "If the situation was reversed, he would never give up on me, not for a moment."

Archie, who had become noticeably more subdued, serious even, since Vince's disappearance, solemnly took her hands within his. "And you have to face the facts that there might never be a body, never find out the truth as to what really happened to him."

"As if he had never existed. Move on, just like that," Hazel said, snapping her fingers.

"No," Suzy said. "But to not mentally stop living either. To stop waiting for a call that may never come. And to stop ignoring a baby because she reminds you so much of him. Beatrice can't be willed away just like Vince can't be willed to magically appear after all these months. You need to accept it, Hazel. Before it's too late and you have a daughter that doesn't even know you."

No matter how much she tried, Hazel couldn't ignore what Suzy had said to her about Bee, before it's too late, before her own daughter wouldn't even know she was her mother. With great reluctance, Hazel could admit to herself there was some truth to this. It was Lin that Bee saw upon first waking up in the morning and it was Lin who put Bee to bed each night. And of course, it was Lin who Bee was constantly with too, Lin's lap that she crawled into when wanting to be soothed, Lin's arms she reached for when wanting to be picked up. Not Hazel. She did say the French word for mom, *maman,* in her toddler babble, but Hazel reasoned it had more to do with the fact that the young woman must have practiced this constantly with Bee. Hazel couldn't believe this was something Bee would have naturally started saying, yet what example of a *maman* had Hazel really been setting since Vince's disappearance?

Hazel tried telling herself that this was to be expected, the life of a single working mother, and that it would be the same whether she was back home in the United States or in Vietnam like she was. The plain truth was she would always need to work, to make money to support herself and Bee; geography wouldn't matter. When it came time to feeding her child, she would never have the luxury to simply stay home and raise Bee.

Neither Archie nor Suzy had outright said it, but she knew they both thought she should go home, take Bee with her and return to the United States. Fourteen months had gone by since Vince's disappearance; the year he had been taken was no more, a year of new and empty blank pages had been ushered in. And Vince had missed out on more than an entire year's worth of his young daughter's life, an entire year that could never be gotten back.

There were days when Hazel truly considered giving up, for what was the point she asked herself. Banging on officials' doors, calling the embassy, meeting with the contacts of contacts, had turned up nothing. She had allowed herself a brief respite of hope when miracle of all miracles, the Australian journalist Kate Webb, a personable woman whom Hazel had met once or twice with Vince, had been kidnapped by the North Vietnamese and held captive for three weeks only to be released. Perhaps the same would happen with Vince. That they would see he was not an American soldier, was simply there to report on the truth. But how can one compare 14 months with three weeks? The thing was, one couldn't.

Prisoners of war were a tragic fate of war. Was that what Vince was? Could that status be applied to him? Rotting away in some prisoner of war camp in some remote corner of North Vietnam, one rife with disease and cruelty on the actions of the guards? Starving? But she knew another cruel truth- she had met and heard enough about foreigners who had gone missing and whose fate had been immediate death. Missionaries, journalists—they were not the ones waging this war and carrying out the orders of their superiors—and yet their purpose, if that's what one could call it, was what, integral? And he was a man. The VC and North Vietnamese army seemed much more apt to kill a foreign man than a woman.

Later that night in Suzanne's luxuriously appointed guest room, lying on top of what were undoubtedly real silk sheets with most likely a 1000 thread count, she thought of "Dites-Moi," a ditty her mom used to sing to her when she was little, the rare instance when Hazel showed any true maternal affection towards her.

Bee didn't know what the words meant, some song from the Rodgers and Hammerstein musical *South Pacific* but she could hear clear as day in her head, her mom's voice singing those simple words to her. And she wondered, why that song? What was its significance she wondered as she finally started to surrender to sleep.

April 1971

"I'm more scared about being killed by a fraggin' than Charlie himself."

If you had only heard the last sentence, one would think it had been said as a joke, considering the source. Captain Francis Neil was a physically imposing man. Over six feet tall and weighing more than 200 pounds, there didn't seem much that could scare him. And yet, here he was on record with Hazel essentially stating that something did. Fragging- death at the hands of a fellow soldier, or more commonly, murder by an enlisted man of a commanding officer.

"I mean, it's gotten so bad that a buddy of a mine, a captain, he actually moves his cot each night because he doesn't fully trust the drafted men within his battalion to not kill him at night when he's asleep by dropping a frag onto his cot if they always know where he is."

Although fraggings had occurred in every war this century, Vietnam changed all that. No longer were they only a case of revolt against an incompetent or maniacal leader, the saying of kill or be killed holding true when a bad commander's call or tactical decision could prove deadly for all the men involved. Today, the "hit" on a commanding officer could be chalked up to a simple case of "just because."

Hazel had seen for herself how today's draftee in Vietnam was different. On the few occasions she still went into the field with a regiment, she kept to herself, she didn't try to ingratiate herself like with Lance Corporal Napoli's men all those years earlier. It wasn't just that they didn't want to be there. None of the drafted men had ever wanted to be sent here. One heard the name Vietnam, and knew the risks associated with it. And you said as much by bitching about the hardships, the emotional and physical depravities on a 15-mile hump through a monsoon or temperatures so high you could cook a burger on the pavement. You protested by writing an anti-war message on your helmet or rucksack. The men who were being sent here today frightened her. She knew many to have been criminals, granted early release on the condition that they were sent here to fight. And many more were drug addicts, hooked on the hard and sometimes lethal stuff like heroin and cocaine. And these men were why the number of fraggings had increased so much lately.

"Another buddy of mine, a major up near Quang Tri, when he arrived, he immediately enforced strict discipline, he filed a slew of disciplinary charges against insubordinate and disobedient men. His second week there, someone rolled a frag into his tent. It was a dud, but he got reassigned to desk duty, so screwed up in the head after that. In Vietnam, if you're an officer, NCO or not, you're a marked man."

"What do you think the Army or the Marine Corps can do about it?" Hazel asked, notepad at the ready.

"If this can be off the record, ma'am, I believe there's not a damn thing we can do anymore. Our army is near collapse here, propped up with dispirited, disillusioned, mutinous men who I won't even disgrace the term soldier by calling them that. We need to get out of this place before we're all sent home in Glad bags and there's no army left anymore to run."

Hazel recalled her time with Captain Neil months later as she sat in the courtroom awaiting the court martial of a Private Bayonne to begin.

The man accused was on trial for the fragging death of his commanding officer, a Major Haggarty. Haggarty had verbally reprimanded Bayonne for being asleep while on guard duty, but that's all that had come of it; Bayonne had not been formally written up and disciplined. But Bayonne didn't take kindly to any of it. So one night when Haggarty was asleep, Bayonne had thrown a frag into Haggarty's tent, killing the man, a husband and father of two small children, instantly. Bayonne's defense was that he had been high when he'd done it and didn't know what he was doing.

A feeble defense considering most of the men currently serving in Vietnam were routinely high but few of them were throwing nightly frags into a commanding officer's tent for the sole purpose of killing them. A harsh speaking to, but nothing on one's record, and that warrants killing someone and ruining the lives of their loved ones back home?

"Hazel!"

Hazel turned to see Archie coming towards her. She hadn't seen him in months, almost as if he were avoiding her, avoiding facing the guilt he felt anytime he saw the faces of his best friend's wife and child. She hoped that wasn't the reason why but what did she know. Hazel could barely process the guilt she felt, Vince wanting to rush back to Saigon to be with her and Bee, Vince taking the risk by going on a motorcycle, walking right up to that checkpoint—she didn't have the emotional fortitude to ponder someone else's.

"What are you doing here?" Archie asked, giving her a light kiss on the cheek as he sat down besides her.

"I could ask the same of you," she replied. "I thought you were still in Cambodia."

"I needed a breather," he told her, his thin, long face drawn and heavy. "Things are really getting bad there. They, uh, they found hundreds more bodies in the Mekong, Vietnamese I mean. Lon Nol's anti-communist forces are just killing them in droves. I think if the tables turn in the favor of the Khmer Rouge, it's going to get horrifically worse."

Hazel closed her eyes at the mention of the Khmer Rouge. Three years ago, the newly arrived to Southeast Asia Hazel would have seen the story there, the story that was Cambodia, the story that was soon going to be just as big if not bigger than Vietnam back home on the pages of American newspapers and in the living rooms of American families. She would have rushed to report on it. But the Hazel of now, the woman whose husband was missing, presumably dead, the mother raising her young child all alone in a war-torn land, she just couldn't. For all of Nixon's valiant efforts and attempts at curbing the communist onslaught next door, it was proving to be as miserable as the evacuation of English forces at Dunkirk in 1940 in World War II. She had come here for Vietnam, not to see an entire region of the world crumble into a heartbreaking mess.

"Hazel?" she heard Archie asking, his voice full of concern.

"Sorry," she answered, opening her eyes once more and plastering on a rich and fake smile for his benefit. "I'm just sorely in need of some sleep. Bee's been having nightmares lately." Hazel felt guilty over using her daughter as an excuse for her distracted state of mind but knew it would work. "I did a story a couple of months back on fraggings and when I heard about the court martial, I knew I would want to be here, especially since I heard they're quite rare."

"Yeah, most never go to trial." Archie said, pulling out his reporter's pad. "I spoke to an army judge and he said that only about 10% of fraggings end up in court."

"That's a disgrace," Hazel said.

"I don't disagree with you there," Archie answered. "But want to talk about a near impossible case to prove? A grenade splinters into thousands of tiny fragments, no evidence there. Not to mention you can't tie a grenade firing pin with a particular grenade. So who are you going to court martial, the entire platoon? Label them all as suspects? It's why for lack of a better word, they're so popular. A perfect instance of commit a crime and never do the time."

Later that night as Hazel worked on the copy of her story on the opening remarks of day 1 of the court martial, she wrote-

This macabre and downright murderous ritual is the troops' way of controlling officers. Even though it wasn't the officers who drafted them, who picked their lottery number, who changed their lives forever, it's their way of saying, we've got control of you in the end.

March 29, 1973
Clark Air Force Base-the Philippines

As Hazel watched the last of the gaunt POWs come down the steps of the C-141 onto the runway at Clark Air Force Base, some of them with ashen faces, all of them outfitted in the same dreary 'uniforms' that the North Vietnamese had supposedly supplied the American POWs before their release, not wanting the world to see the rags they had been living in for years, Suzy's words echoed in Hazel's head-

It's a fool's errand, Hazel. He wasn't on any of the POW lists. If he had been in a POW prison in the north all these years, you would know it. After the Peace Accords had been signed, you would have known it.

Hazel's counter retort that not every American who had been captured in Vietnam would have ended up in an official POW prison camp hadn't mattered to Suzy. And deep down Hazel knew she was right.

Screams of jubilation. Hazel saw a woman older than her rushing to one of the gray pajama clad men who started to hurriedly limp towards her, their arms then closing around the other moments later.

All around her, people were hugging, kissing, squealing in laughter, excitement, disbelief. It truly was beautiful, all things considered. For every single man who had survived as a POW had made it through hell and back. They deserved this, this wonderful homecoming, this long-awaited reunion they had only dreamt of every day, month, and year spent in captivity.

But didn't she too deserve such a long-awaited reunion? Didn't Bee deserve to know her father?

Hazel had come here today, the spot all the POWs were being

flown to following their release from the prisons in North Vietnam, where they would then be examined by doctors, followed by heavy debriefings by a member of their respective branch of service, because she hadn't yet been ready to give up hope. To give up period. Because Hazel knew Vince wouldn't if it were her.

PART III

"No event in American history is more misunderstood than the Vietnam War. It was misreported then, and it is misremembered now."

—Richard Nixon

CHAPTER 22

New York City
2005

"So she, well we, I mean, left Vietnam for good in '73?" Bee asked. "After the Peace Treaty was signed and her futile visit to Clark Air Force Base and American involvement had ended there?"

"Yes and no," Suzanne answered mysteriously.

"What's that supposed to mean?" Bee asked. "Did we or didn't we?"

"You did, she didn't."

"Well, I was hardly living on my own at the age of four. Is there some other relative I don't know about or remember who was taking care of me if you're telling me she didn't leave."

"No, she did leave. But she still came back."

"From where, Butler?" Bee asked, incredulously.

"No, Singapore," Suzanne said, looking Bee squarely in the eye. "Your mom continued to write pieces for the AP that were picked up, continued to bang on the doors of people and places for news about your dad, before the world that was South Vietnam crumbled."

"My God, how much more is there to know about my exotic

secret to my childhood past?" Bee asked. "And how long did I live there?"

"Till the spring of 1975. Till Operation Frequent Wind commenced, and Saigon fell. Once the capital fell, your mom truly knew that it was over and that he would never be coming back."

April 9, 1975
Singapore

"Anything happens to me, I don't come back when I'm supposed to, you take my daughter to the American Embassy here, and have them get in touch with Archibald Stone and Suzanne Quaglio, you understand?" Hazel said to Lin, speaking more harshly to the young Vietnamese girl than was necessary.

But Hazel didn't have time for niceties. She was headed back to Saigon again tomorrow, only this time with the fall of the South Vietnamese capital imminent, it would most likely be her last trip. Her last attempt to reach Vince. She had gone back every month since they'd arrived in Singapore, sometimes for a story, but more to pressure the Embassy and the *Dispatch's* Saigon bureau chief. In the five years since Vince had gone missing, there had been four bureau chiefs who had filled the role; Hazel hadn't liked any of them.

"*Oui*, madam," Lin said, bowing her head reverently, "I will."

Hazel trusted Lin implicitly with Bee. Sure, she had Archie and Suzanne but they were both so inextricably tied to what was going on in Cambodia. And Bee adored the young girl too, which Hazel was thankful for. And to prepare Bee for what was to come, Hazel had started speaking in English almost exclusively when she was around, thus ensuring her six-year-old daughter would be able to speak in her native tongue when they returned to Butler. Soon, she thought. So very soon. It would do her no good if all she knew was French and some Vietnamese, which had been the case until the last year.

As Hazel threw some pieces of clothing into a small suitcase, she studied herself in the mirror. She was almost 30 but looked older. She had been a wife, mother, orphan, and widow all in the span of barely two years. This realization weighed on her heavily, the many white hairs in her dark blond hair a clear testament to this.

"Mommy?" a small voice called out from the doorway.

Hazel whirled to see a sleepy Bee standing there, her damp hair matted to her forehead. As Hazel was still paying for the apartment in Saigon, she'd had to be frugal when it came to finding one here in Singapore. And unlike Saigon, Singapore had been a lot more expensive.

"Beatrice, what did I tell you about sucking your thumb? Good little girls don't do that."

The child looked crestfallen even though she was routinely chided by her mother over things she shouldn't be doing and things she should be doing but wasn't. And yet she still sought Hazel out time and time again.

"I can't sleep," Beatrice said. "Will you read me a story?"

"You're big enough to read to yourself now," Hazel said. Realizing that was a bit cold she added brightly, "And besides, you're a marvelous reader, and marvelous readers don't need their mommies to read to them, that's only for babies."

Beatrice's face showed she was pondering what Hazel had just told her since she absolutely did not want to be called a baby. Taking a moment to apparently find a counter point she then asked, "Will you sing me a song then so I can fall asleep?"

Rushing over to Beatrice she scooped her up in her arms, then pretended she was an airplane until she reached the child's bed where

she gently laid her down. Only pulling up the thin sheet to cover
Beatrice's small arms, she started to sing, gently tracing the outline of
her daughter's angelic face-

Dites-moi

When she knew her daughter was firmly back in the depths of
slumber, she kissed her on her forehead, got up, and gently closed the
door behind her.

✿

April 23, 1975
Saigon

As Hazel flipped through the pages of the booklet the American
Embassy had given out in preparation for the evacuation when, and
not if, Saigon fell, she couldn't believe it had come to this.

SAFE-
Standard Instruction and Advice to Civilians in an Emergency

"Note evacuational signal. Do not disclose to other
personnel. When the evacuation is ordered, the code
will read out on Armed Forces Radio. The code is: The
temperature in Saigon is 105 degrees and rising. This
will be followed by the playing of I'm Dreaming of a
White Christmas."

There was even a map of Saigon pinpointing "assembly areas
where a helicopter will pick you up."

The end was coming and it really had all been for nothing, she thought disgustedly as she shoved the 15-page booklet into a bedside drawer.

April 29, 1975
Saigon

The temperature in Saigon is 105 degrees and rising.

And then the music and lyrics of "White Christmas" filled the air.

As Hazel watched the Marines chop away at the massive tamarind and other trees that had so beautifully adorned the embassy's parking lot but were now being removed to make way for helicopter landing zones, all she could think of was a sinking ship metaphor. Thousands of people were currently huddled inside the embassy's walls, awaiting evacuation by helicopter that would take them to the evacuation armada that currently waited in the South China Sea, while thousands more were clustered around the perimeter of the embassy, desperate to get through the gates before the North Vietnamese army arrived and marked them as traitors.

Although some of the people inside the walls were American civilians, most were South Vietnamese- military and politicians and the like and their many family members, and more South Vietnamese civilians who had worked for the American military here during the war years. No one needed to tell either the South Vietnamese or the Americans what would happen to the former when the North

Vietnamese army arrived. They had placed their bet on the side that had lost and the worst was surely yet to come. Rumors of massive arrests, "re-education camps" akin to Nazi concentration camps, and executions at the hands of the communists had persisted for weeks now.

In the hours since she had first arrived at the embassy, Hazel had seen the infusion of additional Marine battalions. Since American military involvement had ended two years ago, it was only the Marines that had stayed, officially that is, the men who provided security at the embassy, as they did at all embassies worldwide. Only here, tonight in Saigon, was an embassy assignment like no other. Using one's rifle butt to smash the fingers of desperate Vietnamese trying to make it over the embassy's walls, a 15 foot concrete fence. When all they were doing was simply trying to stay alive.

By nightfall, the trees had been removed and now cars and a fire engine were lined up in a square so that the headlights would help in illuminating the helipad.

Hazel watched as the Jolly Green Giants were filled with dozens of people, the Marines ushering body after body into them, undoubtedly taking many more than the weight limit, them yelling at the evacuees to get rid of the baggage and just get on board. She saw people frantically remove thick wads of money from their suitcases and stuff it into their shirts, blouses, pants—anywhere they could put it. That money now being their last hope of a new life when they got to America.

As the hours passed, a new day having dawned, the crowds inside the embassy grew less and less until Hazel realized she was one of the few white faces remaining. And through it all, Vince had never materialized. Had she really thought he would? Missing for five years, nary a word from him, but *White Christmas* playing on the radio is all that was needed for him to surface? She wasn't ready to say goodbye to him, to all that they had shared, to all that he had been to her. She didn't want to tell him *au revoir,* not like this, not here. She'd wait just a little more.

New York City
2005

"A prisoner to the past," Bee said.

"What dear?" Suzanne asked.

"My mom, she lived the rest of her life as a prisoner to the past. She literally and figurately remained inside the mental and emotional prison she had created for herself. She got on that helicopter and it wasn't a case of never looking back. She did nothing but look back, stay transfixed on that particular rearview mirror for the rest of her life. I'm not saying I ever lacked for anything, because I didn't. But she was there in the bare minimum. She was only one step above my dad's mother who essentially abandoned him when her husband was killed. She said she wouldn't do that, but you know something? She did. She emotionally abandoned me. And I know she's dead so what good does it do me to be mad at her now, but I am. I pushed away any serious relationship I ever had thinking I was somehow messed up, that I was somehow **her**. I never once entertained the prospect of having children, thinking I would somehow irrevocably scar them as she had scarred me." Bee's chest was rising, the enormity of the last day and half finally catching up to her. She looked at Suzanne now whose face revealed nothing. The older woman wasn't saying anything but Bee took that to be a good sign, that she wasn't just by default coming to the aid of her deceased friend, scolding Bee for judging her dead mom too harshly over something so painful she would never be able to fully understand.

"And you know something?" Bee continued on, her voice now breaking. "When I was older, if she had just told me any of this, told me about my dad, told me about the unbelievable fact that I was literally born in a war zone, I might have, no, could have understood, or at least understood better. But she never gave me that chance. She made that decision all by herself to keep the memory that was Vincent Cerny all to herself. And for that I can never forgive her," Bee finished and left Suzanne's apartment.

Hours later after Bee had spent the afternoon aimlessly wandering around Manhattan, not having set out with any intended purpose or destination but ironically ending up outside the main branch of the New York Public Library at 476 5th Avenue, she returned to Suzanne's apartment. She was armed with platters of chicken bulgogi and mandu and a bottle of soju she had procured from a small hole-in-the-wall restaurant she had wandered by in the city's Koreatown. She had purposedly avoided stepping foot in the Vietnamese restaurant that was catty-corner, not the least bit in the mood for pho or whatever it was they ate there.

"Good, I was about to call the cavalry," Suzanne said as she opened the door letting Bee enter. "I didn't think you had gone home since all your stuff was still here."

"I brought lunch, or dinner," Bee said, by way of a greeting, holding up the bags of steaming takeout. "And soju, which is apparently the Korean version of sake."

"It's okay to be mad," Suzanne said. "And angry, and confused." She took Bee in her arms now and although she was initially resistant, before long she was sobbing openly in Suzanne's embrace, the older woman's perfectly manicured red fingernails lovingly stroking her back.

Hours later the takeout containers of the spicy chicken dish and dumplings had been finished off, along with an unknown number of shot glasses of soju downed. (This Bee was impressed by.) The two women sat on Suzanne's couch, each armed with a glass of red wine, which the older woman was knocking back while the younger one nursed hers.

"But what was the point of telling me this now?" Bee asked, taking a sip. "She's dead, she's gone, it's not as if I'm ever going to be able to ask her to tell me about any of it. There's no 'first-hand' re-telling of the past. I mean, it was a lot easier thinking I just had an emotionally messed-up childhood, complete with an emotionally distant mom and no dad to boot. Now I have the emotional weight of knowing my dad was probably killed by the Khmer Rouge, the genocidal maniacs of the late 20th century, my mom was a talented journalist and not just some reclusive hermit translator and that I spent the first six years of my life living in Vietnam."

"Would you rather have never learned the truth?" Suzanne said, almost knowingly. "Never learned who you really are and where you came from?"

A long, reflective pause then.

"No."

Hours later in the middle of the night-

"You're still up." Bee said this as more of a statement than a question as she wandered into the dimly lit living room.

"I don't sleep much, too many ghosts of the past- past wars, past loves, past everythings- always haunt me the most at night," Suzanne replied.

"I just don't understand how I never could have remembered any of this?" Bee asked exasperatedly as she threw herself dramatically into the plush sofa as if she were a hysterical woman from the 1800s. "I mean for God's sake, I lived in Vietnam of all places until I was almost six! Not exactly a typical childhood for an American girl."

"I'm no psychiatrist," Suzanne began, taking a long sip of the contents of her tumbler she was holding, "but your mom in her own way repressed those memories for you. She never talked about it— your dad, Vietnam, your childhood- she kept it inside her lock, stock, and barrel, so what child is going to remember that on her own?"

"But how would I not have remembered anything besides the smell of plumeria trees," Bee retorted, putting extra emphasis on the word 'I.'

"For memories to exist, to stay alive," Suzanne said, "they need to be reinforced- brought up, talked about, laughed about. You're putting too much of the onus on you. I remember next to nothing about my earliest years back in Boston except what those around me regularly regaled the family with at holidays and other get-togethers. It was just you and your mom and she said nothing. It's not that you were brainwashed per se-"

"Wasn't I?" Bee cut in bitterly?

May 1975
Somewhere over the Pacific Ocean

"Would you change any of it?" Suzanne asked, as they stood together hugging at Changi's Airport. Hazel was headed home, back to the

United States, back to Butler with Beatrice, a place her daughter had never seen, a home she hadn't been to in almost a decade, while the other woman was headed to Cambodia. The capital city had fallen on April 17, the Khmer Rouge entered Phnom Penh victoriously, the residents hopeful that peace would be long lasting at the hands of the Communist victors. Only time would tell.

Suzanne didn't have to elaborate for Hazel to know what she meant.

"No," Hazel said. And then looking down at her beautiful daughter, a dark haired beauty, so much a mirror image of her father, said to herself again, "no."

December 1979
Butler, Pennsylvania

"Beatrice, stop playing that."

Bee instantly stopped playing, removing her hands from the piano keys as if they were hot coals. The look in her mother's raging eyes at that moment made Bee think that if she hadn't stopped playing immediately her mother might have closed the lid right onto Bee's fingers.

"I thought you'd like it," Bee said, her bottom lip quivering from being scolded by her mother. "Mrs. McIntrye says I've gotten really good, that I could maybe perform it as a solo at the school concert."

"Well, you won't be playing that. It's a terrible song, it's entirely too commercial and doesn't remotely invoke the religious nature of Christmas. So I expect you to learn an actual Christmas carol and not that commercial junk," her mother said, sweeping out of the room just as abruptly as she had entered it.

Bee didn't understand how her mother could hate "White Christmas" so, call it so commercial but then play Brenda Lee's "Rockin' around the Christmas Tree" on repeat.

CHAPTER 23

February 2006

"We're beginning our final descent into Tan Son Nhut Airport," a voice in heavily accented English said over the loudspeaker, waking Bee from the fitful sleep she had been having ever since the plane had left Singapore that morning.

Am I crazy for wanting to go there, Bee had asked Suzanne, barely an hour after she had purchased her non-refundable plane ticket. 'No, you want to see where your story began,' the other woman had told her and then cheekily added, 'maybe you do have a little bit of journalist blood in you after all because I won't lie, I've been having doubts.'

And then while waiting for her flight to Saigon inside Singapore's Changi Airport, using the international calling card she had purchased, she'd dialed Suzanne's number only to get the answering machine. She left a message anyway, although she wasn't entirely sure if it was a question or a statement.

**"If she was still alive today, would she be here with me...
for this."**

Bee was one of a few white people on board the flight; everybody else looked Vietnamese (or she supposed she should say, Asian). She had heard an Australian accent and possibly German, but she didn't hear or spot any other Americans. She wasn't entirely surprised by this. She knew from Googling that the United States had only resumed diplomatic relations with Vietnam, its former foe, the tiny David of a nation that had beaten the mighty Goliath, in 1995. Not to mention for many, Vietnam was still too raw and painful a memory, even though the war itself had ended over 20 years ago. But President Clinton and Senator John McCain too, one of the war's most famous POWs, had both come here, the former perhaps wanting to help reconcile with the past, the latter to help bring about his own personal and emotional reconciliation. Bee didn't consider herself much of an intrepid anything but she supposed in a way that she was today. Well, intrepid for her generation, certainly not of Suzanne or Hazel's…or Vince's. They were truly the fearless ones.

On the ride in from the airport, Bee tried imagining a Saigon, or Ho Chi Minh City as she knew it was referred to today, from a bygone era, an era marked by a decade of war. She tried picturing streets marked by barricades and barbed wire, the scores of military vehicles that drove with abandon at all hours of the day, but found she couldn't. The traffic was unfathomable, the streets chaotic, the roadways filled with nothing but a sea of black motorbikes of varying ages and types, but she couldn't picture war, she couldn't picture the scene that must have greeted Hazel when she'd first arrived back in 1967. But wasn't that a good thing, an inner voice inside her head asked. For a country to bear no visible scars of its painful past? To have been able to move on to something positive, something good?

When Bee had asked Suzanne where she should stay, the older woman had immediately said, "The Caravelle," and then, placing her hand over Bee's, had added, "my treat." As the taxi pulled up in front of the towering modern building, she drew in a sharp breath. This was it, she thought. This is where her parents' story truly began.

"What can I get you?" the bartender asked Bee in European accented English.

"Is it that obvious I'm not French?" Bee asked, laughing.

"I, how do you say, hedge my bets. And most of the French, they are at the Majestic," he said smilingly.

"How about a French 75?" Bee said, feeling at that moment an intimate connection to Hazel, the ardent Francophone and Francophile.

"*Parfait, a soixante quinze* coming right up."

After checking into her opulent room which easily rivaled Suzanne's apartment and which also overlooked the Opera House, a beautiful grand dame of a building left over from the country's colonial empire days, she headed up to the rooftop bar, appropriately named the Saigon Saigon Rooftop Bar. As she took in the view around her, skyscrapers seeming to fill every crevice of the open landscape, she closed her eyes and tried imagining another one, the Saigon of 40 years earlier.

"So what brings you to Vietnam?" the bartender politely asked as he set Bee's drink down in front of her.

Taking a sip of the gin and champagne-based cocktail she said, "My parents were actually correspondents here during the War." What war needn't be said, for it was known by both Americans and Vietnamese. "They got married here, in Vietnam I mean, that's where they met. They even had their wedding reception right here too," Bee added animatedly, excited and proud over telling someone, even if he was a stranger, about her parents' incredible story.

"What, here at the Caravelle?" he asked incredulously.

"Yes," she answered excitedly.

"Super cool," he replied. "Are they here with you too? To go down, what's the phrase, memory lane?"

Bee paused then, instantly realizing this wasn't something she had prepared for. It was one thing to share the happy parts about her parents' love story with a complete stranger but the sad and tragic ones? The complete ignorance of what had truly happened to her father? And was it the North Vietnamese or Viet Cong who had killed him or the Khmer Rouge, as Suzanne had suspected. And what if this young man's father or grandfather had been from the North, fought for them. He didn't seem to harbor an ounce of animosity towards her, towards the fact that she was an American, but the war wasn't that long ago either. One wouldn't necessarily know it from here, but she knew elsewhere in the country, especially in the more rural areas, land mines were still being uncovered, often with devastating results, and Agent Orange, a tactical herbicide used by the U.S. military during the war, was to this day taking and destroying lives here just as it was back home by the men who had been exposed to it, by way of cancer and other heinous physical deformities.

"Um, no, just me," Bee said almost nervously.

"That's too bad," he said sounding entirely genuine. "But maybe one day you return with them. It was not my war, and my generation, we want peace with the Americans. For us to be friends once more."

Later that night while lying in bed, insomnia rearing its ugly head due to the 13-hour time difference between here and Pittsburgh, the bartender's words resonated in her head—

It was not my war

Did every generation feel this way? About a war they were perhaps too young to remember and yet grew up with its painful memories all the same? For her father, whose own father had been killed during the Second World War and whose own mother had abandoned him because of that same war. The ripple effects felt from a bullet that had claimed the life of her grandfather on a tiny island in the Pacific that forever altered the course of her dad's life and history. And what about her and Vietnam. She was born here but she hadn't fought here, she hadn't been a nurse here on the frontlines, she hadn't humped for miles with a platoon of soldiers and Marines as Hazel had done. And yet what transpired during the war forever changed her whole existence, her life's story. One parent lost to the war, the other emotionally destroyed by it.

Bee took another sip of her delicious Vietnamese iced coffee, watching the traffic (comprised mainly of motorbikes) go by, individuals and cars jockeying to go every which way since traffic lights were scant here and even where they were found, seemed to be ignored. She breathed what she realized to be a pleasant and even relaxed sigh of relief. She particularly liked this little street-side outdoor only café that was outfitted with the country's ubiquitous plastic kiddie chairs as she called them, since they were so very low to the ground. She sat near an old man at an adjacent street stall who was happily slurping away on a bowl of noodle soup, his darkened and aged feet clad in white socks and traditional-style sandals. He was completely oblivious to the cacophonous chaos and smells of exhaust fumes and dust. She was becoming accustomed to them as well.

Vietnam itself was hardly a relaxing destination- looking at a map, especially when wandering Hanoi's Old Quarter, the city's oldest section which was more than five centuries old, proved to be a futile and highly frustrating affair, and feeling like she was the chicken who would never cross the road due to her fear and trepidation of stepping out and being struck since no driver ever yielded to pedestrians. Or being the reason an accident occurred, blamed by a gang of angry Vietnamese yelling at her in a language she couldn't understand for having caused said accident. And yet she was still enjoying herself. She could see that even in the throes of war how it was a destination that had captivated her parents so—sucked them in with its exotic and alluring charm, its feeling of being a place like no other.

Bee had enjoyed Saigon- it was after all her birthplace (she still found it crazy to say that, see, Beatrice Cerny of Butler, Pennsylvania had been born in Vietnam)- and of course, her parents' story, of love, loss, and heartache. But just as it had been so Western during the '60s and '70s due to the American culture infiltration, the same could be said in the 21st century, only now it was the infiltration of American capitalism. Although Vietnam was a Communist nation, you wouldn't know it from Saigon's mega skyscrapers and building projects at every corner.

She had come to Hanoi not knowing what to expect. Although the American military had bombed the capital and other sites in the North for the duration of the war and the Hanoi area was home to POW prisons, including the most infamous, the 'Hanoi Hilton,' it had never been infiltrated culturally and commercially in the same way that Saigon had. Driving in from the airport in the taxi with the broken air-conditioning, her hair becoming a wind-blown mess, Bee knew she was in a foreign country when the taxi took the off-ramp from the highway and she got off in the Old Quarter. The streets were narrow and maze-like, the traffic like clogged pores in its arteries. She got lost more than once, even walking in a circle. She would later learn that each of its nearly 40 streets was named for its primary good or service, so there was "copper wares street" and even "bamboo wares street."

As she downed the final drops of her Vietnamese coffee, a strong brew heavily sweetened by the addition of condensed milk, before she planned on making her way to the nearby Tran Quoc Pagoda, she saw an older white couple go by, accompanied by a petite Vietnamese woman, presumably their tour guide. As they came nearer, Bee saw the man wore a hat that said, "US Air Force Vietnam Veteran." The man happened to see her looking at him and nodded his head at her in polite deference, to which Bee smiled back.

She was surprised by this, surprised by the sight of Americans here in Hanoi. Although she had seen many Westerners here in the capital, she had yet to come across many Americans (although this hadn't been the case in Saigon, where she had seen many men who would be her dad's age today who had fought here during the war, wearing those same Vietnam Veteran hats). Would the veterans who had done bombing raids want to come back to the land that they had scorched, the land that they had made red clay ashes of? Would a veteran who had been a POW want to come back to the place of his brutal imprisonment? Where he had endured such physical and mental suffering and depravities? Bee remembered reading once an interview with Senator John McCain and him saying that he could never forgive his captors at the Hanoi Hilton over what they had done to him and his fellow brothers in arms. Vietnam and its people yes, but not those directly responsible.

She thought of a neighbor back in Butler who had been in a Japanese POW camp in the Philippines during the Second World War. The man's wife was an incredibly kind woman, never treating Bee differently because Hazel was or wasn't considered "normal." The man, she knew today, had to have suffered from PTSD although back then he was just called "crazy." Bee remembered a couple of times him sitting outside, completely placid and then all of a sudden yelling and even screaming the most nonsensical of things, but almost always words like 'dirty Jap' and "we should have killed them all in 45." She remembered driving to Hazel's house with the first new car she had ever bought, a 1992 Honda Accord. The man happened to be outside, his wife trying to get him into their car, when he noticed Bee's Japanese made one. He said she was "un-American for buying a Jap car."

What about Jews- did every single Jewish person who had survived the Holocaust or had their entire family killed in it hate all Germans? Could you ever truly forgive the people who had taken everything you loved in such a horrific and unimaginable way, or merely just forget? Where was the line drawn between forgiving and forgetting, or could such a line ever be really drawn? When did a new dawn begin when one forgot about what had happened earlier? From the next generation? When there were no longer any tangible lines to the generation who had lived through it?

From all that she had learned of Hazel, from her articles and of course Suzanne's firsthand knowledge, Bee didn't think for a second that she had hated the Vietnamese people. Bee would never know but she reasoned that for her mom, it was like Senator McCain. Hazel must have hated the men who took her husband from her, but not an entire nation and its people. And being here now, with everything she had learned, Bee didn't think she ever could either. Bee was reconciling the past by coming here. If only Hazel had too.

Saigon

"Hello?" Bee asked to an empty store. Bee had stepped inside after seeing a sign out front that had read 'artisan crafts' on the front facade. Although she'd perused numerous souvenir shops filled with every tchotchke imaginable, (although no shot glass or bobble head featuring the likeness of the revered leader Ho Chi Minh, something she knew wouldn't be the case back home), none had grabbed her enough to make a purchase. Perhaps the adage "make memories not things" really did hold true here. Well, she didn't make memories here but rather she had seen where they had first taken root. Maybe that would be her greatest souvenir.

"Pardon," a young woman said appearing from the back, her arms laden with boxes. She then proceeded to rattle off something else that Bee had no idea about.

"Oh, I'm sorry," Bee cut in "but do you speak English?"

The young woman looked to be biracial and in her 20s. She stopped, put down the boxes she had been carrying on the counter and then smiled kindly at Bee.

"Some," she answered.

"Well, it's more than my French; that's what you were speaking, right?" Bee asked.

"You have a good ear," she told Bee.

And for the first time in her life she felt nothing but pride when saying, "My mom spoke French. She was a professional translator of books."

"Oh, how interesting! My other languages besides French, my non-mother tongue ones, I am not good enough."

"How many do you speak?" Bee asked in wonder. She had always felt inferior around people who spoke more than one language. She had felt this way with Hazel but now knew those feelings were attributed to something else entirely.

"Oh, just two," the young woman said casually but without being arrogant. "English and of course Vietnamese."

"My mom passed," Bee began, "but now I wish I had learned French to speak with her."

"Well, maybe still learn it to honor her," the young woman said. "I am Sandrine by the way," she said extending her hand towards Bee, who shook it.

"Beatrice, but everyone calls me Bee. Your shop is lovely," Bee said admiringly.

"*Merci*. It's actually my aunt's shop. I am here for the summer visiting and helping."

"So France is home?" Bee asked.

"Yes," Sandrine replied. "My aunt returned here, to live I mean, in 1998. She opened the store a few years later."

"The photographs are so neat," Bee said as she looked at each black and white image hanging on the wall in plain white frames behind the counter. "Are they all of your family?" Bee asked as the photographs seemed to be displayed chronologically, the fashions and hairstyles changing with each one. Some seemed to have been taken here in Vietnam, while others presumably in France, a mixture of both Western and Vietnamese faces.

"Me, when I was a petite with my *maman*," Sandrine said, noticing that Bee had stopped on that one in particular.

"You look just like her," Bee said, now thinking of Hazel and how she hadn't remotely looked like her. She looked so much like Vince, Suzy had told her.

"Do you resemble your *maman*?" Sandrine asked politely.

"Um, no. Not at all. In fact, many people were always surprised to hear we were mother and daughter," Bee said, trying to sound casual but unsure how well she was doing masking the pain of this. "Today, people wouldn't think twice about asking if I had been adopted. That no longer seems to be as hush hush as it used to be."

Sandrine looked curiously and then asked, "what is hush hush?"

"Oh," Bee said, not realizing she had used an idiom. "Something that you don't talk about, keep quiet on."

The younger woman nodded but Bee could see she still didn't quite get the significance.

Bee continued scanning her eyes down the row of photographs until she settled on one in particular, that of a Eurasian looking woman and a white man. The man looked familiar somehow, so not asking permission, Bee stepped around the counter for a closer look. Directly eye level now with the photo, she gasped. For the man looked exactly like Vince, her dead father.

"Beatreez?" Sandrine asked, a note of concern in her voice. "Are you okay? *Ça va?*"

Bee tried to speak. She knew she must have been mouthing the words in her throat but no sound was coming out. Finally she heard herself say, "Who is this man?" The man she noticed that was in numerous photos with the same Eurasian woman.

"Which one?" Sandrine asked, coming around now to join Bee behind the counter.

"Here," Bee said, pointing to the image that had left her shaking.

"Oh, that is my Uncle Milton."

And then Bee really started feeling dizzy and lightheaded at the mention of the name Milton, her young uncle who she had never met, who had been killed here almost 40 years ago. Not to mention, it was hardly that common of a name.

"I need to sit down, please," Bee asked.

"Of course," Sandrine said, taking Bee's hand and leading her to a backroom where there was a small wicker chair.

Sitting in it, Bee leaned forward, placing her head between her legs as she had been instructed to do years ago by a school nurse after becoming faint at the sight of a large amount of blood that had gushed from a knee following a fall on the playground. And then she felt a cool damp rag being placed around the nape of her neck. Sandrine didn't say anything, she just rubbed Bee's back in a slow and soothing manner.

Bee wasn't sure how much time had passed but after a while she sat up and adjusted herself, now sitting fully upright against the back of the chair.

"I'm sorry, I'm not crazy but I'm going to tell you something that you probably won't believe and then you will think I'm crazy but here it goes. I think the man in the photograph is my father who went missing here during the war. Everyone thought he was dead but his body was never found. He was a journalist and in 1970 he was taken away by the North Vietnamese army at a checkpoint and never seen again." And then Bee removed from her purse the photograph she now carried with her everywhere. The one of her and Vince. She handed it to Sandrine, whose eyes widened in disbelief.

"I don't think it's a coincidence," Bee said after a moment. "I mean, I know it's said all of us have a twin, a lookalike somewhere in the world, but it's him," Bee added, her voice now choking up. "The same thick dark hair only grayer with age, the profile of his nose, and the eyes." After a pause although inwardly already fearing the answer, Bee asked, "He's not alive, is he?"

Sandrine looked at her, sadness etched all over her face. "No, I'm sorry. He died last year. Back in April. April 8."

Bee didn't remember what happened next. All she knew was that her father had died the week after her mom. It was as if he knew his Frenchie was no longer on this earth. Try explaining that, she thought, before everything went black.

CHAPTER 24

When Bee came to, Sandrine looked especially alarmed and said she wanted to take Bee to the hospital. Not wanting to add the inside of a Vietnamese hospital to the list of places she saw while here, she politely but firmly said no, that she would be fine.

"Is your aunt here, I mean in Saigon?" Bee asked, hopefully.

"Yes," Sandrine replied. "I've already called her. I hope you are free because she's cooking us dinner."

Bee didn't know how she could possibly eat but knew it would be rude to not accept.

Seeing Bee's anxious face, she said, "Don't worry, it's not far, just a few blocks away. It's still in District 1 so you don't have to go on my motorbike."

Bee did blanch at this. The city's thousands of motorbikes going every which way terrified her. She was amazed she still hadn't gotten hit.

"Your aunt won't mind you closing early?" Bee asked, as the younger girl turned off the lights, set the alarm, then locked the door.

"Believe me when I say she's an anxious to meet you as you her," Sandrine said, smiling.

Sandrine's aunt lived on a small side street, a quiet one (at least by Saigon's standards) that was lined with plumeria trees, the smell of the flowering scent being the one rare memory of her first years staying with her.

As they traveled up the building's antique wire cage elevator, Bee heard the sound of a door opening. Upon stepping out of the cage, an older woman rushed over, the woman from the photograph, and immediately embraced Bee. Bee, not accustomed to physical affection, remained stiff at first but then felt her body relaxing and hugged the woman back.

Leaning back from Bee, she said, her voice emotional, her eyes brimming with tears, "You look so much like him."

That night they enjoyed a delicious feast prepared by Manon. It was by far the best Vietnamese food Bee had eaten the entire time she had been here- plate after plate of dishes whose names she would never remember but whose incredible taste she would never forget- pho, the ubiquitous noodle soup eaten at every meal; cha ca, a fried fish; banh xeo, a crepe bulging with minced meats and bean sprouts; and cha gio, her favorite, crispy spring rolls. Only then did Bee learn some of Vince's story after he was led off into the tree line by the North Vietnamese on that spring day in April of 1970.

"He had been shot, left for dead," Manon said. "He had a scar here," pointing to her lower abdomen, "and in the back of his head. He was always self-conscious of that one, never wanting to cut his hair too short for fear that it would show."

"But how did he survive, I mean, God, if he was shot in the head?" Bee asked in disbelief.

"I'm not entirely sure," Manon said. "We believe villagers saved him after discovering he was still breathing. They had been tasked with burying the bodies. Someone removed the bullets, perhaps a sympathetic medic or doctor, I don't know. But he lived. But he had no idea who he was. He didn't know his name, the villagers had found no identification of him of any kind on his body. He stayed in this village for almost two years. The villagers protected him. After the Peace Treaty was signed, he made his way to France with some French missionaries he had met."

"But I don't understand, why he didn't go to the American Embassy. And why France? I mean, did he speak French? Just why he didn't make an effort to remember who he was!" Bee said, upset now, thinking he could have come back to them, she could have had a father. She could have had a mother who hadn't been broken.

Manon reached over to Bee now, covering her hand with hers. "I'm not sure, *cherie*. I met him in France. You see, I had left Saigon for good in '71. My mother was Vietnamese, my father French. What I've told you now is what he told me."

"Surely the missionaries could see he wasn't French, didn't speak French," Bee said in response.

"*Mais non*," Manon said. "He did speak French. I mean not as a native Frenchman but yes. He was the man without a name, simply called *l'homme blanc,* the white man. When they got him a passport in order to leave the country and travel to France, he chose Milton. He always said this name was the only one he could remember."

"My uncle, my mom's younger brother," Bee said. "He was killed here during the war. He was a Marine."

Manon gasped, understanding the significance behind the name now.

Sandrine, who had been quiet through all of this, mused out loud, "I wonder why he remembered that."

And then asking what Bee considered to be a painful question, "How long were you married?"

Manon looked at Bee then, studying her, appraising the young woman who was the daughter of the man whose unknown past had always troubled her, sitting here now in her living room. She was exactly the reason why.

"We were never married. We lived together as man and wife all those years but were never married in the eyes or God or the courts of law."

"But why not? I mean, he didn't remember he was already married so it's not as if either of you knew."

"One of his favorite movies was *Gone with the Wind* and so when people would ask him, ask us this, he would respond, 'as Rhett Butler would say, I'm not the marrying kind' which would make everyone laugh. At first this bothered me, but over time, I more wanted him and our life together than some certificate. I knew what we were."

"And besides *Tante* Manon, it's more chic today to just live together than marry; marriage is passé," Sandrine chimed in.

"Whether it is or isn't," Manon continued, "I don't know, but now I know that he knew he couldn't. He didn't know who he once belonged to and still did, but he didn't entirely betray them."

"He always stayed married to my mom," Bee said. "He was always true to her in his heart."

After Bee had learned all there was to tell about Vince, it was Bee's turn to tell Manon about her mom. It wasn't a case of jealously about the 'other woman' since the other woman was never known or even existed in her and Vince's life. But Bee could tell Manon genuinely felt saddened now learning that Vince's other life had always been out there, if only he could have remembered.

"Where is he buried?" Bee asked, standing at the door, waiting for Sandrine, who was going to walk her back to the Caravelle.

"He was cremated, as he wanted to be," Manon answered.

"And his ashes?" Bee asked next.

"Hawaii, in the Pacific Ocean. Another thing I never understood since we never went, but he said he knew he went there once and loved it. So I honored his wish and spread them there."

Bee smiled at this. So much he had never remembered but then the few fleeting yet beautiful and meaningful things he did.

"Talk with Sandrine, but please, I would love to see you one more time before you go home."

"*Bien sûr*," Bee said smiling, then leaned down to kiss the older woman on each cheek.

Saigon
January 1969

"Hey, where'd Vince go?"

Hazel looked up at Suzy's question. She saw Archie flirting, or attempting to flirt with a red-haired woman who was paying him no mind, but she didn't see her husband anywhere.

The music, which only moments before had been blaring to compensate for the loudness and excess that was Saigon, both indoors and outdoors, had abruptly come to a stop. A new record was put on, Love Affair's "Everlasting Love" by the sounds of it. And then she heard a person's voice start to tentatively sing the words.

"Well, I'll say this. He should stick to his day job," Hazel said, taking a drink of the club soda she had been nursing ever since they'd arrived. "Even if it is Tu Do Street, I'm not impressed."

"Um, Hazel, darling. I think I know where Vince is," Suzy said, trying to hold back a smile or a laugh, or both, gently elbowing Hazel in the arm to look towards the stage.

Hazel turned in her stool, with some difficulty considering she was eight months pregnant. And then she saw him and she could not have loved him any more than she did at that very moment.

There standing on a stage in a seedy bar in Saigon's even seedier Tu Do Street, she saw the man she loved more than life itself. She saw the man who had irrevocably turned her life upside down and altered her heart and mind forever.

Their eyes locked then, and the pure love and adoration she saw reflected in those dark onyx pools of his made her tear up. How was it possible to be so deliriously happy in the midst of war? How had she been allowed to find love and happiness in a place that had brought so much sadness and tragedy to others?

"Did you know he was going to do this?" Suzy asked, laughing when she saw Vince mimic him opening his heart.

"I had no idea," Hazel replied, her face aglow in sheer joy.

How had she been so lucky?

Butler, Pennsylvania
April 2005

Hazel woke up, her nightgown drenched in sweat, her heart racing as if she had just run for miles without stopping. She had been having that dream again. She picked up her watch from the nightstand. His watch. Well, one of his two beloved ones, the one he hadn't been wearing when he had angrily left their apartment forever in 1970. 2:33AM was the time. Then she reached into the bedside table drawer and pulled out a worn paperback of *Le tour du monde en quatre-vingts jours*.

Swinging her legs over the side of the bed, she got up slowly and walked towards the calendar that was hanging on the wall, a small 7 x 7 of black and white scenes of Paris her daughter Beatrice had gotten her for Christmas. The Bouquinistes of Paris, the booksellers who display their used and antiquarian wares in historic stalls along the banks of the Seine, was March's image.

But she realized that it was a new month now. That today was April 1.

Turning the page she saw April's image was of a couple kissing against the backdrop of the Eiffel Tower.

She returned to bed now, the book still in her hands and fanned open to the page that contained a yellowed handwritten note.

October 28, 1968

To my little Frenchie. You'll have to translate this for me one day when we're on our own journey around the world, although our journey will last a lifetime, not just 80 days. I love you baby, buku.

Although she knew the contents of the message by heart, she still read it. She still read it after all these years. Thirty-five years today of him being gone.

EPILOGUE

BEE

Saigon
February 2006

As Bee took another sip of her Saigon Sunset cocktail, taking in the night sky that was illuminated with a bedazzling array of lights and colors, she paused, thinking how different this very same view would have been for her mother. Illumination would have come not from the futuristic looking 21st century skyscrapers before her but rather from bombs being dropped in the distance, Cu Chi perhaps. Now, there were no sounds of gunfire or explosions, just the cacophony of street life- car horns blaring, the engines of motorbikes revving, people just happy to be out and about. The promise of life was here, the threat of death long forgotten.

When she boarded her flight home tomorrow, she would go a changed woman. Coming here hadn't altered the past- hers or Hazel's. It hadn't changed that fateful day when Vince had been marched off into the tree line at gunpoint, never to be seen again by his wife or daughter. On the day Saigon fell, when Hazel left Vietnam for good, never to look back, he hadn't come back when she thought he still might, when she still fervently held out hope.

Growing up, Bee had never understood why her mother was the way she was towards her, never hugging her just because, never telling her she loved her, not even saying how proud she was of her. Bee had always thought it was her, something she had done, something she wasn't. But it was none of those things. It was that she had been a daily reminder of Vietnam, this exotic land that had given and then painfully taken so much from Hazel. Her mother had never been able to forgive Vietnam or its people. But Bee would, for her life was inextricably tied to this place, both the good and the bad. Her story had started here, in a place thousands of miles from where she had grown up, a land where exotic plants like plumeria and jasmine were as common a sight as dandelions back home, and a country where her looks pointed out that she was considered the outsider, not them. Yet her heart belonged here for it's where her father had lived all those years.

"*Bonsoir, madame,*" the Asian James Bond of bartenders said to Bee, suddenly appearing before her. "I didn't know you were still here."

"Oh," Bee said, blushing over the fact that he had remembered her, considering he must serve dozens of people on a daily basis. "I was in Da Nang, then Hue, Hoi An, a few days in Hanoi, and now back here before I start the long trek home."

"Wow, you've seen more of my country than a lot of my fellow countrymen," he replied jokingly.

"It's a beautiful country," Bee answered honestly. "I, um, so much to tell, er, write about when I get home."

"Oh, are you a journalist too like your parents?"

"No, a librarian actually. But I think I'd like to try my hand at writing a book, telling my parents' story as wartime correspondents."

And then feeling slightly bold she added, "Americans know so little about what actually went on here during the war."

The Asian James Bond nodded in polite agreement.

Bee thought to herself, writing a book for the incredible memory and experiences of two intrepid human beings- Vincent and Hazel Cerny, my parents.

"Beatreez!" Bee heard her name being called.

She turned around to see Sandrine and Manon coming towards her, both of them smiling. And going home with the knowledge that it was no longer just her, alone in this world anymore. She had two people she could call *ma famille* Bee thought as she smiled back at them.

THE END

AUTHOR'S NOTE

I was born in 1985, ten years after the fall of Saigon. Because of how recently the Vietnam War occurred, it was not a topic covered in school. It was not, at that point in the 1990s, "history" in the traditional sense as the American Civil War or even World War II were. My knowledge of the Vietnam War more or less comprised hippies who were against it, the Hanoi Hilton, whose ironic nickname I didn't fully understand until I was older, and the (brief) history presented in the musical *Miss Saigon* which premiered on Broadway in 1991. I remember my parents seeing it and talking about the life-size helicopter complete with a whirring rotor blade that was on stage depicting the fall of Saigon, when South Vietnamese desperately tried to escape the oncoming North Vietnamese army by trying to jump onto the helicopter that was theatrically operational. When I was a little older I would go on to see *Miss Saigon* four times on the stage. It's one of my favorite musicals, not just for the incredible music but also its haunting spin on *Madame Butterfly*. To this day, there's very little done on the Vietnam War when compared to other wars, even though the conflict claimed the lives of more than 58,000 Americans and was a decisive turning point for the United States.

I'm not sure when but at some point in my young adult years I became obsessed with visiting Vietnam. Although I had been to Asia once before, a summer study abroad experience in South Korea, I hadn't been back since, although I told myself that the next time I traveled halfway around the world and endured grueling jet lag, it would be to visit Vietnam. Although most Americans seek out China or Japan or more commonly amongst the young backpacker demographic, Thailand, I wanted Vietnam. I adored its cuisine and although I am at best a feeble speaker of French, I also loved its French colonial past.

When the opportunity arose for me to finally have that experience, I jumped at it. At the age of 34, I planned my long-awaited return to the Asian continent, to the country I had dreamt of visiting for years. I began my time in Hanoi, the capital of Vietnam, which is in the far north and flew south to Saigon, today known by the international community as Ho Chi Minh City, where I embarked on a river cruise along the Mekong Delta, ultimately finishing in neighboring Cambodia. On a side note, I actually traveled to Southeast Asia in February and March 2020—mere weeks before the COVID pandemic lockdowns started. But that's perhaps an idea for a future story.

I didn't travel to Vietnam with the intention of becoming ingratiated with the ghosts of the past, in the war that the Vietnamese people refer to as "the American War." But I did. There were many moments throughout my time "in country" that indirectly inspired me to write this book. When walking the streets of Hanoi, a city very much tied to its past with its crumbling French villas from its colonial empire days and dearth of Western enterprises (at least in the Old Quarter), I witnessed a smattering of American veterans there. (White faces, especially older ones who are not flip flop backpackers, are not as common a sight in Hanoi as they are in Saigon.) They were coming back all these years later to finally put to rest the ghosts and demons of their past. And I recall my own tour guide, a middle-aged Vietnamese man who had been a child during the war and remembered fleeing his home in the countryside to escape the bombs, telling me that he harbored no resentment towards the American veterans who come back here if, like him, they are united in their quest for a forever peace.

My visit to the infamous Hanoi Hilton, or as it's known in Vietnamese, Hoa Lo Prison was mind-blowing. Its most well-known prisoner, Senator John McCain, was imprisoned for five and a half years although a compatriot of McCain's, Navy pilot Everett Alvarez Jr, the first United States pilot to be shot down and detained during the Vietnam War, endured over eight years in captivity there. The Communist propaganda on display, let's just say, decidedly favored one side. But keep in mind, Vietnamese political activists who campaigned against French rule and occupation of their country were jailed there originally and under equally horrific conditions. Although I didn't visit Con Son Island, site of the horrific tropical paradise prison, reading up on it did make me think of the film and book, *Papillon*. And just like at Con Son Prison, there were *cachots,* the French word for dungeons, to visit at Hoa Lo Prison. I based Hazel's visit to Con Son Island on the real-life visit of two United States Congressional representatives who really did "sneak away" from the official tour in order to see the whispered about tiger cages. The men who exposed them were quickly retaliated against by both the South Vietnamese and American governments, neither of whom wished to lose face in the ever-mounting troublesome storm that was Vietnam. The real-life photographs of the tiger cages can be seen in the July 17, 1970 issue of *Life* magazine.

Going from Hanoi to Saigon, which is in the far south (study a map of Vietnam sometime, you'll see that it is an incredibly long country) was in its own way a form of culture shock. Although both cities are incredibly chaotic, the traffic simply unfathomable for lack of a better word (and in many streets, there are no traffic lights, you simply just 'go', not to mention as pedestrians, you have zero rights), Hanoi was like a decrepit Sleeping Beauty. I imagine its Old and French Quarters are similar to Havana's Old Town, crumbling buildings from a bygone era where the past is nursed like a wonderful book you don't want to end. Saigon was everything Hanoi was not, at least in its ultra-Westernized districts 1,2, and 3 (Saigon is comprised of districts which are essentially neighborhoods). Every Western food chain, convenience store and hotel brand can be found here. And while the fashions and cars look different, along with music blaring from shops and eateries, and a few more insanely high skyscrapers, it was also easy to imagine this Saigon from the war years. Soldiers and Marines no longer prowl the streets in search of illegal drugs and booze and at that time, girls. Today those same soldiers and Marines are now old men wanting to put their ghosts to rest once and for all, to show their wives and children where they once were young men, to relive past times and remember the memory of their fallen comrades. I saw many of these American men.

But it was at the Rex Hotel, site of the infamous Five O'Clock Follies, where falsehoods and lies were told and spread on a daily basis, while patrons nursed a delicious cocktail known as the Saigon Sunrise (and this was also well before the hands on the clock were 'straight up' as my pop pop would say) that the idea came to me to write a book about the war. My protagonist would be a female correspondent, or as Hazel, Ann and the many other real-life figures who were there during the war, a correspondent, no gender designation necessary. The Vietnam War was a war of firsts in so many ways-most notably, it was the only war in American history that allowed journalists to have essentially 'free rein' on the battleground—reporters were generally allowed to go anywhere and report anything that wasn't classified. (That of course was a one-time deal. American journalists have never had that freedom since, military officials long feeling that it was the journalists covering the Vietnam War who ultimately turned the American people against them.) But it was also the war where female journalists were on the frontlines too. They were the ones with the bylines, with the photo credits, with the on-air TV reporting; they were no longer relegated to the role of fact checkers back home in American newsrooms.

Although the character of Hazel is entirely fictitious, she's inspired by many real-life intrepid female journalists who covered Vietnam (and then Cambodia) during the war years. Kate Webb, an Australian who went on to have a long and illustrious career as an award-winning journalist, really was kidnapped by the North Vietnamese army and miraculously was released a few weeks later; Anne Morrissy Merrick, a trailblazing fighter who went up against General Westmoreland and the Pentagon, actually met her husband, a fellow journalist in Vietnam, and gave birth/raised their daughter there until the bureau office was closed in 1973. (Hazel and Vince's marriage and Bee's birth is based on Merrick's marriage.) And then of course, there is the indomitable Ann Bryan Mariano. By all accounts, she was a mentor to many of the newly arrived young female journalists to Vietnam who were without credentials and often gave them their shot at being able to stay in-country by letting them write for the military tabloid she ran, *Overseas Weekly* (it really was beloved by the men and loathed by Washington).

Many journalists really did go missing and/or were killed during the war, the most famous being Sean Flynn, son of Hollywood leading man Errol Flynn, who I based Vince's disappearance on. He and his compatriot, fellow photojournalist Dana Stone, went missing together in 1970 and were never seen again, presumably meeting their deaths at the hands of the Khmer Rouge. Tragically, to this day, their remains have never been found. And a sobering statistic- there are still 1,246 Americans unaccounted for in Vietnam according to the Defense POW/MIA Accounting Agency's website.

Aterbea was a real French restaurant that existed in Saigon during the war. However, I changed its location to be on Rue Pasteur as I remember walking on Rue Pasteur myself during my time in Saigon. Aterbea was actually located on Tu Do Street in its entertainment district. And it really is called the Saigon Saigon (that was no error), the rooftop bar on the top floor of the famed Caravelle Hotel.

Operation Frequent Wind, the final evacuation of Saigon, really did occur as described in the book. *"White Christmas"* was chosen as the song that followed the coded message being played on the Armed Forces Radio. United States military aircraft was pushed into the South China Sea in droves from the carriers that they landed on. Contrary to popular belief, the iconic image of people desperately trying to get aboard a waiting helicopter on a rooftop building was not the American Embassy, but rather one tied to a CIA front. And last but not least, thousands of desperate South Vietnamese civilians, many of whom had helped and were affiliated with the American military and government presence there, were left behind, forced to await a cruel and unimaginable fate at the hands of the oncoming North Vietnamese victors. Their contributions so soon forgotten once it was clear the end had come.

A visit to the War Remnants Museum in Saigon is emotionally jarring (and also a bit heavy on propaganda), but one of the exhibits featured journalists that had been killed during the war, journalists from all nations, not just North Vietnam. I found this to be an eloquent memorial to them because not only does it demonstrate the known risk a journalist takes when he or she travels to a war zone but also the simple truth that the most important role of that profession is to tell the people back home the truth about what is going on. And for that simple truth, one's nationality is irrelevant.

To say I have received an education by writing this book is an understatement. But the void that was my lack of knowledge on the Vietnam War, one of modern history's greatest tragedies, has now been filled. And I will forever carry a deep reverence for the young men who were sent there- the lucky ones who made it back, and to those who didn't. May their memory and service to their country forever live on through the pages of history.

Julie at the Rex Hotel's rooftop bar in February 2020

ACKNOWLEDGEMENTS

I want to extend a sincere thanks to Martin Albritton of Louisiana, Vietnam War veteran of the United States Army. He was an invaluable help when writing about the Tet Offensive as he was stationed in Hue, the epicenter of it all, arriving there in 1967 and serving with the MACV Team 3. Although there is much written on Hue about the offensive and siege and its aftermath after six weeks of brutal street to street fighting, there's a dearth of information on what it was like before January 31, 1968. That's where Mr. Albritton offered his firsthand memories of the "sleepy imperial city" that instantly became a household name for American families once the sneak attack began.

I consulted many books and resources but here are some of the most useful ones:

Bartimus, Tad, Tracy Wood, et al. *War Torn: Stories of War from the Women Reporters Who Covered Vietnam.* Random House, 2002.

Becker, Elizabeth. *You Don't Belong Here: How Three Women Rewrote the Story of War.* Public Affairs, 2021.

Bowden, Mark. *Hue 1968: A Turning Point of the American War in Vietnam.* Atlantic Monthly Press, 2017.

Hastings, Max. *Vietnam: An Epic Tragedy, 1945-1972.* Reprint ed., Harper Perennial, 2019.

Kautz, Barbara. *When I Die I'm Going to Heaven 'Cause I've Spent My Time in Hell: A Memoir of My Year as an Army Nurse in Vietnam.* Independently published, 2018.

Nguyen, Lisa. *We Shot the War: Overseas Weekly in Vietnam.* Hoover Institution Press, 2018.

Nguyen, Viet Thanh. *The Sympathizer: a novel.* Grove Press, 2016.

Pisor, Robert. *Siege of Khe Sanh: The Story of the Vietnam War's Largest Battle.* W.W. Norton & Company, 2018.

Rottman, Gordon L. *Grunt Slang in Vietnam: Words of the War.* Casemate, 2020.

"The Tiger Cages." *Life Magazine*, 17 July 1970, pp. 26-29.

Book Club Discussion Questions

1.) Has your reading of *Red Clay Ashes* changed your perception of the Vietnam War?

2.) Do you have a greater sympathy towards the men who were sent there to fight, even though it was not "their fight" and a great many of them were barely out of high school? Knowing that American politicians considered their lives expendable? Boys that were sent to fight a man's war, as the saying goes?

3.) Were you surprised to learn that journalists during the Vietnam War could just show up there and that if they had proper accreditation from a newspaper (or three newspapers if you were a freelancer), you could get a press badge and travel anywhere/travel on American military transport to report on the war?

4.) Do you think Hazel was a bad mother to Bee after Vince disappeared? Do you think she betrayed her word to Vince that she wouldn't do to their daughter what his own mom had done to him after his dad was killed during the Second World War?

5.) Should Hazel have left a letter for Bee to read upon her death, explaining the past? Explaining the truth about her father and her earliest years? Even in death, should Hazel have made one final attempt to restore a personal connection with her daughter? Instead of Bee learning about it by chance, and then hearing the full extent from Suzanne, a woman she had never known? Do you think she owed her daughter that?

6.) Do you think Hazel hated Vietnam and its people for what was stolen from her? Or do you think it was a case of, she hated the men who stole her husband and her child's father from her?

7.) Do you think Hazel ever really reconciled with her past or rather, simply mentally blocked out the years she had with Vince?

8.) Were you shocked when you learned that Vince had survived? Or would you have preferred his story to have ended when he was marched into the tree line?

9.) Do you think the journalists who reported on the war and told the truth about what was actually going on there contributed to the ultimate downfall of the American and South Vietnamese military might? Caused them to lose? Or do you think the South Vietnamese capitulation to the North was inevitable?

10.) How much do you feel today's female journalists owe to the female reporters of the Vietnam War? Do you feel their story is acknowledged as much as the infamous "Cronkite bombshell" of 1968, considering he only ever visited, and didn't live in the midst of a war zone as many of the female reporters did for months and in some cases, even years?

Julie Tulba is the author of the historical fiction books *The Dead Are Resting* and *The Tears of Yesteryear*. It was series like Dear America, Little House on the Prairie, and American Girl books that instilled in Julie at a young age her lifelong love and fascination with history. And a childhood spent growing up in Philadelphia, colonial America's foremost metropolis, further cemented this love affair. She lives in the Pittsburgh area, passport always at the ready for her next international adventure, but also brainstorming ideas for her next novel. For more information, please visit her website, www.julietulba.com.

Made in the USA
Middletown, DE
14 November 2022

14972227R00203